Maya came out of the building and almost tripped down the steps, the door swinging shut behind her and smacking her backside. Vic stood in front of a Kawasaki 1100, looking like a 3-D advertisement out of *Black Men* magazine. No lie, she wanted to pin him up on her wall like when she was a kid and would tear out the centerfold photos from *Right On*. He had on a brown leather jacket and held a helmet tucked underneath his arm. There was another helmet hanging from the back of the seat.

With a baseball cap cocked to the side of his head and a pair of rather large, brown Timberland boots on his feet, Vic's presence made Maya's knees tremble. His stance had a sort of power in it that made Maya feel confident in his ability to take care of her and show her a good evening.

"Whassup?" he asked.

"Aren't we prompt?"

"Well, I know how you women hate to be kept waitin'." Vic smiled back. "You ever rode before?"

"Nope."

"Are you game?"

"Sure, but no Evel Knievel crap."

"Don't worry, I got you." Vic helped her tighten her helmet and settle comfortably on the bike. Just as he started the engine and shoved the kickstand back with his heel, he yelled over his shoulder, "Hold on to me tight now. I wouldn't want to lose you."

And, always having been an obedient girl, she wrapped both arms tightly around him.

BOOK YOUR PLACE ON OUR WEBSITE AND MAKE THE READING CONNECTION!

We've created a customized website just for our very special readers, where you can get the inside scoop on everything that's going on with Zebra, Pinnacle and Kensington books.

When you come online, you'll have the exciting opportunity to:

- View covers of upcoming books
- Read sample chapters
- Learn about our future publishing schedule (listed by publication month *and author*)
- Find out when your favorite authors will be visiting a city near you
- Search for and order backlist books from our online catalog
- Check out author bios and background information
- Send e-mail to your favorite authors
- Meet the Kensington staff online
- Join us in weekly chats with authors, readers and other guests
- Get writing guidelines
- AND MUCH MORE!

**Visit our website at
http://www.kensingtonbooks.com**

Pack Light

KIM SHAW

BET Publications, LLC
http://www.bet.com
http://www.arabesquebooks.com

ARABESQUE BOOKS are published by

BET Publications, LLC
c/o BET BOOKS
One BET Plaza
1900 W Place NE
Washington, DC 20018-1211

All Kensington Titles, Imprints, and Distributed Lines are available at special quantity discounts for bulk purchases for sales promotions, premiums, fund-raising, and educational or institutional use. Special book excerpts or customized printings can also be created to fit specific needs. For details, write or phone the office of the Kensington special sales manager: Kensington Publishing Corp., 850 Third Avenue, New York, NY 10022, attn: Special Sales Department, Phone: 1-800-221-2647.

First Printing: October 2004
10   9   8   7   6   5   4   3   2

Printed in the United States of America

To black love.
It is real. Embrace it, believe in it, revel in it,
for our children/people desperately need to see it.

Acknowledgments

To my husband, Donald, through thick and thin. Thank you for believing in me without question. To my children, Niyala and Na'im, you are my greatest joy. Thank you guys for keeping me laughing. To my mother, Eugenia, the most giving person I know. Thank you for holding it down. To my brothers, Kevin and Kyron. Always believe that the best is yet to come. To my Nana, Eartha, love you, beautiful.

Thank you to my in-laws, Ditha, Raymond, Dentya, Dwayne and Dave—a fabulous extended family.

To my girls, Lisa, Tamirra, Phyllis (#1 cuz), Ingra, Cynthia, Brenda, Lorna, Sue, Karen—you ladies keep me sane in this crazy world. While your drama provides great fodder, none of you are getting a cut! Ladies, I appreciate what each of you have been to me over the years.

To authors Donna Hill, Lori Bryant-Woolridge and Nathasha Brooks-Harris. Thank you for sharing your talents with the world, but more specifically, for sharing your knowledge and experience with dozens of aspiring writers. The craft is made better because of your efforts.

To my agent, Patti Steele-Perkins, thank you for teaching a "newbie" the "business" of writing.

To the rest of my friends and family, too numerous to name—remember, love really is the cure-all.

Chapter One

A New Beginning

The gradual lightening of the sky was a welcome sight for Maya, even on this dull gray morning. She'd passed the night tossing and turning over twisted sheets, wet with perspiration. She'd watched the shadows of passing cars cast against the venetian blinds in the city that never sleeps. She'd counted sheep, counted pigs, counted the stains on the ceiling above her head. And, as was inevitable, counted every moment of sorrow since she'd lost her parents.

Maya's long legs were heavy as she struggled out of bed. A thick fog coated the city sky, limiting her view from the open window of her fifth-floor walk-up. She stretched both hands outside the window and upward, aiming to clear away some of the thick moist air and allow her mind's eye to catch a glimpse of her parents. A futile but compulsive routine, she knew. Ironically, there were times when, if the sun shone brightly and if she stared long enough, she'd see a slip of her mother's favorite red silk scarf dancing across the sky. Memories of her father's last days flooded her mind, causing her anger to rise to the surface again. She would never forgive Andrew Payne for his role in her father's death. She thanked God every day that the man was behind bars where he belonged. She also doubted that she would ever be able to look back without the ghosts of her past taunting her.

The rumbling din of a garbage truck lumbering down West 58th Street pulled her from her revelry. Maya took a deep breath and blew it out, knowing she'd have to go it alone today. She shut the window.

Well, this is what I wanted. I worked for it, prayed for it and now it's up to me what I do with it. With that, she pushed open the creaky, half-off-its-hinges door and stepped inside the cramped bathroom. She lingered in the shower, wanting the hot water to work out the kinks in her neck and back. Maya was relieved to find that in spite of a sleepless night, there were only slightly visible bags under her eyes, nothing a little Revlon cover-up wouldn't cure. From the vanity beneath the bathroom sink she retrieved the cosmetics bag she'd been toting around since age eighteen. It was the last present her mother had given her—a green alligator-skin bag with her initials embossed on the outside in golden script. Her mother had given it to her filled with makeup. She smiled as she remembered Pauline's words that day.

"I can't understand why you want to paint your face all up. You're a natural beauty."

"Mom, all my friends . . ."

"I know, I know, all your friends wear makeup now. I guess you're at that age. Anyhow, you've got to be careful, 'cause I've seen some of your friends." Pauline shook her head. "Some of them look like they're eighteen going on ninety-nine!"

"Mommy, you're so dramatic."

"Yeah, that's what your father says. Here . . . I understand these products are the best for black skin. The last thing I want is to see your skin turn into shoe leather."

Maya's smile soon melted, the memories of better days still too much to bear. She sighed, wanting today to be different. She was determined to shake off the blues. Her parents would be proud of her—due to their love and encouragement Maya had graduated with honors from Howard University, then Albany University School of Law. Now, just two months after acing the bar exam, she'd landed an associate position with one of the most prominent criminal and civil litigation firms in New York City. She was on her way to living her dream of changing the American justice system so that it worked for *all* its citizens. No, today was not a day for sadness. No matter what, she would not cry. She would enjoy this day for her parents as much as for herself.

By eight o'clock in the morning Maya was dressed and raring to go. Her shoulder-length hair with its black-cherry tints was styled in a tight bun at the nape of her neck. Her slim, curvaceous figure was conservatively complemented by a black rayon-and-silk-blend skirt and jacket accompanied by an ivory cotton blouse and sensible, black Adrienne Vittadini pumps. The suit was an Anne Klein number she'd found at a warehouse sale.

She planned to save her other suit, a gray lightweight wool pantsuit, which she'd worn on the second interview, for the end of the week. The rest of her business wardrobe consisted of a few simple skirts and blouses and two blazers, which she'd mix and match over the next few weeks. Then there was the black coatdress she'd worn to both her parents' funerals and a couple of other dresses that could either be dressed up or down with the right accessories.

Meager as it was, this wardrobe would have to suffice for a while. With more than eighty thousand dollars in student loans to pay back, Maya was not headed for any shopping sprees in the near future. The remainder of her six-figure salary would go toward fixing up her apartment. Although the purchase had been a wise investment because the block was under major renovations and would soon be considered a high-rent district, the apartment itself was in desperate need of repairs.

Home was just a ten-minute subway ride away from midtown Manhattan where her new job was located at 438 Fifth Avenue. It had been a long time since she'd had a reason to be in Manhattan, but the hustle and bustle hadn't changed a bit. Early September meant that there was just enough summer left to keep the air humid and warm, which in Manhattan translated into oppressive and irritating.

She arrived in front of the office building at twenty-five minutes after eight o'clock, wired from her travels. The murky-colored lobby, which had been decorated in hues of deep burgundy and gray, gave the building a Bates Motel feel. Maya escaped the gloom for a quick bite to eat in a coffee shop at the rear of the lobby. As she picked over a cheese Danish, Maya asked God to help her to be the kind of lawyer whose advice people valued and whose knowledge of the law was unwavering.

After spending a few years gaining practical experience, Maya hoped to be able to provide low-cost legal services to people who couldn't otherwise afford quality representation. Most importantly, she wanted to prove that, affirmative action aside, little black girls and little black boys could hold their own in the Good Old Boy Network. Maya wanted nothing more than to rid herself of the haunting childhood memories of being ridiculed by her classmates. The predominately white classmates had so much as told her by their words and actions that her blackness made her dumb. For the longest time she believed they were right as she struggled with an undiagnosed learning disability. It wasn't until long after her mother discovered her problem and worked diligently to address it that Maya began to see herself differently. The damage to her self-esteem had never been fully repaired, and Maya still vowed to prove them wrong.

Chapter Two

New Kid on the Block

"Good morning. Maya Wilkins to see Samantha Rhodes," Maya said to the woman at the front desk. She was a young African-American woman with jet-black, blond-streaked hair that had been tortured into a tight ponytail with cascading curls. While Maya secretly wished somebody had schooled her on the importance of toning it down in the workplace, seeing a sistah at the forefront of any business was still comforting.

"I'll let her know you're here. You can sit over there if you want," replied the receptionist, never taking her eyes off Maya.

Maya followed the direction of the two-inch, air-brushed fingernail and took a seat on a cranberry-colored leather sofa. The astonished gaze did not surprise Maya at all. She'd received the same response from the Office Services staff, whom she'd met during the three-hour interview at the firm the previous month. The employees, all of them black or Hispanic, practically fell out of their shoes when they saw her. It would've been a big ego stroke to attribute this response to her good looks, but Maya knew better. It was quite evident after meeting with several partners and associates, reviewing the austere faces in the framed photos that lined the foyer and office walls, and hearing about the practice itself, that at Madison, Pritchard & Fusco there were no African-American (or African anything for that matter) attorneys employed there. Maya would be the first, which was causing a stir amongst the staff, both legal and non-legal, most of whom had become accustomed to the lack of color on the attorney roster. Initially this worried Maya, who didn't want to be considered a token hire. But she quickly realized that if such was indeed the case, she'd show them what a wise choice they'd made.

Before she had a chance to second-guess her decision to join the firm, the head of recruiting approached.

"Good morning. Bright and early—we like that, we like," Samantha chirped.

"Good morning, Samantha, how are you today?" Maya answered, shaking Samantha's extended hand.

"Not bad, for a Monday. The partners are busting my chops this morning over some health-care issues, but what else is new? Let's get you settled. Have you met Rashon? Rashon, this is Maya Wilkins, our newest associate. Rashon is the best receptionist this firm's ever seen. She's been here for, oh, Rashon, how long *have* you been here now?"

"Four years," came Rashon's dry response.

"Four years?! Way to go! That's longer than any other staff member. Just goes to show, there are still people who know how to hold on to a job."

The slight was not lost on either Maya or Rashon. Maya smiled at Rashon as she shook her hand warmly. "It's nice to meet you, Rashon."

"Likewise." Rashon returned her attention to the computer monitor behind her.

Maya followed Samantha down a long hallway as the latter chatted incessantly. The walls were lined with framed black-and-white photographs of turn-of-the-century Manhattan and color photos of the firm's present and past attorneys. The tiny brass nameplates affixed to the wall outside every office spoke to the affluence of the firm. Samantha explained that the office space had been redesigned about four years ago to accommodate the growing practice. Madison, Pritchard & Fusco was the largest tenant in the building, operating on the top fifteen floors of the forty-story structure.

Samantha was a likable, fortysomething-year-old bottle blonde who still wore spike-heeled shoes and sky-blue eye shadow. While she wasn't unattractive, she was definitely out of style. She also smelled like she'd just climbed out of a pack of Marlboro Lights.

At the end of the hallway, Samantha stopped in front of a closed door. She adjusted the brass nameplate bearing Maya's name next to the door.

"This is you," she announced, unlocking the office door and stepping aside.

Maya entered the windowless office, her smile widening as she looked around. On the center of the oak desk sat a small basket of gladiolus and tulips, with a sunburst rose in the middle.

"Just a little something I like to do to welcome the new soldiers—especially the women," Samantha whispered conspiratorially.

"Thank you, Samantha, they're beautiful." Maya leaned over the desk to sniff the fragrant flowers.

"You're very welcome. Now listen, I've got a couple of fires to put out this morning. Why don't you take a few minutes to get settled, have a cup of coffee—the pantry is four doors down on the left. One of the junior partners, Ted Brody, will assign you to your first case, so look him up. Oh, and later today you and I will need to process your paperwork—you know, IRS stuff. If there's anything you need, give me a ring, okay, Maya?"

"Yes, and thank you again, Samantha."

"No problem. Ta-ta."

The skinny heels quickly departed, leaving Maya alone. Maya leaned against the closed door, surveying the room. The desk was L-shaped and at the bottom of the "L" rested a black Dell computer with a flat panel monitor and compact modem. She found a box of supplies including a desk calendar, a Rolodex and stationery. In front of the desk were two spruce armchairs, matching the carpet. There was a metal file cabinet with three drawers next to the door and a couple of cardboard boxes containing documents resting at the side of the desk.

Maya sat in the black leather swivel chair behind her new desk. From her briefcase she removed a silver framed photograph of her parents taken at their 25th-anniversary celebration. Their faces smiled back at her as she positioned the photo in its new home between the computer and the telephone. An attractive couple, both Milton and Pauline Wilkins appeared to be a lot younger than their years. Her mother's shiny dark hair was styled in a French roll and she wore the diamond studs which her father had just given her moments before the picture was taken. Pauline looked regal in a Tracy Reese black cocktail dress. A hint of white at the base of her father's temples and lightly sprinkled throughout his wavy hair and close-cut beard did not age him in the least. He wore wire-rimmed glasses and the easy smile of a man completely satisfied with his life.

Maya remembered how much her parents had danced that evening. Watching them together had made everyone believe in love everlasting. Theirs was an unshakable love, built on solid ground, and for that Maya was truly grateful. Six months later her mother died. To this day Maya wondered if her mother had known that she was ill and chose to keep it a secret. She'd never know.

For the next hour Maya played with the computer,

sifted through the files in the boxes and pretended not to notice her new co-workers sneaking peeks at her as they passed by her office. She figured that eventually one of them would be brave enough to introduce themselves. Or, she reasoned, maybe they were waiting for some sort of formal introduction. She tried not to think that it was the color thing, but of course, those thoughts were never far away. Maya longed for that unlikely day when she did not have to pay attention to race. To not have to question every action or inaction would be ideal. To meet someone and know, without a doubt, that that person saw her as Maya and not as "the black woman."

Things remained relatively quiet that first day. Ted Brody did not respond to her phone message requesting to meet with him until after lunch.

"Maya, it's Ted Brody."

"Yes, Mr. Brody. Thanks for getting back to me."

"It's just Ted, Maya."

"Yes, Ted."

"Listen, George Bramwell and I are in my office, on thirty. Why don't you pop in and we'll bring you up to speed on a few things."

"Sure, Ted, I'll be right there."

When Ted Brody neglected to release the call at the end of the conversation, having mistakenly pressed the SPEAKER button, Maya guiltily listened on.

"She's on her way," Ted said.

"Fine," responded George Bramwell.

"I still don't understand why I have to have her. I don't want her screwing up my case," Ted said.

"Relax, Ted, just give her the simple stuff, like cover letters and file organization."

"Hmph. You know they don't follow instructions well."

"She apparently graduated at the top of her class. . . . She might surprise us," George reasoned.

"Whatever. All I know is Marjorie needs to lay off

the save-the-world kick. First she had us take on all those pro bono, hoodlum criminal cases and now she's filling associate spots with just anybody. What next?"

With a trembling finger, Maya softly pressed the release button on her phone. Chewing her bottom lip, she replayed the conversation. *Who in the hell did this Brody guy think he was?* She blinked several times, forcing the tears surfing the rims of her sockets not to fall, snatched a legal pad and a pen off her desk and marched out, prepared to introduce herself to ignorance, yet again.

Chapter Three

Dig In

"No, thanks. I'm swamped today," Maya said into the handset tucked between her shoulder and chin. "Sounds good. . . . Okay. . . . Bye-bye."

Maya hung up, swept aside a stray bit of hair which kept tickling her forehead and continued proofreading the brief she was working on. It was the end of her third week at the firm, and the "go light on the new kid" period was over. Ted Brody's contract dispute case was headed toward arbitration, necessitating cumbersome research and document production, which required Maya to become more heavily involved in the case than Brody desired. In addition to Brody's case, Marjorie Chapman had seen to it that Maya was assigned to a very active, high-profile tax-evasion case with a partner named Richard Griesler for which a brief was due in a week. She also was supposed to attend a deposition the following Monday, although she was still uncertain what exactly her role there would be.

All this was part of the reason why she'd begged out of going to lunch with the group of associates headed to a Japanese spot nearby. Another part was that she hated sushi, and it seemed that was all the attorneys at the firm liked to eat. Obviously, they had no idea what a sushi lunch did to their breaths because many of them walked around for the rest of the day smelling like hot garbage.

Her main reason, however, was that she wanted to avoid getting hooked up with a clique there, which seemed to be the practice. The group heading out today consisted of two first-year associates like herself, Michelle Morrison and Peter Sealig. They'd both been with the firm for less than six months but they fit in quite well with the rest of the yuppie crowd. Also in the group were two guys Maya could not tell apart, although they were unrelated. They were both short and dark-haired, with blue eyes hidden behind brown horn-rimmed glasses, and were always clad in the customary attorney uniform—white or pastel shirt, sober tie and dark suit. "Nerd" would be the word to describe Jeff and John, if this were high school. The final member of the group was a big blond Swedish woman named Giova, who reminded Maya of the Sasquatch character from the late 1970s television series *The Bionic Woman*. She wore at least a size-thirteen shoe and the backs of her hands had a noticeable layer of blond hair on them.

Maya had eaten lunch in the conference room with that particular group on two occasions, and although she tried to reserve judgment, it was obvious that she had nothing in common with most of her fellow associates. They were, in large part, the type of people she and her best friend, Katrina Brewster, had distanced themselves from during law school. They were sheltered kids who came from wealthy homes, whose connected dads made one phone call and landed their kids cushy jobs in whatever fields they chose. These kids had no ideas apart from the ones belonging to their parents. They lived by some blind-eyed, upper-class code of ethics, their universe confined to making money and rubbing elbows with the *right* people. It wasn't that they were bad people. They'd just been brought up with little knowledge of or concern for how the rest of the world lived. All they talked about during lunch was what they did at their parents' weekend cottages or condos and the latest *Friends* episode.

One day Michelle Morrison noticed a snapshot of a young child named Anna from Blantyre, Malawi, on Maya's desk and she assumed the child was a relative. When Maya explained that her mother had been sponsoring this child's family over the years and that Maya was continuing the assistance in her mother's memory, Michelle responded with a polite "That's nice," while her expression read that she'd suddenly developed a bad taste in her mouth.

Another favorite lunch topic was how some of the rich clients represented by the firm had managed to amass their fortunes and to evade the law—at least up until now. Now that these clients had criminal and/or civil accusations mounting against them, the associates, still in obvious awe of these criminally rich people, dedicated a great part of their working day and leisure time saving their butts from the fire.

Although Maya was also dedicated to being the best attorney that she could be for each and every client, she could not and would not bring herself to feel sympathy for them, and she definitely didn't feel any awe or respect for their practices. Her colleagues, on the other hand, acted as if it was the government who was out of line for even suggesting that these people had committed some improprieties. So what if they'd fudged a few numbers on their income tax returns? Who did it hurt if they occasionally made a killing off of inside tips from someone about a company's stocks? They were rich people—translation: they were good people, so a slipup every now and then should be excusable. For Maya, this was all a crock. She knew from firsthand experience who could be hurt by it. She also knew that no one should be above the law, no matter what their net worth.

"Hmmn." She sighed, drumming her split nails on the table and wishing she could afford a weekly manicure, pedicure and facial. She'd set a strict budget for herself and the best she could do might be a monthly pampering session. Besides, she had greater concerns than skin and nails. Here she was three weeks on the job and seriously doubting whether she belonged at Madison Pritchard. While people had been generally nice to her thus far—aside from Brody's derogatory remarks—it was she who felt out of place. She told herself that their world and their interests just didn't correlate with her own. However, a stronger truth was that she couldn't let her guard down and get comfortable enough to give it a real try.

It was reminiscent of her first few days at Albany University School of Law. When she pulled the rented U-Haul into the student parking lot, she found herself searching frantically for a face that mirrored her own. The picturesque campus grounds and surrounding quaint town were populated about ten to one, white to black. Maya's roommates were both white, her classmates were all white and the few black students she'd seen around campus couldn't figure out exactly who they were. She experienced strong feelings of isolation, especially in the first few weeks, which could not be dismissed as normal away-from-home jitters.

During her undergraduate studies at Howard she'd served as vice president of the Students For Multi-Cultural Understanding Association, aka SMCUA, because she believed in its mantra of breaking down barriers between the races in an effort to denounce prejudice and promote a positive exchange of cultures. She felt that people should have the freedom to love whomever they wanted to love, regardless of color, go wherever they chose to go, regardless of color, and express themselves in whatever fashion they chose to express themselves, regardless. However, in spite of her queen-sized righteous attitude, she still couldn't deny the fact that at Albany she felt like a fish out of water.

In walked Katrina Brewster when they were both in their first few days of law school. Katrina was a Southern-bred, no-nonsense sister of African-American and French descent. She wore her toffee-colored skin, frizzy light brown hair and green eyes with pride. Meeting Katrina made Maya feel as though she now had an ally, a kindred spirit. From then on it didn't matter if they were swimming in a sea of white faces: Maya felt at ease. Maya regarded Katrina as a very adaptable sort of person, worldly and approachable—the type of person people naturally gravitate to. Because she had been raised by a Caucasian mother from France and a Southern-born black father, she knew a lot about both worlds. She helped relieve some of the tension Maya experienced in situations where she was the minority, and they became lifelong friends.

Maya made other lasting friendships during her three years at Albany, including a naturally blond bombshell named Shelly Kolatch (but nicknamed Fudge by Maya and Katrina because she was the blackest white girl ever), and Bonnie Persaud, a mousy immigrant from Guyana who would've been a knockout if she had stopped hiding behind her thick glasses, oversize sweatsuits and floppy hats. Shelly hated her figure, which was a little thick by European standards but by no means overweight. An intelligent, analytical woman, Shelly was filled with a double serving of self-doubt.

The women recognized their cultural and physical differences, but these things were never an issue between them. They could discuss race and religion unabashedly; no one left feeling defensive or insulted.

The four of them had spent hours upon hours debating the wrongs and rights of the world, the wrongs and rights of academia and the wrongs of men (they'd agreed that there were no rights in this regard). Those days spent sprawled out on the soccer field's manicured turf—Katrina, Maya and Bonnie pigging out on Twinkies or Hostess cupcakes, Shelly chewing on a celery stick— seemed so far away from Maya now that she'd begun to wonder if they'd really happened.

Maya sighed again as she thought of her friends, hating the fact that they were all separated. Shelly was in California working at her father's law firm, and Bonnie was in Bolivia, living like a pauper. During their last year of school, Bonnie had met and fallen in love with a man who worked for the Red Cross, so she'd decided to do a stint as a missionary, working with underprivileged communities. Katrina—well, Katrina had decided that although she'd graduated in the top five percentile, she didn't really want to practice law—or, at least, not just yet. She skipped the bar exam and was now teaching at a community college in D.C. and trying to "find" her true calling. At least D.C. was just a few hours' drive away and Maya had made a promise to Katrina and to herself that once she got settled she'd hop on the first thing smoking and spend a few days in Chocolate City. Otherwise, Maya was all alone in the Big Bad Apple.

Just then, as if she were sending out some sort of telepathic wave, the phone rang.

"Maya Wilkins," she answered.

"Didn't I tell you you're supposed to say, 'Maya Wilkins, attorney-at-law'? Damn, girl, can't you follow simple directions?"

"Nope, especially not coming from you." Maya laughed. In an instant, Katrina waved her magic wand and Maya's anxiety lifted.

"God, you're going to live a long time. I was just thinking about you," Maya said.

"Good thoughts, I hope," Katrina replied, standing in front of the full-length mirror on the back of her bedroom door. She was re-dressing after a forty-five minute workout at the gym and a quick shower.

"I was thinking about you, Shelly and Bonnie . . . about the good old days. I miss us all hanging out together."

"What's wrong?" Katrina asked intuitively, buttoning a cardinal-colored sweater across her considerable bosom.

"Nothing. Why do you always ask me that?" Maya retorted, clearly annoyed. She wasn't sure if she was bothered most by the fact that Katrina was always so suspicious of her moods or because Katrina was usually right on the mark.

"I don't always ask you that. Just when you have that whiny, nostalgic tone in your voice like you lost your best friend—which can't be because I'm right here—or your dog died or something."

"Oh, so now I'm whiny?"

"Cut the crap, Maya, what's up?"

"Nothing really. I just miss you guys. Can't I say I miss you without there being something wrong with me?"

"Are you feeling like the black Lone Ranger again?"

Maya shut her eyes, not responding while she rubbed her temples. She didn't need to say anything. Katrina always seemed to know what was going on with her without her having to spell it out. Katrina took Maya's silence to mean that her assumption had been correct.

"Look, Maya, you knew this going in. White-collar crime is one of the least-integrated areas of law, hence the name. You're gonna have to just get over it. Sometimes you're gonna be the majority—like if you came down to D.C. for the National Black Family

Reunion Celebration. But sometimes you're going to be the minority, like right now."

"I know. It's just that it's so hard sometimes fitting in when you really don't fit in. You know what I mean?"

"Yeah, I hear you, girl. But listen to me. You've got to stop being so self-conscious. Everybody in the whole wide world does not have race on their minds every waking moment."

"Seems like it."

"To you, maybe," Katrina said, turning sideways to admire her profile in the mirror. "Listen, Maya, you made the grades, right?"

"Yeah."

"You got the job, right?"

"Yeah."

"You're on top of your game, right?"

"Yeah."

"And you are just basically all that and then some, am I right?"

"Heck yeah." Maya laughed.

"So lighten up and get your corporate card-carrying self back to work."

"All right, girl. Enough about me. How's school going?"

"It's a little strange being on the other side of the classroom, but I'm adjusting. I just wish I had less freshman students and more seniors. These kids are just not ready to deal with real life. They whine when you give them assignments, whine when you give exams, whine when you ask them a question. It's like they just expect to hang out in your class all day doing nothing and then end up with an A at the end of the semester. Wasting their parents' hard-earned money. It pisses me off!" Katrina ranted.

"You know how it is when you're fresh out of high school. All you really want to do is just chill," Maya answered, as she printed the memorandum she'd been working on. She skimmed it, realizing that it still didn't read the way she wanted it to.

"Well, they need to chill on somebody else's time, not mine." Katrina huffed, pursing her thin lips so that she could apply a coat of stoplight-red lipstick.

"Come on now, Kat, take it easy on them. They'll get into gear soon enough. It's still early in the semester."

"Yeah, right," Katrina prepared to hang up. "Anyway, girl, I've got a class in twenty minutes."

"Okay, I won't keep you. I've got a memo to revise and a ton of other stuff to do myself."

"You remember what I said, Maya. You don't have to feel out of place, just be yourself. You know everyone loves you anyway—once they get to know you, that is."

"All right, smarty-pants, I'll talk to you over the weekend."

"Bye-bye," Katrina oozed.

Maya hung up the telephone, laughing to herself; she felt better from just five minutes of Katrina's craziness. But there was really no time for her to dwell on all that stuff anyway. She had a ton of work to do, and she knew it didn't matter if she was the color of split-pea soup—she was the new jack and all eyes were on her right now. Her game had to be tight and that's exactly how she was planning on keeping it. Some of her peers may be content with just getting by, just doing enough work to get over and nothing more, but Maya had never settled for mediocrity. Her parents taught her to strive for excellence at all times, meet all challenges head on and never quit. Her father died living up to those ideals, and she would use her last breath to follow in his footsteps.

Chapter Four

Getting to Know You

Maya opened the door and stepped into the cafeteria. The firm's small but well-equipped eating area was located on the twenty-fifth floor, along with office services, accounting, human resources and the paralegal offices. Inside were eight small round tables with five seats at each table and a counter with ten high-backed stools on the right wall. There was a refrigerator loaded with beverages, and along the counter on the far wall sat a microwave, an ice maker, a coffeemaker, condiments and paper goods. Maya looked around the room as she entered, carrying her brown-paper-bag lunch, noting that all eight tables were occupied by at least two to four people at each table and a couple of guys were seated at the counter.

"Hello," she said to Brie and Susanna, two associates seated nearest the door. Across from them at the next table sat three women from accounting. The table closest to the refrigerator held four people Maya did not recall having met, all associates. At a table in the rear sat Rashon, Denise (who was Marjorie Chapman's secretary) and a guy she assumed worked in the mailroom. Maya smiled and nodded at every table as she made her way toward the back, ignoring the sideways glances she got from some of them.

"Hi," she said, pulling out a chair. "Is anyone sitting here?" Denise and Rashon both looked at her blankly, then shifted their eyes to look at one another as the guy from the mailroom filled the silence.

"No, it's empty. Sit, sit." He shifted his lunch over to the left to give Maya room.

"Thanks," Maya answered. She smiled again as she sat down. "I don't think we've met yet. I'm Maya." She extended her hand.

"Vic," he answered, shaking hands. Hazel eyes smiled at her as he added, "This is Rashon and Denise."

"I know. What's up, ladies?" she asked.

"Nothin' much," Rashon answered.

Denise shook her head in agreement as she chewed a mouthful of food.

"That looks good," Maya said to Denise as she peered into the Tupperware bowl that held Denise's food. She was eating white rice smothered with pepper steak in a thick gravy. Maya could tell it was homemade, not warmed-over takeout.

"Mmm-hmm," Denise answered in between forkfuls. "I threw down on this one."

"Damn, everybody's lunch looks better than this," Maya said, dropping onto the table the egg-salad sandwich she'd hastily prepared at home that morning, and looking around at Vic's Chinese spareribs and fried rice and Rashon's meatloaf and potatoes. "Oh, well." She sighed, unwrapping her sandwich.

"So, Maya," Vic asked, "how do you like it here so far?"

"So far, so good," she answered as she held a napkin over her egg-filled mouth. "The firm's not quite as uptight as I thought it would be—you know, white-collar criminal defense and all."

"These guys are a pretty okay bunch," Denise answered.

Rashon coughed. "Humph." Maya looked up, catching her eye before Rashon turned away. It was long enough for Maya to see the disdain.

"I hear the firm has a pretty decent softball team. Do any of you play?" Maya had been thinking about joining the team, softball being one of her favorite sports. Growing up in Westchester, she'd led the Tarrytown Tigers, a local softball team, to numerous championship seasons over the years. At that time she was her most confident self whenever she was in front of a mound.

"Who's got time for that mess after work?" Rashon said, sucking her teeth.

Talk about negative vibes. Maya started to ask Rashon if she was always this ornery or if it was just for Maya's benefit, but she stopped herself before getting started. She checked the homegirl twitch rising in her neck and took a big bite of her sandwich.

"Nah, softball's not my game," Vic said, once again filling the awkward space.

"So what's your game?" Maya said, looking at Vic.

For the life of her, she didn't mean to say that the way it'd come out. Everyone looked at her and she blushed. Then Vic cracked a smile and Maya noticed how attractive the brother was. His skin was a reddish-brown color and he had small, baby-smooth lips, a dominating, bone-straight nose slightly flared at the tip and sleepy eyes, like the alarm clock hadn't gone off yet. His hair was cut into a low Caesar. When he smiled she noticed that one of his front teeth had a very small chip in it, which gave his otherwise innocent-looking face a sly edge.

"Basketball," he answered.

"Mmm. Did you watch the game last night?"

"Did I?! The Nets were in the house last night. Everybody sleeps on that team, but they're gonna prove the world wrong. Watch."

"I don't know about all that, but you've gotta admit, Chicago still spanked them. In a clinch, we always pull through."

"Oh, please, you women are all alike. Always talkin' about Chicago, Chicago, when all you guys ever really cared about was Michael, Michael. After Michael left Chicago, ninety percent of their fans went with him. What are you still hangin' on for?"

"For your information, yes, MJ is the man, no doubt. However, I was a Chicago fan when he was still at North Carolina, back when both Bill Cartwright and Horace Grant were running things. And my daddy introduced me to Artis Gilmore once. Second, I'm from Chicago and even after we moved to New York, Chicago remained our team. Third, Chicago has repeatedly led the league in—"

"All right, all right. You got it." Vic smiled, as amused with the woman's basketball knowledge as he was with her no-nonsense attitude.

By the time lunch was over, Vic and Maya had exchanged witty commentary on everything from sports to world affairs. The rapport between them was incredibly effortless and magnetically charged. Maya returned to her office pleased at having a lunch filled with good conversation. Vic was a little too cute for comfort, but that she could handle. She did enjoy the fact that she didn't have to pretend she was interested in what was being discussed—she actually *was* interested. All this reaffirmed her belief that she would always be more comfortable with her own, no matter what the situation. By the same token, Maya also was acutely aware of how the game was played, and she was willing to admit that it was important for her to be a part of the team. She'd just have to work harder at letting down her guard and getting to know her colleagues, despite the divide.

Chapter Five

Midnight Oil

"Alright, Vic, Joseph. Here are the exhibits, lettered A through M. We're going to need to make about thirty copies and insert the exhibit tabs. But don't bind it or anything yet, obviously," Maya said as she dropped a stack of papers onto the counter in the mailroom. It was already ten o'clock at night and Richard Griesler, the partner in charge of the case, was still making revisions to the brief. Maya swept a piece of stray hair from her brow and sighed. So much for catching some Zs tonight.

"These are going to be VeloBound, right?" Vic asked, taking the pile from Maya.

"Yeah."

"Okay. Joe, start copying these onto VeloBind paper," Vic said, handing the pile over to his assistant. Maya pulled out a chair and sat down.

"Tired?" Vic asked, leaning against the counter in front of her.

"Beat. I can't wait until this weekend," Maya responded wearily.

"Big plans, huh?"

"Actually, no plans. None whatsoever and that's fine with me. I'm going to sleep all day, eat all night and not do a damn thing that requires me to use my brain."

Vic laughed. "Borin'."

"Yeah, well, just call me boring then. I've worked almost sixty hours this week and it's only Thursday. Believe me, I could use a little boring."

"Nah, life's too short for borin'." A wicked smile played at Vic's lips.

"So what are you doing that's so exciting this weekend? Bungee jumping or something?"

"Nope. Saturday mornin' I'll probably work out at the gym. Then maybe go down to the park and shoot some hoops or get into somethin', you know. And I've got two tickets to the fight at the Garden Saturday night."

"Oh, Prince Salam Salam, or whatever his name is?"

"Yep. Oh, don't tell me you're a boxin' fan, too?" he mocked.

"Fan? No, I'm way more than a fan. I love boxing. I especially love watching the life-story profiles of the veterans, like Joe Lewis and Muhammad Ali."

"Damn, girl, you're into basketball, boxin'—you're a perfect date. How come you don't have a man?"

"What makes you think I don't have a man?" Maya asked indignantly. *How dare he make assumptions about my love life, even if he is right.*

"I'm sorry, didn't mean to offend you or nothin'. I'm just sayin', it seems to me that if you had a man, you wouldn't be spendin' one of the last mild weekends of the year holed up in your crib all alone." Vic looked her dead in the eyes when he said this, and if she didn't know any better, she would swear there was something there. But, of course, that was impossible. They worked together, co-workers, employees of the same firm. He was a cool guy and all, but as far as she was concerned, you should never mix the business with the personal.

"There's absolutely nothing wrong with being alone with yourself every now and again. That is, if, like me, you enjoy your own company. Now, if you can't stand yourself, then I could see why you'd want to spend every waking moment in the company of others." Maya smiled. She knew she'd gotten him back with that one. Or so she thought.

"True, true. But if you really love yourself, you'd feel obligated to share some of that good stuff with others," Vic retorted.

"Oh, please! On that note, I'm going upstairs to check on the brief," Maya said as she walked out of the mailroom, Vic's laughter tickling her ears.

The brother really did have it going on, despite the fact that Maya was trying hard not to think of him in that way. He was cute, funny, intelligent and, and . . . he worked in the mailroom of the firm she'd just started working for. A definite no-no. It wasn't that she had a real problem with a brother who was not part of the professional staff or anything. But she could tell that everyone else there would have a problem. Maybe if he worked in the mailroom of another firm, that'd be okay. Besides, office romances of any type were definitely not a smart thing to do. Whether the relationship was good or bad, everybody was in your business and, before you knew it, you were spending more time trying to maintain some privacy than focusing on the relationship. She could just imagine the looks and comments from the associates and partners. No, she did not want to open that can of worms. No way, no how. Besides, her last jab from Cupid's arrow had left her with an infectious contusion.

Gerald Milfred had been Maya's first love. They met

in freshman English class at Howard, but had maintained a platonic relationship their entire first year there. By the time Maya's mother had fallen ill, she and Gerald's relationship had become more romantic. Gerald was supportive and reassuring during that painful period.

After Maya buried her father, she tried to resume her normal activities, but she had changed, and while Gerald was patient at first, he eventually tired of trying to deal with Maya's anger, mood swings and impenetrable sadness. Ironically, it was at the moment when Maya did, in fact, start healing that she learned of his betrayal.

Walking into Richard Griesler's office, Maya almost screamed. There he was seated at his desk, pen in hand, hacking away at her brief. The few remaining strands of black hair at the front of his balding head shook as he scratched furiously at the pages before him. At this rate it would be ten o'clock tomorrow night before they got out of there. Maya understood that it was just and proper for the partner to revise a brief to make it more in tune with his or her personal style. That she could accept. But what she could not fathom was— even after she had given him, at his request, a draft of the brief every night that week to take home, and all he'd done was come back the next day with one or two comments and a general "Looking good"—why he would wait until the night before the damn thing had to be filed to decide to take it apart, stitch by stitch. What sense did that make?

"Oh, Maya. Glad you're here. Listen, there are a few things I need you to take a look at. In Point Two there's a reference to the properly prepared nineteen ninety-one tax returns, but, remember, we'd decided not to refer to anything other than the years in question, nineteen ninety-two through nineteen ninety-five."

No, she didn't remember that conversation, but Maya knew enough already to keep quiet and let the partner recall what he recalled.

"In Point Four we've got to elaborate on this section here," Richard said, pointing to a paragraph around which he'd drawn a red circle. "Now, even though this is not the crux of our argument, we've got to make this a strong follow-up point, understand?"

Maya nodded.

"Oh, and let's make the conclusion a little more succinct. Okay?"

"Sure, Richard," Maya answered, her voice tacitly measured.

She'd been made to understand by her fellow associates that no matter how well written and unabridged her work was, no partner at the firm could resist what they liked to call "a little fine-tuning." It made them feel like they were actually doing some of the work, when, truth be told, it was the associates who did the research, the writing, the editing and proofing. All the partner really did was put his or her John Hancock on the finished product. When and if a case made it to trial, however, it was the partner who stood before the court arguing that case, questioning witnesses and giving summations. If a case received media attention, it was the partner who got interviewed. Becoming partner, especially at a prestigious law firm, entitled one to captain the ship, so to speak, on every voyage, and it also entitled you to a large part of the loot. So, associates toiled away into the wee hours of the morning, writing and rewriting to satisfy a partner as part of the necessary groundwork, as did Maya with mild irritation.

"Otherwise, we're looking good. Looking good." Richard handed the marked-up, fifty-five-page brief to Maya and swung his chair around toward his telephone. He began dialing as Maya trudged out of his office. As she passed Elizabeth, Richard's secretary, she met her questioning stare with her fingers pointed in the shape of a gun resting against her own temple. Elizabeth got her meaning and dropped her head onto her desk with a thud. With her head down, the top of Elizabeth's thick, heavily sprayed hairdo sticking up like a porcupine was the only thing Maya could see over the ledge of her desk, causing her to laugh inside, in spite of their plight.

"I'll call you soon," Maya said to Elizabeth over her shoulder. She made her way down the hall, into her own office, plopping down at the desk. It was an hour before she had plodded through all Richard's changes. She then spent another fifteen minutes seated in front of Richard's paper-strewn desk as he reviewed the edits.

"Perfect. This is good. This is really good. Okay, so we're all set on the exhibits, right?"

"Yes, they've been copied and collated."

"Okay, good. Have you arranged for the brief to be delivered first thing tomorrow morning and the other copies by noon?"

"Yep. The Affidavit of Service is ready. Elizabeth took care of all the labels and envelopes and the mail-room has two guys on standby to make the deliveries. The ones that are going to Washington will be sent via overnight mail."

"Okay, then. We're done. I'm going to head on out and leave the rest in your capable hands. It shouldn't take you guys much longer." Richard picked up his briefcase and headed for the door, Maya following behind. With a quick goodnight to Elizabeth, he was gone. Maya handed Elizabeth the brief with a menu to the nearest all-night deli. She felt bad for the woman because after working all day, she had to go home and do the whole mommy thing with her two-year-old twins. Elizabeth would tell everyone who would listen that the only reason she was willing to work so much overtime was because she and her husband were saving to buy a house out in some ritzy part of Suffolk County.

"There's no way any of us can do another thing without some food. I'll run out while you make the changes."

"Fab," Elizabeth said, quickly selecting something from the menu and giving it back to Maya. Maya read the menu on the way down to the mailroom. Inside, she found Vic talking on the telephone, his back to her.

"Nah, I'll be here for a while. Maybe I'll see you tomorrow night. . . . Come on, don't be like that. . . . Look—" He stopped midsentence when he realized Maya was there. "Hey, I gotta go. More work just came in the door. Cool. I'll hit you back later." Vic hung up the telephone.

"Sorry, didn't mean to interrupt your call," Maya said wryly. She immediately chided herself, hating the fact that she was annoyed to have found him having a conversation with what was obviously someone he was dealing with.

"That was nothin' . . . it's okay. Is the brief ready for me yet?"

"Elizabeth is making the last set of revisions," Maya answered.

"Now where have I heard that one before?" Vic asked sarcastically.

"No, I'm serious. Richard is gone. So all that's left after that is for me to proof it and then you can do your thing. In the meantime, I'm going to the deli across the street. You want something?" Maya asked as she handed him the menu.

"Yeah, as a matter of fact, I do," Vic said, not looking at the menu at all. His eyes remained on Maya's and for a minute neither of them could or would disengage. All Maya could think was that she didn't need a safe to fall on her head to know that the man was flirting with her. Finally, it was Vic who spoke.

"I'll go with you."

"Fine." Maya turned on her heels. Her mind was tossing around a million thoughts as they went to the twenty-four-hour deli, none of them making much sense. She could feel his eyes on her and prayed that her skirt was straight and not twisted to the left with the split on the side of her leg, the curse of being a woman with a healthy derriere. Even though she chalked it up to exhaustion, she couldn't erase the one persistent thought that this guy was doing something to her.

Neither of them spoke much while they purchased their food and returned to the office. Elizabeth was still working so they set up dinner in the conference room near her desk. From opposite sides of the brightly polished cherry-wood table, Maya and Vic ate in silence, intermittently broken only by the sounds of Vic's complimentary moans of delight.

"So, Maya, what made you decide to become an attorney?" he asked suddenly.

Maya snapped back from the less-than-professional thoughts she'd been entertaining about Vic. Pondering the question at hand, she admired the room around her. The glow from the track lights on either side of the ceiling was romantic, a contradiction to the staunchness reflected by the massive conference table, twenty black leather chairs surrounding it, and the countertop in the corner of the room dressed with legal pads, writing utensils and lawyerly publications. Even the framed black and whites depicting various New York City business districts in the early 1900s screamed stability and affluence. How could Maya explain why she was so driven to gain a place at this table? She doubted someone like Vic would understand her motivation.

"I don't know, really. I was a freshman in college and it just sort of came to me one day. I was like, 'Lawyers make good money; there's always a criminal or

two out there, so why not?' " Her answer, while not entirely truthful, was not completely a lie either.

"Mmm, I thought you were goin' to say somethin'
like, 'My daddy's a lawyer and his daddy was a
lawyer.' That's the story behind most of these attorneys
you see up in here."

"No, my daddy was actually an entrepreneur—
owned one of the largest import/export businesses in
Westchester County," Maya answered quietly.

"Retired?"

"He and my mother died a few years ago."

Maya answered so quietly that Vic wasn't sure he'd
heard her right. He looked at her for a moment and the
look on her face told him that she had, in fact, said
what he'd thought she'd said.

"I'm sorry," he said, feeling truly apologetic for the
loss experienced by this woman he didn't even know.
He understood the veiled look across her face, thinly
covering a sadness that was always present. He too
would wear that look if he allowed himself to feel his
pain at losing his own mother at a young age. Although
the circumstances were very different, he understood.
But to share that amount of hurt and sense of loss with
someone was something he hadn't yet been able to do,
so he looked at Maya sympathetically and said nothing.

"Thanks," Maya answered. "So what about you?
What made you decide to become Office Services supervisor? That is your title, isn't it?"

"Please," Vic said. "You don't honestly think this is
what I want to do with my life?"

"Well, why not? Many a brother would love to have
your job."

"Well, I'm not many a brother. Some of us do have
real goals, you know?"

"Don't get salty with me. Now if I had assumed that
this was just a pit stop for you, you would have thought

I was putting the job down or something. I, of all people, know that some brothers have goals. Some sisters
do too, you know."

"Can't argue that."

"So, what are your goals?" Maya asked earnestly.

"Music."

"Music? What, are you a rapper or something?"

"Why all the brothers got to be rappers?" Vic asked,
annoyed again.

"Sorry," Maya said sheepishly. She could kick herself for playing into a stereotype that she despised
hearing from other people.

"Not that there's anything wrong with the rap game,
if you've got the talent for it. But for your information,
Ms. Attorney, I am a songwriter. I write songs, have
ever since I was in high school. Now I'm studying creative writing at NYU, minoring in music history."

"Get out of here. Are you serious?" Maya checked
Vic's face for any sign that he was gaming her. His face
was choirboy earnest as he swallowed a forkful of
food.

"Straight up. That's why I fly out of here at five
o'clock most days. I've got classes beginnin' at six,
Monday through Thursday."

"So why aren't you in class tonight?" Maya asked,
still somewhat suspicious of him.

" 'Cause a brother's got bills. I skip sometimes
when there's a good amount of overtime to be made."

"Ooh, I'm telling," Maya joked.

"You've got a piece of lettuce on your top lip." Vic
smirked.

Maya laughed sarcastically. "Thanks for pointing
that out."

Vic laughed with her and for a moment there was
that thing again passing between them. And, once
again, Maya pushed it aside as an impossibility.

It was after one o'clock in the morning when

Elizabeth got into the cab waiting for her. They let her take the first car since she had the farthest to travel. Vic lived uptown on 138th Street, so he and Maya decided to share a car. They rode in silence until a couple of blocks before Maya's stop.

"You know, for an attorney, you're pretty cool," Vic said as he leaned against the window.

"If that's a compliment, thank you," Maya responded.

"It is."

Maya got out of the car, closing the door.

"Good night, Vic. See you tomorrow."

"Good night, Ms. Wilkins." He smiled. Then as he watched her walk away, his eyes drawn to her slim ankles, sexy stockinged calves and promising rear, he impulsively leaned out of the window.

"Hey, Maya?"

"Yeah?" she said, turning around at the bottom step of her building.

"I was just thinkin' that, I don't know, maybe you and me could hang out sometime?"

Before her mind had a chance to compute all the implications, Maya responded, "Sure, why not?"

"Cool. I'll see you tomorrow."

"Good night," Maya said again and then headed up the stairs, into the building. She turned around just as the car sped away, baffled at how expertly those worms had managed to get the lid off the can without her knowing it.

Chapter Six

Round One

Maya stopped by the mailroom the next morning to make sure the brief had gone out as scheduled. She was relieved to find Vic nowhere in sight. Satisfied, she went up to her own office where she remained in solitary confinement for most of the day, buried beneath transcripts of witness testimony. By shortly after five o'clock she was spent and ready to go home. She'd made enough headway that day so that she wouldn't have to even think about work over the weekend. As she packed her briefcase and prepared herself to leave, there was a knock at her door.

"Come in," she said, silently praying that it wasn't Richard or one of the other partners with some last-minute, *can you review this over the weekend* crap. It wasn't. However, she wasn't sure if that wouldn't have been such a bad thing, considering it turned out to be Vic cautiously filling the doorway.

"Oh, hi. I brought you a couple of faxes."

"Thank you," Maya said as she continued straightening her desk.

"So, you, uh, headin' out to that big borin' weekend you've got planned, huh?" Vic asked.

"Yep and happy about it."

"Well, I wouldn't want to throw a monkey wrench into your program or anythin' so don't feel like you have to say yes, I mean, unless you want to," Vic stammered.

"Yes to what?" Maya asked.

"Well, my man was supposed to go to the fight with me Saturday night but he has to go out of town for the weekend, so I was thinkin', uh, since you claim to be such a pro, why not let me see what you're workin' with?"

"Excuse me?"

"I mean, you know what I mean . . . what you know about the sport?"

When Maya answered him with a blank stare, his embarrassment multiplied.

"Do you want to go?" he sputtered, his cool, confident demeanor visibly shaken for the moment.

"With you?"

"No, the other guy with the tickets. Of course with me."

Maya laughed then because it was obvious this whole thing was difficult for Vic and she wasn't making it any easier. Not knowing how to respond to her laughter, he walked out of the office, pulling the door behind him.

"I'd love to go," Maya yelled before the door banged shut. She wasn't sure if he'd heard her, and for a moment she was scared that she'd really hurt his feelings. But then the door opened a crack and he stuck his head in.

"I'll pick you up at six o'clock." He smiled, closing the door again.

Maya sank down into her chair, grinning like a Cheshire cat. She'd just made a date with the supervisor of the mailroom at the firm where she'd been working for little more than a month. She'd just broken her number-one, *no romance in the office* rule, her number-two, *no romance until she got her career off the ground* rule, and her number-three, *no romance with guys who make your stomach flutter* rule. They were always the hardest ones to get over. What was she doing? Beaming like it was Christmas morning. Why? Because he was funny as hell, witty, smart and fine. Too fine, as a matter of fact. So now what? A date. One little date. They'd probably both realize they didn't have very much in common anyway and it would all be for naught. Yeah, one date and then back to reality. *Did he say he'd pick me up at six o'clock? In what?* She headed home for the night still wondering.

Maya awoke Saturday morning feeling well rested, but famished. She'd taken a long hot shower the minute she walked in the door the night before, lathering herself with the Avon Raspberry Royale shower gel purchased from one of the secretaries at the office. She wished she could take a bubble bath, but since that was out of the question until she had the bathtub reglazed, she settled on a steamy, fruity shower. The scent reminded her of Jell-O gelatin with berries in it. That had been her dad's favorite dessert, so as soon as she was old enough to use the stove she used to make it all the time for him, always trying to come up with a different combination of Jell-O flavor and fruit. Then they'd sit in her father's study, sharing a big bowl of the stuff while he talked about the places he'd visited, such as Senegal, Great Britain and France.

It was during those times that Maya's own thirst for exploration and travel broadened. Her father could make a trip to the local park sound like a soul-quenching pilgrimage, and Maya soaked it all up like a sponge. By the time she was seventeen years old, she'd traveled both with her parents and with classmates to Paris, London, West Africa and several Caribbean islands. Afterwards, seated in her father's study, they'd compare notes over berry-flavored Jell-O for hours on end. This was one more on the long list of bittersweet memories Maya clung to desperately.

After the shower Maya gave herself a manicure and a pedicure, and let her freshly scrubbed hair air-dry. She dined on leftover grilled chicken and pasta with Alfredo sauce and found herself wondering what Vic was doing at that moment. By ten o'clock she'd brushed her hair out until it was reasonably straight, applied some hot-oil lotion to it and tied it down with a worn scarf. She'd had that raggedy scarf since high school and it looked that way. But it was the only one that fit her head just right and stayed on all night long, no matter how much she tossed and turned. Every time Katrina saw it she would beg Maya to throw it away and get a new one, but Maya refused and even threatened to do bodily harm to anyone who messed with it.

Maya sprung out of bed with a burst of energy and went straight to the window. Flinging it open, she looked down at the already awakened street below and then up toward the sunny sky above. Without having to stare or strain for more than a minute she caught a glimpse of a cinnamon-colored hand waving just before it disappeared behind a thin baby-blue cloud.

By noon Maya had cleaned her apartment from top to bottom. She had to admit that in spite of the tired flat white paint, the mismatched kitchen appliances and the cheap, worn linoleum tiles, the apartment looked a lot better than it had the day she moved in. She'd hung sheer teal curtains on the living room windows, draping a hunter-green scarf across the top and down the sides. The two ferns in front of the window provided an almost tropical feel. She didn't have a sofa, but she'd picked up two recliners from an antiques shop in Tribeca which she'd covered with floral fabric. In between the chairs sat a wicker table, which she'd painted hunter green, holding the most current issues of the essential three Es—*Essence, Ebony* and *Black Enterprise* magazines. On the living room wall facing the armchairs hung one of her mother's paintings. It was a landscape of a sandy beach with the bluest ocean imaginable and different shades of little afro-wearing children standing at the shoreline. Since there were no closets in the apartment besides the one in the bedroom, Maya had found a coatrack at a surplus shop downtown and on it hung her two coats and an umbrella.

The apartment's kitchen wasn't really a kitchen. It was more like a little nook off the living room that contained an olive-green stove and a yellow refrigerator and sink. Two dozen magnets taken from back home covered the refrigerator. They reminded her of childhood, as she had spent many years arranging and rearranging the magnets while her mother cooked. Maya hung colorful pot holders, dish towels and oven mittens on hooks throughout the kitchen but that was about all she could do to spruce up the otherwise drab area.

In the bedroom she covered her queen-size platform bed with the patchwork quilt she, her mother and her grandmother had made one summer when they stayed at the Wilkins' family house in Orangeburg, South Carolina.

Grandma and Grandpa Wilkins' house was a typical Southern home, having once been part of a plantation owned by a replanted English family, the Smythes. By the time Grandpa Wilkins, a physician, bought the place at an auction, it was an eyesore. Having been neglected for many years, it needed a new roof, new plumbing and extensive grounds work, among many other things. Maya's father and grandfather worked on that house for years and by the time the younger Wilkins left the south for his first job as a warehouse manager for a shipping company in Chicago, Illinois, the house was stunning. Maya spent summers and

Christmas vacations there, mesmerized by the high vaulted ceilings, numerous columns and spacious windows. That place became home to her as much as her family's residences, first in Chicago and then Westchester County, New York. When Grandma died and Grandpa's Alzheimer's advanced, they'd reluctantly sold the house. Grandpa didn't want to leave Orangeburg, so they placed him in a nursing home where he lived comfortably until his death a year later. Maya missed that house and all its beauty just as much as she missed her grandparents and her parents.

On a shelf above Maya's bed sat four of her mother's handsewn "Chocolate dolls." Pauline had started making the dolls shortly after Maya was born, inspired by her newborn baby. Before she passed away she'd made hundreds of dolls, selling most of them to the women in her numerous clubs for a cost of next to nothing. Each doll was unique, with its own quilted dress and colorful head wrap, ribbon or scarf. Pauline called them Chocolate dolls because their colorful faces made out of different shades of fabric ranging from off-white to brown to blue/black represented all the colored girls and women she'd ever known in her lifetime. After her mother's death, Maya gave away what remained of Pauline's collection to a couple of black-owned craft shops, a small museum down in Orangeburg and to her mother's dearest friends, keeping four of the most exquisite dolls for herself.

Maya flipped the radio dial to Hot 97 and landed in the middle of Ja Rule and Jennifer Lopez's hit, which happened to be her number-one jam. She turned the volume up to ten and began dancing around her living room as if she were in the middle of the Shadow, a hot nightclub in lower Manhattan. By the time the song ended she'd worked up a sweat, so she decided to just go all out. She stretched for ten minutes, reacquainting herself with muscles she hadn't heard from in months, knowing that she'd probably be full of regret tomorrow. She imagined that she was in aerobics class at the local gym and that she was the bubbly instructor, minus the dental floss masquerading as a leotard. Over the next twenty minutes and five hip-hop songs she shouted out combinations and steps and then, acting as the class, followed the instructions. By the time she turned the radio down it was one-thirty and she was spent. She was sweaty and tired but invigorated at the same time. She promised herself that she would try to work out like this three or four times a week, no matter what.

Left with four and a half hours before the big date, she wasn't sure what to do next to keep from thinking about it. She tried curling up in one of the recliners with a paperback mystery she'd been reading a while back but had never finished. After struggling through the first three pages she gave up, unable to focus.

Thinking about how long it had been since she'd had so much free time on her hands, she decided to fish out her special stationery—the eggshell bond paper with the flecks of brown throughout—and write her college friends, Shelly and Bonnie, each a quick note. Those quick notes turned into two-page letters, filled with the 411 on the new job, the progress on the apartment and the Big Apple.

Upon graduation, Shelly had begged Maya to apply for a position at her father's law firm in California, but Maya had declined. She couldn't see herself on the West Coast and she was scared to death of earthquakes. Besides, she thought that with her parents buried here in New York, she would feel like she had abandoned them somehow.

In her childhood fantasies, she had always imagined herself working in Manhattan, either down on Wall Street or elsewhere. Shelly was a California girl and, similarly, it had never occurred to her to live or work elsewhere. Shelly's father was a big-time entertainment lawyer out there, his practice providing legal services to many well-known film, television and recording artists. While Maya respected Mr. Kolatch's work, she wanted to serve in a legal capacity which would be more meaningful to her.

She caught Shelly up on the routine of her days at Madison Pritchard, inquired about Shelly's family and requested a prompt update on any new love interests on which Shelly may have set her sights.

In her letter to Bonnie, Maya inquired about the living conditions in Bolivia, expressing concern for Bonnie's safety. She had heard that between the government's antidrug efforts and the deep-seated poverty there, corruption was rampant. She told Bonnie how much she admired her selflessness and assured her that she prayed for her daily.

She reminded both of them of their promise that they'd all get together sometime in the coming summer or as soon thereafter as their schedules permitted. The telephone rang as she signed off with hugs and kisses and stuck a couple of stamps on each envelope.

"Hello?"

"Hello, Maya darling. It's Betty Armstrong. How are you, dear?"

"Mrs. Armstrong? I'm great. How are you? How's that hip?"

Mrs. Armstrong had been one of her mother's oldest and dearest friends, and it was Mrs. Armstrong who had stepped in as surrogate mother after Pauline's death. She still sent Maya birthday and Christmas presents, called every so often and regularly visited the cemetery where the Wilkinses were buried.

"Well, child, you know I don't like complaining. When you reach your golden years as I have, you certainly don't heal as quickly. But it's coming along, I suppose," Mrs. Armstrong said, rubbing her left hip, still a sore reminder of the fall she'd taken climbing out of her swimming pool this past summer.

"That's good. Did you get the book I sent you?" Maya asked as she filled a glass with water from the pitcher she kept in the refrigerator.

"Yes, sugar. I got it one day last week. You were right—it is one of the better productions from the Harlem Renaissance period. I'm so enjoying it. Thank you again, dear."

"Oh, you're welcome. I'm glad you like it."

"So tell me, how's city life treating you?" Mrs. Armstrong asked.

Maya took a sip of water before responding. Should she tell her how lonely she'd been or how scared she was of not doing a good enough job at the firm? Mrs. Armstrong was a lot like her mother had been, in some respects. She took on other people's problems as her own and was always making sure everyone she loved was doing okay. Not having any children of her own, Mrs. Armstrong fussed over her nieces, nephews and Maya, too. The last thing Maya wanted to do was worry her.

"Everything's going pretty well, Mrs. Armstrong. I'm crazy busy at work. You wouldn't believe the hours first-year associates like me have to keep just to stay on top of things. But I'm managing and I'm truly enjoying the work. And then trying to fix up this place is like a second full-time job," Maya said, waving her hand around the kitchen.

"Uh-huh," Mrs. Armstrong said skeptically. "Well, I hope you're not spending all your time working. You know, if you died tomorrow, them folks would get along just fine without you. You've got to take some time to enjoy your life. You're a young, pretty girl. Don't waste this time, sweetheart. You need to find yourself a beau and make a little love. It'll keep you young."

Maya laughed. "Mrs. A, you are too much."

"It's the truth. You do what I say now. Hear?"

"Yes, ma'am," Maya answered. She thanked Mrs. Armstrong for calling and promised for the umpteenth time that'd she come up to Tarrytown for a visit soon. She felt a little guilty that she hadn't seen Mrs. Armstrong in person in more than two years, but she just couldn't bring herself to visit the old neighborhood. Mrs. Armstrong lived half a block from the former Wilkins home and Maya didn't want to see it or its new owners. She thought it would be too painful. Still, she knew that spending a little face-to-face time with her would probably be worth it.

"That woman is still just as crazy as ever." Maya laughed.

At two-thirty, she felt like she needed to take a nap, but when she lay down she couldn't close her eyes no matter how hard she tried. She tossed and turned for a while, thinking about work, about her parents, about life and, against her will, about Vic. At three-thirty the telephone rang and, tired of tossing and turning, she was grateful for the distraction.

"Hello," Maya answered, scooting backward on the bed until her shoulders rested comfortably against the wall.

"Hey, chick, what's going on?" Katrina sang out. There was loud music playing in the background and Maya could barely hear her.

"Katrina? Is that you? I can't hear you," Maya yelled.

"Hold on a minute," Katrina yelled back. Maya could hear the sound of a door slamming and then the music became a quieter background noise.

"Better?"

"Yeah. Don't tell me you're having a party at this time of day?"

"Sort of. Some of Dominic's friends are here drinking beer and making too much damn noise. You know it's that dreaded time of the year when Dominic eats, sleeps and breathes football." Katrina huffed.

"Well, why isn't he entertaining in his own apartment?"

"Because his apartment, like yours, is a dump, and he claims the games look better on my wide-screen, high-definition television. Besides, they're actually an all right bunch, when they're not being loud and obnoxious."

Maya laughed. "If you say so."

"Anyway, girl, I called to tell you something juicy!"

"What?" Maya squealed as she folded her legs beneath her, preparing herself for a good story. Whenever Katrina said she had something juicy to tell, you could bet your last buck that it would be good. Katrina was not a gossiper—at least, not an ordinary, run-of-the-mill, talk-about-any-ole-thing type of gossiper. She knew how to separate the regular dirt from the good and dirty dirt and she was almost always accurate.

"Guess who I saw last night?"

"Who?" Maya asked, hardly able to stand the suspense.

"Well," Katrina said dramatically, knowing she had Maya hooked now, "Dominic and I went to the opening of this new club in Maryland last night called the Jook Joint. I was all set for some bamma folks listening to some whack music and thinking this was the place to be, but it was actually bumping. So we're in there, what, an hour or so, and out of nowhere this girl sashays past our table like she was on somebody's runway. Homegirl was about four-eleven and that's counting the Space Mountain clogs she was wearing. Beyond retro."

"Eew," Maya said.

"Eew is right. She had to be at least a size twenty-two, all booty, and had the nerve to be wearing this little tube top, not quite a dress."

"Yuck."

"Double yuck. So now you know I couldn't help but check her out, right? Her hair, what little she had, was heavily gelled down all over her head. Girlfriend was tore up. And I won't even tell you about the face. Mmm, mmm, mmm. But the best part is this—guess who she was with up in there?"

"Who?" Maya screamed, unable to hold back any longer.

"Gerald."

Maya didn't answer. The smile on her face froze and she felt the hairs stand up on her arms and at the nape of her neck. Her heart beat like a conga drum for a few seconds before she found her voice.

"Gerald?"

"Yes, girl, Gerald."

"Gerald who?"

"Gerald-Gerald. Your Gerald. Gerald Milfred."

"He's not my Gerald," Maya said quickly.

"He used to be your Gerald," Katrina reminded.

"Why are you telling me this?" Maya snapped.

"Because, girl, I thought you'd want to know that the man who you thought you were going to marry but had to dump because he was about as dependable as a press and curl in the summertime was truly so pathetic an individual that he was now dating anything with two legs and a—"

"Katrina, please. Do you always have to be so crass?" Maya didn't even try to keep the exasperation out of her voice.

"Please what, girl? I'm trying to tell you that your ex is scraping the bottom of the barrel where he belongs. I would think that would make you smile a little bit."

"I don't care what Gerald does, and I certainly don't want to know about it. So in the future, keep all references to him to yourself, okay?"

"Well, excuse me." Katrina sighed, her previous excitement completely deflated by Maya's response. "I'm sorry. I guess you're not as over him as you claim to be, huh?"

"Yes, I most certainly am over him. That's precisely why I don't want to talk about him."

Maya raised an arm above her head and pulled one of her mother's dolls from its perch. She fingered the yarn hair and blinked until her eyes were no longer hazy.

"So, whatcha got going on this weekend?" Katrina asked, deliberately changing the topic of the conversation.

She knew that despite what Maya said, Gerald was like that place in your finger the day after you'd removed a splinter from it: a soreness that just wouldn't go away.

If Maya had ever given her the chance, Katrina would have loved to share her own anger at the way Gerald had treated Maya. But Maya never wanted to discuss him or the situation. It had been more than a year since the engagement-party blowout, and Katrina had never really gotten the whole story. All she knew was what Maya had told her after everyone left the party. Gerald could never give her what she needed, he was incapable of loving her the way she wanted to be loved and she'd rather roller-blade through hell than be hitched to the man. After that, the subject was closed.

On her own, however, Katrina did a little investigating and found out that there had been a physical altercation of some sort. This alone made Katrina want to go and box Gerald around a bit. She also discovered that Gerald had made some disparaging comments about Maya's father, which added fuel to Katrina's burning urge to punch his lights out. Anyone and everyone who knew Maya knew how sensitive she was about her father.

What else went on between Maya and Gerald Katrina never knew. Maya made her swear that she'd drop the subject and never confront Gerald about it, which Katrina did for two reasons: one, because Maya was her best girlfriend in the whole world, and two, because Katrina had walked that road a time or two herself. So she shut her mouth, canceled the floral arrangements and the band and dropped the whole thing.

"Nothing much." Maya tried to regain her cool. She was sorry she'd snapped at Katrina but sometimes the girl acted like she had stir-fry for brains. She, of all people, should know that Gerald was not a subject Maya wanted to discuss.

"So I see you're not working this weekend. That's a plus. Got plans?"

"I was actually taking a nap when you called," Maya lied.

"A nap? What, did you have a late night? Oooh, give me the dirt."

"Nope, not at all. I came home early and stayed here."

"Alone?"

"Yes, alone."

"So why are you taking a nap in the middle of the damn day?" Katrina asked.

Now it was her turn to be annoyed. Maya hesitated for a moment more, trying to think of a way to switch gears. She wasn't sure she wanted to tell Katrina about her date with Vic. Katrina was so unpredictable, Maya wasn't sure how she'd react. She might make more out of it than it really was since she was always trying to get her hooked up with somebody. Or she might tell her that it was a bad idea, and half of Maya was sure that she wanted to be talked out of this. Finally, she took a deep breath and blurted the truth.

"I've got a date tonight with a guy from work."

"Hmm, sounds interesting. Tell me more."

Maya spent the next few minutes telling her about Vic. She talked fast, not leaving anything out, and when she was finished she waited patiently for the proverbial shoe to drop.

"Are you sure this is a good idea?"

"No, Katrina, I'm not sure. All I know is that he's a nice guy, and he asked me out. So why not go?"

"There's a million reasons why you shouldn't go but then there are a million reasons why you should, starting with the fact that you're sprung."

"Sprung?"

"Did I stutter? Yes, sprung. Open, turned out, you know the word."

"I am not sprung. What gives you the idea that I'm sprung? All I said was that he's a nice guy," Maya replied indignantly.

"No, that's not all you said. What you said was that he's funny, intelligent, witty and gorgeous."

"Damned gorgeous," Maya corrected, giggling.

"Damned gorgeous," Katrina repeated. "Look, I say go. Have a good time and worry about the consequences later."

"You think?"

"I think. Now let me get back to these Neanderthals in my living room before they break something. You'd better call me the minute you get home . . . unless you're otherwise engaged. Love you."

"Love you, too, Kat." Maya hung up and leaned back against the wall, thinking. Katrina was right. She should just go and have a good time and worry about silly little things like meaning and implications and consequences later.

The alarm clock on the nightstand grabbed Maya's attention. It was already going on four-thirty and she hadn't decided on what she was going to wear. She hopped out of bed and sifted through her closet. Her options were limited, to say the least, her wardrobe consisting only of work clothes and the sweat suit/holey jeans ensembles she'd worn throughout her college years. She finally settled on a pair of jeans that were only slightly worn, had no holes and only a few faded spots.

Shoes were next. She dug around the mountain of shoes, sandals, sneakers and other footwear at the bottom of the closet until she found a pair of black boots. She had to rummage through the nightstand to find a can with just enough black shoe polish left in it to properly cover the scuffs. She buffed the well-worn boots until they shone and then, satisfied with her work, began looking through her dresser for a top. It took a while, but she finally decided on a multicolored, button-up shirt which wouldn't need ironing.

By the time she'd coordinated her entire outfit it was pushing five-thirty. She hopped into the shower, brushed her teeth, washed her face. She applied gingerbread lotion to every reachable part of her body and then, using the hot curlers, styled her hair into a cute bob. A minimal amount of fawn eye shadow and a light cocoa lip gloss were enough because, date or no date, the weekend was take-a-break-from-makeup time.

When the intercom rang, Maya had just slipped into her jeans and top and was lacing up her boots. With a bit of admiration she noticed that it was six o'clock on the dot. Okay, two points for the brother. She pushed the speaker button and let him know she'd be right down.

Maya came out of the building and almost tripped down the steps, the door swinging shut behind her and smacking her backside. Vic stood in front of a Kawasaki 1100, looking like a 3-D advertisement out of *Black Men* magazine. No lie, she wanted to pin him up on her wall like when she was a kid and would tear out the centerfold photos from *Right On*. He was wearing blue jeans that sort of hung down low enough to tell you that he was from around the way but not so low that they looked like they would fall off any minute. He also had on a brown leather jacket and held a helmet tucked underneath his arm. There was another helmet hanging from the back of the seat.

With a baseball cap cocked to the side of his head and a pair of rather large, brown Timberland boots on his feet, Vic's presence made Maya's knees tremble. His stance had a sort of power in it that made Maya feel confident in his ability to take care of her and show her a good evening. Hoping he couldn't see her legs shaking as much as she could feel them, she walked down the short flight of stairs and gave him her best *in no way do you faze me* smile.

"Whassup?" he asked.

"Aren't we prompt?"

"Well, I know how you women hate to be kept waitin'." Vic smiled back. He extended the helmet beneath his arm to her and, as she took it, asked, "You ever rode before?"

"Nope."

"Are you game?"

"Sure, on one condition."

"Name it?"

"No Evil Knievel crap."

"Don't worry, I got you." Vic helped her tighten her helmet and settle comfortably on the bike. He sat down in front of her and started the engine. Just as he shoved the kickstand back with his heel, he yelled over his shoulder, "Hold on to me tight now. I wouldn't want to lose you."

And, always having been an obedient girl, she wrapped both arms around him and did as she was told.

"Mmm, this is good," she said through a mouthful of honey-glazed baby-back spareribs. They were seated across from one another at the Hut, located uptown in Manhattan. It was a small, discreet little diner-type restaurant with dim lights hung from a low ceiling and tiny tables for two crowded together so that any intimacy was one shared by the entire room. A jukebox played some Ruth Brown, B.B. King–kind of blues, where women moaned about no-good men and men swooned over out-of-reach starlets.

It was a cheaply crafted place by any measure, yet it was very rich in ambience. It was the kind of place that would keep your secrets tucked inside its walls, and no matter how infrequent your visits, welcome you like a great-aunt down South.

"Yeah, they get busy in here," he answered.

Vic watched Maya eat, mesmerized. He liked the way she chewed, carefully, not allowing her mouth to open, even slightly, to reveal its contents. Maya watched him as well, amused by the way he licked his thumbs every so often and grunted in approval. Even the way he chewed his food was hardy, giving him this Herculean air beneath a gentle exterior. Maya was moved by the man, so much so that she found herself giggling and flirting like a pubescent schoolgirl. What's more, for once she didn't really care if he knew how attracted she was to him. She was enjoying herself, remembering how good it felt to let a man be in charge of her for a little while.

"This was nice. I had a really good time," Maya said as they stood in front of her building, Vic leaning on his bike and she standing in front of him. The fight had actually ended a little early, with the champ retaining the belt in a fourth-round technical knockout. Vic had suggested that they do something else but Maya declined, having become too aware of her strong attraction to Vic and thinking it best to call it a night.

"Me, too," Vic answered shyly. They smiled at each other for a few moments, until the cool night air prompted Maya to pull her jacket in a little bit closer.

"You'd better get inside."

"Yeah," Maya agreed.

"Well, goodnight, Vic," she said, turning away. In a moment of daring she turned back to him, leaned close and kissed him lightly on the cheek.

"I had a really nice time," she said again and disappeared inside the building before Vic had a chance to respond.

He watched the door as it closed slowly in front of him and continued standing there for a few minutes more. When he saw a light go on in one of the windows on the fifth floor, he turned away. Jumping on his bike, he let the good vibe that had been coursing through him all evening propel him home.

Chapter Seven

Kansas City Blues

"Hey, Maya, I heard you got the Haynes case," Bob said, sticking his head into Maya's office.

Bob Dallas was one of the junior partners at Madison Pritchard. He was one of the most laid-back attorneys Maya had ever met, a stark contrast to most of the other partners there.

"Yep," she answered, looking up from the files she'd been reviewing.

"This should be a relatively simple one. Peter says all we need to do is play a little ball and get our client to come out with a slap, maybe two, on his wrists," Bob said as he stepped a few feet into Maya's office.

He surveyed the photographs on her credenza, and picked up the one of Maya and Katrina, taken the previous month at Katrina's birthday party. Her parents had thrown her a surprise party at their summer home in the Hamptons, and it had been a blast. In the picture, the two women were seated on the dining room table, and with forks serving as microphones, they tried to outsing CeCe Winans and Whitney Houston on their duet, "Count on Me." Katrina's mother, Mrs. Brewster,

had snapped the photograph as the rest of the partygo-
ers clamored for an encore.

"Is this your sister?" he asked with interest.

"No, just a dear friend," Maya answered. The fact
that the two women resembled each other about as
much as night and day seemed lost on Bob.

"Oh. Nice picture." He returned the frame to its
place on the shelf and continued. "Well, anyway . . .
this case should be a piece of cake for you."

"I hope so. The government has already hit us with a
document production request, which I understand
Roger had been trying to get shortened. I'm heading
up to Boston next week to meet Mr. Haynes and to go
through the files. Hopefully, I'll get things organized in
one trip."

"Good luck. If you need any help, I'm around," Bob
said.

"Thanks, Bob," Maya answered to his retreating
form. She was pleased by his show of support and
looked forward to the opportunity to work directly
with him. Bob Dallas had a reputation for being an
easygoing yet highly astute guy. He was also known
for his willingness to pitch in and work equally as hard
as, if not harder than, the associates assigned to his
cases. He believed that if one person on the team had to
work around the clock, then so should the rest of the
team. His behavior differed from many of the other
partners, who dumped the brunt of their cases on the
associates as they were often too busy politicking.

Maya returned to the files in front of her. She'd been
given this case yesterday when Roger Perkins, the
third-year associate who'd previously been assigned to
it, announced he was leaving the firm. During the bi-
monthly litigation luncheon, Roger had announced his
decision to return to his hometown of Overland Park,
Kansas, and open his own law practice there. Roger

was a quiet man who spoke in a slow, deliberate manner, reminiscent of summer days spent on wraparound
porches, waving to passersby on a dirt road. He said
he'd been away from the Midwest for too long, ten
years to be exact, and that the big city was not where
he wanted to spend the rest of his days.

Roger's eyes had shifted uneasily around the room
as he'd made his unexpected announcement yesterday,
never settling on any one face for more than a moment.
His abrupt resignation brought a solemn mood into the
room. Oddly enough, Peter Fusco, a senior partner,
took center floor to wish Roger well on behalf of the
entire firm and to thank him for his years of service. It
was as if while the other partners appeared shocked by
Roger's announcement, Peter already knew about it.
Since Peter Fusco was not a supervising partner, nor
did he and Roger appear to share any special relationship other than working the Haynes case together, it
was strange that Roger would have confided in him
alone.

Peter's impromptu speech had been followed by a
not-so-discreet exchange of querying looks around the
room, especially amongst the other partners in atten-
dance. Even Maya, who'd not had much dealings with
Roger in the time she'd been with the firm, felt there
was something a little off-key about the situation. He
was planning to make a quick exit, giving only the
standard two weeks' notice. He and Maya arranged to
meet later in the day to go over the case; thus Maya had
spent the latter part of the day before and most of the
morning going over the files delivered to her by the
records department at Roger's request.

At first glance, the case seemed pretty straightforward to her. The client, Allen Haynes of Wexton &
Haynes Securities Trusts, Inc., had not yet been indicted,
but it was rumored that the government was considering charges of securities fraud, insider trading and crim-

inal misconduct. Wexton & Haynes was a retail brokerage house. The stocks were sold by the company primarily to domestic clients, although they did have a small foreign market. Allen Haynes had founded the company six years earlier with the father of a colleague from business school, Kevin Wexton. Kevin Wexton, a fifty-eight-year-old man, was semiretired and had left the day-to-day operations of the company in the hands of Haynes.

The government's case had originated with a tip received by the Securities and Exchange Commission from an as yet to be named source, who reported that Haynes had allegedly been selling the stocks short. This shorting of stocks devalued the securities, leaving the company's unwitting clients holding stock certificates to securities worth half of what they had paid for them. Wexton & Haynes had made a killing while its clients suffered tremendous losses.

When the government first began its probe earlier that year, they contacted Kevin Wexton. While Wexton firmly defended both the company and Haynes, and categorically denied any wrongdoing, he did begin to resume a more active position in the company. As of June of this year, the company instituted a new policy which required both Wexton's and Haynes's signatures on every transaction. Thus, for the past year there were no questionable transactions made. However, for the time between January, 1998, through May, 2000, Haynes had put the company in serious jeopardy—another example of a person having to watch his back, even amongst his friends.

It was almost a sure bet that some sort of indictment would be handed down in the near future, which was why the firm had advised Haynes to cooperate as fully as possible with the government's investigation. In this way, Haynes could hope to reach some sort of plea agreement. It was Maya's job to get the case files in order, oversee the production of documents to the government and prepare the employees to provide testimony. With a mountain of work already on her desk, Maya hoped against hope that this case turned out to be as straightforward as everyone seemed to think.

The muscles in Maya's neck ached and she attempted to rub away some of the tenseness. She closed her eyes and shook her head vigorously, trying to will away the memories causing her to become so tense. She couldn't let all that resurface again, wouldn't let it affect her thinking or her work. The circumstances of this case were eerily familiar, reminiscent of the worst time in her life.

Five deep breaths. Despite her best efforts, the memories she'd so craftily kept at bay flooded in, present and past colliding in undulating motion until she felt seasick. Five more deep breaths. She was sweating, her blouse sticking to her back, her bangs pasted to her forehead. Ten deep breaths. The anxiety began to lift.

"Shhh," she whispered. "Shhh." Finally, she began to regain her composure. Leaning back into her chair, she let go and felt the tension seep from her pores, her thumping heartbeat slowing.

"You've got this. You can handle this," she told herself. When she felt herself in control again, she continued poring through the files.

When Roger arrived in Maya's office to go over the case, he handed her a relatively empty manila file.

"What's this?" Maya asked, scanning the folder from cover to cover in less than ten seconds.

"My working file," Roger replied slowly.

"This is it?" Maya had expected him to come with a carton or two of notes. This was a big case, one that should have a paper trail a mile long, and he'd been working on it since its inception.

"Well, most of the notes I'd taken have been typed up and included in the files," Roger answered, and again Maya got a unsettling feeling that something was not quite kosher about Roger.

"Roger, I've gone over everything the file room has on the shelves on this case and it seems like things are incomplete. I mean, we've had this case for quite some time. . . . I would have expected more . . . corporate tax returns, trading records—"

"Well, that's all I have. Look, Peter expects that we'll enter a plea with the government in the near future. All you'll really have to do for now is stay on top of Haynes's people to organize whatever documents they have, bearing in mind that some of the records have been destroyed."

"Destroyed how?" Maya asked.

"Uh, Wexton & Haynes have changed office space twice in the past three years and things were lost or thrown out accidentally during the moves. So anyway, what they have, they'll turn over to the government. What they don't have and what can't be re-created is just lost."

"Hmm," Maya said, more to herself than to Roger, whose discomfort seemed to increase with the passing of each second. While Maya didn't like making him feel uneasy, she was perplexed by the carelessness with which the case was being handled.

"When the time comes, you'll help draft the settlement papers, the presentencing report, etc. . . . Just keep it simple and defer to Peter Fusco. You, of course, are angling for no jail time and for Haynes to keep his license, but I doubt you'll get both." Roger stood up to leave.

"Well, Roger, thanks for your time. I'm sure I'll have more questions. Will you be reachable once you leave?"

"Uh, well, not really . . . not right away. I'm going to take some time off for a while, travel a little. I'm sure you won't need anything from me." Roger turned the door handle and stepped out into the hallway. He turned and said, "Good luck, Maya." His tone was as somber as an undertaker.

Maya was dumbfounded as she tried to process the whole conversation. The hairs on the back of her neck were raised like a Doberman's ears, and since that only happened when intuition told her she'd just stepped in something foul, she dared sneak a peek at her shoes.

Heading home for the evening, Maya shared an elevator down with Peter Fusco.

"So, Maya, did Roger bring you up to speed on the Haynes case?" he asked.

"Somewhat. Strangely, it doesn't appear that he completed much due diligence on the case. I'm going to have to put in a lot of time organizing files and pulling together documents to make some sense of things."

"Well, it's really a no-brainer. Besides, the client doesn't have a lot of money, so we don't want to spend too many billable hours on this." Fusco, standing a full 6'3", smiled down at Maya. The iciness of his steel-blue eyes caused goose bumps to spring up along her arms.

"I see. Well, I'll, uh . . . I'll do the best I can to get it done in as little time as possible," she stammered.

"Yes, yes. I'm sorry, but this isn't one of those cases where you'll make a name for yourself. I know that's important to you."

"Excuse me?" Maya asked.

"Oh, we partners hear things, too. It seems you've developed a reputation as being a bit of a dogmatist. I guess that's youth." He chuckled. "Well, anyway, just keep your work to the bare bones and leave the rest to me. As I said, you don't need to try so hard on this one. I promise, no one's paying attention anyway." He laughed again. "Have a nice weekend, sweetheart." He stepped off the elevator behind Maya, briskly pushed

past her and proceeded through the lobby without
looking back.

She never responded, not that he'd notice anyway.
Several elevators opened and closed, other tenants brushing past her, anxious to get on with their evenings, before Maya could move. Besides the fact that Peter's
condescending attitude angered her, it was crystal clear
that she had just been put on a leash like a disobedient
dog.

Chapter Eight

Round Two

Maya pumped the pedals hard on the stationary bike, keeping her speed above sixty mph. She'd set the bike to the rough-terrain course, the resistance at a moderate level, and her muscles were straining to live up to the challenge. She had been at it for almost an hour and she gave no appearance that she'd be stopping soon. Vic had long since left the bike at her side and was across the gym lifting weights.

He could easily tell there was something wrong with Maya from the vigorous way she'd been working out that morning. He'd asked her if there was something she wanted to talk about, but she'd said no. Not knowing her well enough to push, he decided to give her a little space and hoped that her mood would change.

Meanwhile, Maya's head raced as she pedaled, sweat dripping from her forehead and armpits and settling between her breasts. She wanted to talk to someone about what had happened the day before at work but she didn't know who she should talk to. She didn't trust any of her fellow attorneys enough to talk to them, even though they often confided in her about work-related problems. She figured if she called

Katrina, she'd just tell her to stop being paranoid. Ted Brody's comments about "them" not being able to follow instructions still rang in her head, although she'd never mentioned it to Katrina. The latter would probably tell her that she'd misconstrued what he was saying. Katrina was always encouraging her to lighten up on the "black/white" issue. And part of Maya did want to apply some other meaning to Brody's words. But now, with Peter Fusco all but telling her to just play dumb and not ask any questions, how could she ignore the slights? If these partners really thought they'd hired some *yes, master, right away, sir* girl, they were mistaken. She just needed to figure out a way to make them respect her. She needed to talk to someone objective about the situation, but again, the list was very short.

Then there was Vic. He seemed genuinely interested in knowing what was bothering her but she'd told him she didn't want to talk about it. It wasn't that she didn't feel comfortable talking to him, because she did. Very much so. And she trusted that he wouldn't spread her business all over the office. As far as she could tell, he hadn't told anyone they were seeing each other. True, this was only the fourth date—if you could call spending a morning working out at the gym a date. Still, somehow she trusted that he would be discreet about anything she told him. The problem was, she wasn't sure what his response would be to the situation and she may not want to hear what he had to say. It was obvious he kept a certain distance from the attorneys at the job. He didn't socialize with any of them, other than brief discussions about sports. Maya was uncertain if it was the race thing or if it was because he worked in the mailroom. In any event, he didn't seem interested in anything about the attorneys other than what was required of him workwise. On top of all that, she was leery of dumping her problems on a guy she was just starting to get to know. The last thing any guy would want was to deal with somebody who had a lot of issues.

Maya got off the bike and pulled her towel from the handlebars. She was determined to push it all aside for now and enjoy her time with Vic. She was certain that by now her sour mood had him wondering what he'd let himself in for. Vic was lying on his back on a workbench, lifting hundred-pound weights. Maya stood facing the top of his head and waited. His forehead was covered with sweat and two tiny veins were visible on the left side of his head. When he finally opened his eyes, she laughed.

"What a weakling. Is that all you've got?" she joked.

Vic huffed as he returned the weights to the resting bars. "Woman, please, I did about two hundred repetitions. Feel this," he said, curving his arm and making his hand into a fist. He pointed to his biceps. "That's iron, girl!"

Maya squeezed his muscled bulge and giggled. "That's all right for a beginner. But see that?" she said, motioning to a hulking, ponytail-wearing guy who walked by in a tank top and shorts so tight, his bulging muscles threatened to tear them to shreds. "Now that's what I'm talking about. That's the kind of guy that gets me going!"

She exploded with laughter as she watched Vic look from her to the guy and back to her with the face of an abandoned puppy. When he realized she was joking with him, he grabbed her in a bear hug and squeezed until she apologized. Being that close to him, inhaling his Ivory soap–scented sweat made Maya feel high and giddy, like she'd had a couple of margaritas. The brother definitely had an appeal that she could bottle and sell for considerable profit.

By now neither one of them were in the mood to continue working out, so they hit their respective changing rooms and a short time later met outside the gym. The remainder of the day was spent window-shopping, followed by lunch at the Olive Garden on Broadway. Vic was appreciative for the change in Maya's mood, glad to know that it was nothing he'd done or said to upset her.

They parted as dusk fell, Vic heading for a meeting at a studio with a track producer interested in working with him, and Maya off to continue trial preparations for the coming Monday. She watched as Vic disappeared into the crowded Times Square scene. Knowing she was starting to like him a lot more than she cared to, Maya made a decision to put a little space between them. Hard as that might prove to be, she was just not looking for a relationship. Next chance she got she'd have to get some advice on how to love 'em and leave 'em from her girl Katrina, aka the relationship guru.

Chapter Nine

Round Three—Knock Out

"Want a soda?" Maya called with her head stuck in the refrigerator.

Vic was in her living room, lying comfortably on the hardwood floor. It had been a couple of weeks since their last date. Surprisingly, it was Maya who had suggested they hook up. Despite her decision to slow things down, she'd found herself missing his company.

"Yeah, thanks."

Maya returned from the kitchen with two glasses of Pepsi and two large bags of potato chips.

"Hot or plain?" she asked as she handed Vic a glass.

"Which one do you like?" he asked.

"Both."

"Okay, so I'll have both."

Maya joined Vic on the floor. "Thanks again for helping me pick this out," Maya said, indicating the stereo system Vic was fiddling with. They'd met after work two nights ago and he'd gone with her to the Wiz where she bought the equipment. Vic tried to talk her into getting a television, calling her strange for not having at least one in her home, but she decided against the purchase for now. As she explained, television had never been a constant activity in her life. She and her parents had always found other ways to amuse themselves.

"No problem. So what do you wanna hear?" He spread out a few CDs he'd taken out of his knapsack on the floor between them. Maya sifted through Vic's array, which consisted of Tupac's latest, DMX, Jay-Z, the Roots, Lauryn Hill and Deborah Cox, among others.

"I can't believe these people are still releasing Tupac albums. I mean, they act like the man ain't dead and buried," Maya said, scanning the track listing on the back of the disc.

"Maybe he's not. You've heard the rumors," Vic said.

"Yeah, okay. I suppose he's living with Elvis down in Memphis, huh?"

"Nah, but you've got to realize, Tupac was a lyrical genius."

Maya continued going through the pile, setting aside those albums she wanted to listen to.

"I gotta confess, I'm not really into rap too much. I mean, I like the party stuff that people like Will Smith and Busta Rhymes put out. But all that heavy, dealing-crack-in-the-hood, baby-mother, drive-by-shooting crap . . . I just don't see the point behind it," Maya commented.

"People write about what they know. A lot of these guys are living that lifestyle, be it wrong or be it right. And they gotta write about it, sing about it 'cause they don't know about nothin' else," Vic said passionately.

Music had been the one constant in Vic's life. Growing up on the streets of Harlem, Vic was a product of the hip-hop generation. As a teen, he hungrily devoured the music put out by rap artists. It was his music teacher in high school, Mr. Dunham, who got him to open up to other types of musical expression. Now, while his tastes ranged from hip-hop and rock to neosoul and alternative, his admiration for artists who—like Tupac—were poets remained unchanged.

"That's all fine, but I refuse to believe that every rapper that rhymes about that hard-knock ghetto life is really living that way. I mean, I know there are a lot of people down and out, struggling to survive, but do you honestly believe that all these rappers are telling the truth?" Maya countered with equal intensity.

"No, no, I don't. I think you can separate the ones comin' from the heart from the fakers. Like Biggie—he was legitimate. Now, true enough, some of these guys are just out here tryin' to make a buck, sayin' whatever they have to say to do that."

"But why do so many of them have to write about all this depressing stuff? It makes outsiders think that's all there is to black folks—violence, sex and whatnot. My dad hated rap music. He said it was causing the death of poetry," Maya said.

"Tell me about your parents." Vic asked suddenly. He didn't notice Maya bristle at his question.

"What about them?" she responded.

"Anythin' . . . what were they like? Were they strict? You strike me as the type of girl who was always gettin' into stuff . . . givin' your parents wrinkles."

"Not hardly. I was a good kid. My mother never had so much as a worry line." Maya was silent for a moment, painting a mental canvas of her mother. "She was a natural beauty—her skin was the color of roasted chestnuts and she never wore makeup, just kinda glowed."

"Hmm, that's a nice picture," Vic said. "Who do you look like more?"

Maya's mind searched its archives for a picture of her parents and strangely the first one that came to mind was of the three of them in a private room at Westchester

County Hospital a few days before her mother died. Pauline was resting comfortably, the combination of painkillers temporarily freeing her body from the overwhelming agony she'd experienced just hours before at home. She was talking to Maya in a soft voice, not wishing to disturb her husband, who had fallen asleep in the armchair next to her bed. The room was quiet except for the occasional beep of the heart monitor connected to Pauline's chest. The walls were painted a sunny yellow in an effort, Maya assumed, to brighten the room.

But even coupled with the bright floral curtains and painting of smiling children at the circus, the room could not mask the illness and death which hung in the air all the time. The nurses' station could be seen through a large window near the foot of the bed and Maya glanced up to see that Nurse Mitchell, her personal favorite, was on duty tonight. Maya knew that Nurse Mitchell would come in soon to check her mother's vitals. She would examine the three bags of liquid—two clear and the other yellowish-colored, which hung from a pole and were fed intravenously into Pauline's arm—while chatting exuberantly with Maya.

"You need to get your daddy home. He's worn-out," Pauline said.

"I know, Mom, but you know him . . . he wouldn't budge from that chair if his pants were on fire." Maya smiled.

"Oooh, that stubborn old man." Pauline laughed, her eyes bright, the laughter filtering its way down from her eyes into her cheeks and finally her lips. Maya was amazed at how beautiful her mother looked at that moment, as if God himself were truly resting on her shoulders. They both looked at Milton, slumped on his left side in the too-small-for-his-frame chair. Even unshaven and stuffed in a tiny seat in crumpled clothes, his sturdy build and defined features made him handsome. A light snore rose from his lips every so often.

"Uh-oh, Mom, he'll be calling the hogs soon." Maya laughed again, before noticing that her mother had drifted off to sleep, a smile still dangling on her soft, parted lips.

"Maya?" Vic called.

"Huh? Oh," Maya said. "My dad . . . I look like my dad. I've got his complexion, his nose. My dad had, like, a . . . a casual attractiveness. Very distinguished-looking. And my mother, she was ageless, you know? Just always beautiful. A beautiful baby, a cute little girl and a striking young woman. She grew into a classic older woman. They were beautiful together."

"I'm sorry," Vic said quickly, suddenly aware of Maya's discomfort.

"No, it's okay. You know, sometimes it's not so bad to remember. My parents were everything to me. We were so close. They always made time for me no matter what . . . whether it was to help with homework or listen to my corny jokes or come to my softball games. They were always there."

"Only child, huh? I bet they spoiled you rotten." Vic laughed.

"I'm not rotten—well, maybe a little bit," Maya agreed, a grin playing at her lips. For the first time in a long time it didn't hurt too badly to talk about her parents. Maybe enough time had passed. Or maybe it was Vic who made it okay to remember.

A silence, equally sexual and curious in nature, cloaked them. Their faces inches apart, both Maya and Vic were aware of the importance of the next movement. One scintilla of a second held the power to change everything. Vic inhaled a mixture of spicy potato chips and Pepsi on Maya's breath and found it intoxicating. Her breath hit his nose in tiny, hot bursts and for a moment it took his mind away, causing him to forget everything else. He wanted to taste her more than he wanted to breathe himself, but he could not remember how to make his body move. So he just stared at her, moving his eyes ever so slowly across, around, up and down her face, wanting to memorize every beautiful feature.

She had a tiny scar on her hairline that he'd never noticed before, probably because he'd never allowed himself to look too closely at her for fear that she'd look at him with equal scrutiny and discover his overwhelming attraction for her. The scar was the length of half a finger and it started at the center and ran down to the left side of her head. Her nose was flat at the bridge and rounded at the tip and it made him want to bite it. Her thick, silky eyebrows looked like they'd just been brushed. And then there were the lips surrounding the sweetness into which he wanted to climb—soft supple lips that were moist and inviting. He moved his hand to her face and with one finger traced the scar along her hairline.

"I took a dive off my bunk bed when I was six," she said in a small voice, and he could see her, as a child, sitting on the floor holding her hands over her head, screaming in pain.

"Poor baby." His finger finished tracing her scar and traveled down to her chin, where he cupped her face and finally, after what seemed like hours of hesitation, gave in to the urge to taste the sweetness. He leaned forward and kissed her, feeling a shudder but believing it to be her body, not his. He pulled back then, afraid that he'd upset her in some way. When he felt the shudder a second time, he realized it was coming from somewhere inside him. He'd never felt anything like that before and the feeling confused him.

Maya leaned toward him, covering his mouth with hers and cutting off any further thoughts. Her kiss was soft but firm at the same time, like it was politely asking for something and wouldn't take no for an answer. He began leaning backward, pulling her by the arms with him until he was lying flat on the bare floor. Her upper body covered his and she explored the insides of his mouth so thoroughly that he couldn't tell which tongue was his, which teeth were hers. When they finally came up for air, her face still just inches from his, the shudder came again and he closed his eyes until it was over.

"What's wrong?" Maya asked.

"Nothin'," he said. He couldn't tell her that she had moved something inside him and that it excited and frightened him at the same time. She'd think he was a punk or something. He opened his eyes again and smiled at her to reassure her as much as himself that everything was okay.

"So now what?" Maya asked. She hoped he hadn't heard her voice crack.

"I don't know. You tell me," he answered, sounding a little bit more serious than he had intended.

"What's wrong?" she asked again, this time with an edge to her voice. She raised herself.

Vic sat up, too, then and sighed. "Why do you keep askin' me that?"

He was trying not to sound annoyed but was failing miserably. His left eye began twitching, imperceptible to someone looking at him, but he felt it all the same. It was a nervous condition he'd developed as a kid which continued to plague him as an adult in tense situations.

"I don't know. Maybe because all of a sudden you seem a little . . . I don't know . . . weird."

"I'm fine. Why wouldn't I be fine?"

"I don't know. That's what I'm trying to figure out myself. What went wrong. One minute we were sharing the most wonderful kiss I've ever had and the next —" She stopped then and looked away from him.

He sighed again, not wanting to argue with her but

not knowing how to express what he was feeling. He stood up and then reached down for her hand, which she gave to him freely. He pulled her to her feet and into his arms.

"Wonderful?" Vic smiled, and seeing those sexy lips part and that slightly chipped front tooth glisten made her smile, too.

"Well, something like that."

"Oh, now, it's just somethin' like that, huh?" he teased.

"Yep."

"I put it on you and now it's just somethin' like that?"

"Oh, you put it on *me?* Is that what you think? Negro, please!" Maya laughed.

Vic loved the way she laughed, her whole spirit in on the act. "Laugh for me again," he pleaded.

"I can't just laugh on command," she said. "Say something funny."

"Okay, somethin' funny."

"Ha ha ha. Very amusing."

"You're amusin'."

"Why, thank you."

"You're welcome."

"What are we doing?" she asked, referring to the direction of their relationship and not the fact that they were embracing in her living room, trading witty commentary.

Shaking his head, Vic couldn't answer. All he knew was that it felt good to him, too good to try to figure it out.

"I don't know, Maya, and I don't want to know."

"But we need to talk about this. About what we're doing. This is complicated, you know—"

"It doesn't have to be, Maya."

"But it is," Maya said. She wanted to warn him that everything for her, her life, in fact, was complicated. She wanted him to understand that she had long ago given up on happy endings. But looking into his eyes now, she couldn't find the right words.

"Come on, baby, don't do this. Not now. I . . . I just . . . damn, I don't know what to tell you. I don't want to think about complications or direction. I just want to stand here and feel you and smell you and I don't want to talk about it."

Maya was quiet for a while, listening to the sound of her heart beating loudly against her chest, but not loud enough to drown out the warning bells that had started to ring.

Chapter Ten

Stonewalled

The offices of Wexton & Haynes were located on the corner of Berkeley Avenue at the edge of a bustling business district in downtown Boston. After a three-and-a-half-hour ride on Amtrak, Maya took America's oldest underground train system, commonly referred to as the T, to the spacious, modestly decorated offices. She was kept waiting in the reception area for nearly thirty minutes, and it was only after she insisted that the receptionist ring Mr. Haynes a third time that he sent a young broker out to meet her.

"Ms. Wilkins. Hello. I'm Charles Carberry. How are you?" a freckled-face, redheaded kid greeted her.

"I have to say, I'm a little confused," Maya responded. "My appointment with Mr. Haynes was scheduled for noon, a half hour ago. Is there a problem?"

"No, no, not a problem, exactly. It's just that Mr. Haynes has been tied up in an emergency shareholders meeting all morning. It appears that he won't be able to meet with you today. I do apologize for any inconvenience."

The ingratiating grin Carberry displayed did nothing to squash the growing anger rising from the pit of

Maya's stomach. She took a deep breath, checked the attitude creeping across her face and assumed a lawyerly tone.

"I'm not certain if Mr. Haynes recognizes the seriousness of his situation. The request for documents by the government is not something we can drag our feet on."

"Yes, Mr. Haynes is—"

"While I respect that Mr. Haynes is a busy man," Maya interrupted, "we are putting forth our best efforts on his behalf in order to produce a favorable outcome for both Mr. Haynes and the company. Therefore, we're going to need to get on the same page, so to speak, quick, fast and in a hurry." Maya huffed.

"Yes, well, Ms. Wilkins, I'm sure Mr. Haynes will be in touch with you to schedule a more appropriate . . . uh, a better time for him to meet with you. May I show you out?"

"No, I won't be leaving just yet. I'd still like to start reviewing the documents in question. Is there a workroom or empty office I can use?"

"Well, uh, well . . . I'm not sure . . . uh, I think the plan was for you to meet with Mr. Haynes first before doing any document research." Carberry had begun to sweat, his shocking red hair pasted to his forehead. He was agitated and eager to get away from Maya.

"Yes, well, Charles, that was the plan. But I don't see any reason for my three-hour train ride to be in vain. Besides, you seem to be available." Maya gave Carberry a sweet smile which belied the irritation she felt within. "So, where shall we set up?"

For the next four hours Maya wallowed knee-deep through the most disorganized, poorly maintained file room in existence. Every question she posed to Carberry was met with a stuttering, unintelligible response. The 1998 and 1999 trade records, hard copies of which were kept in big log books, were incomplete. Some of the pages were completely illegible and some were just missing. Correspondence between the company and shareholders indicated there had been concerns expressed from as early as 1997 regarding stock performance and access to funds. Carberry, who had only been at the company for six months and who, as Maya later found out, was Haynes's son-in-law, knew next to nothing about anything. Maya was glad when he excused himself and left the room.

Maya realized that many of the letters from shareholders had been written either directly to Mr. Haynes or to a Kyle Rota, vice president of operations. Because this was the type of day Maya was having, her desire to meet with Mr. Rota was unmet. He was apparently away in Paris on vacation.

A sharp knock on the door startled Maya.

"Come in," she responded.

"Brett Davis," said the young man who entered the room, extending his hand.

"Nice to meet you, Brett. I was beginning to think you guys had heard that I have a case of leprosy or something. You're the first person to come in here since I arrived this morning."

"Oh, no, you shouldn't feel that way. It's just . . . well, this is a tough business we're in and, well . . . let's just say that people tend to keep their noses to the grind and in their own business, so to speak."

"I see. Well, what brings you by?" she asked.

"Well, you're the first person from your firm, besides Mr. Fusco, to have come down here."

Maya silently waited for Brett to get to the point of his visit. She was anxious to wrap things up after what had proven to be an unproductive day.

"Yeah, so . . . well, I know that things are a bit of a mess in here and I thought maybe you could use some help."

"That's thoughtful of you, Brett. How long have you

been here?" Maya asked. She removed the stack of documents from the chair next to her.

"Thanks. Almost five years," he answered, sitting down.

"So you were here during the office moves and the fires?"

"Yep. It's been crazy."

"No, crazy is trying to gather support for a defense out of this," Maya said, indicating the boxes of disorganized documents surrounding her. "I can't find anything. I can't get anyone to talk to me. I guess you guys don't understand that I'm on your side. I work for you."

"I think everybody's hoping this thing will just blow over," Brett said.

"Not likely. The government is under serious public pressure to put up safeguards against securities fraud and insider trading. They're not about to let this go without at least slapping someone on the wrist."

"This whole thing is so unfortunate. I mean, Mr. Wexton is a good guy, a decent human being. You know, he gave me a job right out of college, no experience. Said I had an honest face."

"What about Mr. Haynes? What kind of man is he?"

Brett became visibly tense at the mention of Allen Haynes, clearly unwilling to say too much.

"Let's just say if it weren't for Mr. Wexton, I probably would have left here a long time ago."

"Is that a widespread sentiment, in your opinion?" Maya asked.

"I don't know about that, but it's how I feel," Brett answered.

"Well, Brett, what do you say you help me go through some of these trade records for the period in question and see if we can't make sense of things? The better prepared we are to face the government, the better chance this company has of staying in business."

* * *

A tired, frustrated Maya left the offices of Wexton &
Haynes after five o'clock. While Brett had been able to
shed some light on the climate of the company over the
past few years, he seemed to be holding back. She assured him as best she could that she was only interested in knowing the truth so that she could best serve
the company. She handed him one of her business
cards, imploring him to get in touch with her if he
thought of anything that could help.

Other than Brett, she had received zero cooperation
from the employees of Wexton & Haynes. Maya didn't
care what Peter Fusco thought of her. She had every intention of marching into his office on Monday morning
and demanding that he intercede. How Haynes expected the firm to protect his interests and defend him
if he wasn't willing to cooperate was beyond her.

Her mind raced and her head ached as she struggled
to maintain her objectivity. The last thing she intended
to do was let this case ruin the fragile footing she had
created for herself. Knowing that Allen Haynes's misdeeds could result in financial ruin for Kevin Wexton,
who by all accounts seemed to be uninvolved, struck a
chord with her.

The pain of watching her own father lose everything
because of the treachery of a friend was still too fresh.
Her role in that loss was something she would never
get over and, as such, her guilt had made the loss of her
parents all the more overwhelming. But that was then
and this was now. She knew she'd have to keep remind-
ing herself of that fact in order to keep the walls from
closing in on her.

Chapter Eleven

A Quiet Place

"So where are we going?" Maya asked as she blew on the wet fingernails of her freshly polished left hand. Vic had practically dragged her out of her apartment door, leaving her scarcely enough time to brush her teeth. She was dressed in a pair of sweatpants and a long-sleeved T-shirt, Nike sneakers on her feet, a ponytail sticking out of the back of a Yankees baseball cap. To clean up her grunge look a little, in the car she'd applied some lip gloss and had just finished sprucing up her dull nails. She looked over at Vic, who was looking good as usual, wearing a pair of jeans, a football jersey and a cap tipped to the side. A sly smile was his only response.

"Come on, tell me where we're going. You burst through my door at the crack of dawn and you won't even tell me where you're taking me? You know, this could be considered kidnapping," Maya teased.

Vic laughed. "Call the cops on me."

"Don't tempt me."

"You've got to trust somebody, sometime." Vic winked at Maya, which made her blush as much as a chocolate girl could. They were riding in Vic's father's car, a shiny gray Lincoln Town Car. They drove for half an hour up Interstate 95, not speaking. The radio was tuned in to WBLS. The jams they played like Toni Braxton's "Un-Break My Heart" and Brian McKnight's "Anytime" took Maya back to her days at Howard. When they lost the station, Vic popped in a classic soul cassette. Maya hummed along with the music, her head thrown back against the seat and her eyes closed. There was such a nice vibe that she almost wished it didn't have to end when Vic stopped the car, announcing their arrival.

Maya squinted at the rising sun in front of her. It was unseasonably warm, a gentle breeze stirring the air. Vic had parked in a virtually empty car lot. Maya tied her jacket around her waist as she exited the car, seeing nothing of particular interest around her. She turned completely around and stopped. About fifty yards away from where she stood, past a large fence, sat a wooded area with trees so tall and dense that she could not see past the first few of them.

"Where are we?" she asked Vic, who was now standing beside her.

"Poughkeepsie. On the east side of the Hudson River. My dad used to take us fishing in this spot when we were kids. At dawn, it's one of the most peaceful places in the world. Come on," he extended his hand, "I wanna show you somethin'."

Maya followed skeptically. For a fleeting moment she wondered if Vic was really some Jeffrey Dahmer wanna-be taking her to his secluded killing field, miles away from any sort of rescue or salvation. As she walked hand in hand with him, she noted that there were two other cars in the parking lot. *At least we're not alone* was her first thought, but then she wondered if maybe the other cars belonged to his accomplices. It could be one of those cult deals out in the southwest she'd heard about.

Her imagination sent her on a Clue mystery as she began examining her surroundings while they made their way down a narrow, rocky path. She planned her escape route and was going over the moves she learned in the defense class she and Katrina had taken at Albany when Vic stopped walking. They were at a clearing in the woods. There was a small brook running directly in front of her and every so often there was the glimmer of a colorful fish making its way upstream. Two white dogwood trees planted very close to one another near the brook provided a patch of luxurious shade in the otherwise sunny area. For the first time Maya noticed the bundle which had been tucked under Vic's arm as he unrolled a beige blanket and laid it out in front of the trees. At his invitation, Maya sat down and Vic joined her on the blanket.

"So, is this your special place?" she asked quietly, afraid to speak too loudly and disturb the peacefulness surrounding her.

"Yep. Until a few months ago, I hadn't been here since I was a kid. But I always remembered how peaceful it was," he said, his voice just as low.

"It's nice," Maya said, still looking around. "Ooh, what kind of fish are those?" she squealed, bending over the brook.

"Which ones?" Vic asked beside her.

"That one. See it?" She pointed toward the water. "The white and black one?"

"I don't know. Kinda looks like an angelfish."

Maya's breath was taken away as she looked around her. The lush green of the trees and grass, the air smelling like honey and cream made her senses come alive. As the water rushed over the rocky bed with a swooshing sound, Maya's mind was a million miles from briefs and depositions, illnesses and death, success or failure. She felt uncomplicated, like she was playing with one of those baby jigsaw puzzles consisting of only five huge pieces. It took only seconds for her to come together inside this perfect picture.

"This place is easy," she said, looking at Vic. "It's just like you."

"I can be difficult, too, you know," Vic said.

"No, I don't think so. You make it easy to be with you and talk to you. Like, you know how sometimes when you meet somebody and you sit there racking your brains to think of something else to say? It's like a chore trying to keep the conversation going."

"Well, that only happens when you and the other person are too different."

"You and I are different."

"Yeah, but not that different."

"What do you and I have in common?" Maya asked.

Tiny wrinkles appeared in Vic's forehead then. He watched the fish in the brook while trying to find the right words. He had never met anyone like Maya. True, he hadn't known her long, but he felt like they were connected. Without even trying they shared something deeper than similar tastes in sports and entertainment. They shared the same sort of hollowness that comes from loss.

"Have you ever wondered why I don't talk about my mother?" he asked finally.

"Yes," Maya answered honestly. She had assumed the woman was dead.

Vic sighed, like he needed to lay down a heavy burden but couldn't find anyplace for it. He leaned back against a dogwood. Maya joined him.

"She left . . . when I was ten. We never heard from her again." Maya's shock creased her brows. They were both silent, Vic's heavy words hanging in the air. The clearing was quiet, save for nature's occasional murmurings.

"She abandoned you?"

"Yeah, just broke out one day. So, like you, I don't have a mother anymore either."

"So I guess we do have something in common." Maya placed her hand over Vic's, stopping him from nervously pulling at the blades of grass beside him.

She noticed for the first time a spiral notebook on the grass next to Vic. "What's that?"

"This," Vic said, holding the book against his chest, the cover facing Maya, "this is my heart and soul. This is where I pen my songs or ideas for songs, poetry, catchy phrases. This is my baby," he said dramatically.

"Let me see it." Maya reached for the book.

"Hold up . . . not so fast, Miss," Vic said, raising the book above his head and out of Maya's reach.

"Oh, come on." Maya laughed.

"First you have to take the oath."

"The oath?"

"Yeah, the oath. You have to make a pledge before you can view the treasure," Vic said. The look on his face was choirboy earnest.

"You're serious, aren't you?"

"Yes, I am. Are you ready?"

"Okay," Maya said hesitantly.

"Raise your right hand and repeat after me." Vic paused until Maya did as instructed.

"I Maya, do promise and swear . . ."

"I Maya, do promise and swear . . ."

"On all that I hold sacred . . ."

"On all that I hold sacred . . ."

"That I will never share what I have read today with another soul . . ."

"Vic, really—" Maya whined.

"Say it," Vic demanded.

Maya rolled her eyes at him.

"This had better be worth all of this. All right . . .

that I will never share what I have read today with another soul . . ."

"And if I should break my oath . . ."

"And if I should break my oath . . ."

"I will gladly hand over for immediate destruction my Denzel Washington photograph collection."

"Wait a minute, now you're tripping. I ain't handing over Denzel," Maya said defiantly.

"I ain't? What kind of grammar is that for a high and mighty attorney?" Vic teased.

"I repeat, I ain't handing over Denzel." Maya laughed.

"Okay, then I ain't handin' over my notebook," Vic answered.

Maya thought for a minute. She was dying to see what kind of lyricist Vic was.

"All right, all right. If I breach your oath, I'll surrender my Denzel Washington photograph collection. Now give me the book."

Vic hesitated for another moment before handing his notebook to Maya.

"Can I read it aloud?" Maya asked.

"If you want," Vic answered, suddenly very shy. Ordinarily, he loved to share his work. Family and friends had always been supportive and impressed with his songs. But now, for the first time, he was worried that this girl, this magnificent, intelligent woman for whom he was falling more deeply than he would ever admit to anyone, might think his stuff was mediocre. Or, worse, just plain old corny.

If time could stand still,
I wouldn't want it to,
All I want is to spend my life
My days, my nights with you.

If happiness is an illusion
Then I'll settle for make-believe

'Cause without this thing right here
Without you there is no me.

If oceans covered the land
And washed away every man
I'd close my eyes and gladly go
As long as I held your hand.

Maya stopped reading. "Wow, you're really good," she said.

"You sound surprised."

"No, not surprised—well, maybe a little. I mean, I didn't expect your stuff to be so . . . so real. You know how guys are always trying to front like they don't feel like this or like these things don't happen to them."

"Not all guys."

"Yeah, well, all the ones I've ever known," Maya said. She read on, awestruck by the beauty of his words and inspired by their candor.

"Do you only write love songs?"

"Nah, I write about what inspires me. Sometimes it's love, sometimes it's hate. You know, it depends on what's going on in the world . . . or in my world."

"Have you ever read Pablo Neruda? Some of your lyrics remind me of him."

"Yeah, he's 'bout it."

Maya thought about the day her father gave her *Twenty Love Poems and a Song of Despair.* She'd curled up on the sofa and read it from cover to cover. By the time she'd finished, the sun had set and her head and heart were reeling.

"His work makes you want to fall in love. Made me believe in the power of love, you know?"

Vic nodded.

"Unfortunately, the guy I was dating at the time was the wrong person for me to be feeling that way about." Maya laughed.

"So what happened?"

"Well, a little of Neruda's poetry had me believing this guy was Mr. Right. I fell hard and fast and, let's just say, I landed on my behind with a thud."

"You know, Maya, I've got a confession to make, Vic said suddenly.

"Uh-oh. Here it goes. You really brought me up here to skin me alive and sacrifice me to Hari Shamu, your cult leader."

"What?" Vic's genuine confusion knotted his eyebrows. "Your imagination is really overactive, you know, borderline warped."

Maya laughed because he was right.

Vic took her hand in his and stared out into the clearing for a minute, wondering if this was the right time to say what he was feeling. Was it too soon to let her know that she impressed him? That their conversations made his head buzz and he couldn't wait to see and talk to her every day? Should he tell her that she had inspired the writing of his latest song about a brother who, against his better judgment, had fallen for yet another woman everyone said was out of his league. Vic worried about what she would think of him. But he also knew that he couldn't help the way she was affecting him.

"Look, here's the deal. When I first met you, I was sure that you would be one of those superficial, stuck-up, wanna-be yuppie types. You know, like ninety-nine-point-nine of the associates at the firm. And when we started kickin' it, I figured that you were just frontin', tryin' to act like you were down and all. People were tellin' me that you were probably only talkin' to me as, like, I don't know, an experiment or somethin'."

"What people?"

"A couple of the guys on the job, my man Malik. They weren't tryin' to put you down or nothin'. It's just that, you know, how often does an attorney go out with a guy from the mailroom?"

He had a point so Maya didn't respond, even though she was pissed off that people she didn't even know were making assumptions about her behind her back.

"So is that how you feel, too?"

"No, no. At first I really wasn't sure what to think. I guess I had my own insecurities about why you'd give me the time of day. But then I figured, well, she doesn't have any people in town so, you know, maybe she really is trying to make friends. So we started kickin' it, and I realized that you're really cool people, that it's not an act or anythin'. You're just as down to earth as anybody else I know."

Maya knew that Vic meant what he was saying as a compliment, but she found people holding preconceived notions about her irritating.

"Look, I am who I am. I don't put on airs and I don't pretend to be something or somebody I'm not—never have and never will. And what's more, I don't really care who thinks differently," she snapped.

"Damn," she continued, "that's what's wrong with us now, brothahs and sistahs always hating on each other."

"It's hatin', not hating," he said, her perfect diction making him laugh. Even she had to crack a smile.

"Whatever. You get my drift."

It was silly to get all bent out of shape over what somebody she could care less about had to say. No matter what she did, there would always be someone with something negative to say. That was one of the first lessons life had taught her and it stuck with her.

"I didn't mean to get you all fired up. The point is, I like you and I've enjoyed these past few weeks, hangin' out with you and everythin'. And I just want you to know that if strictly friendship is what you want, then I hope we can be friends for a long time."

"Hmm," Maya said, not sure how to respond. She looked at Vic and felt that quiver in her stomach that had become a familiar feeling whenever she thought about him lately. Part of her felt like friendship was probably all she could handle, but part of her wanted more. But admitting that would leave her open to all sorts of possible outcomes she wasn't sure she was ready to deal with. Maybe he was saying this to really give himself an out. Maybe he wasn't interested in her in that man/woman sort of way. And if he wasn't, maybe that wasn't such a bad thing, considering the circumstances. There were just too many maybes for her to make sense out of any of it. She'd have to come out and say what was on her mind and let the chips fall where they may.

"Vic, I've enjoyed being with you, too, and yes, I hope that we can remain friends." Maya saw a flicker of what appeared to be disappointment in his eyes and that fleeting look gave her the courage to continue.

"I also want you to know that I think you and I . . . this has the potential to be more than just a friend-ship."

There, she'd said it. The ensuing silence was deafen-ing as she held her breath, waiting for his response. When she found the courage to actually look him in the face, he was smiling that half smile he had, where the outside of his lips curled up on one side and parted slightly, making you wonder if he was laughing with you or at you, but then his eyes would tell you he was definitely with you.

She leaned forward then, not caring about playing herself in the least. She put her hand on his cheek and let the smile that was bubbling up inside her belly part her own lips and then join her smile with his. And the quiver in the pit of her belly began doing double-time and her arms involuntarily slipped around his neck just as his tightened around her waist, and it was as if his sweet words she'd just read aloud were written for her and for this moment.

It was unclear how or when they wound up lying

down, Vic's body partially covering Maya's. All Maya knew was that the hand that had opened her blouse and was running across her belly made the quivering quiet until it was a warm ripple of water lapping against the brook's edges.

The only thing Vic could think about was the beauty and the sweetness of this woman that was filling every orifice of his body until he was sure that if he broke away from her and tried to breath on his own, he would suffocate for real. The bulge in Vic's jeans pressed against Maya's thigh, making her aware of the waters flowing between her own legs, and it was then that the bells went off and the lights came on. She stopped kissing Vic, pushing him back gently with her hands as she sat up.

"Whoa. I think we're in trouble here." She stumbled, trying to straighten her clothing.

"I'm sorry, I . . . I didn't mean to," Vic stammered, embarrassed now.

He sat up, too, running a hand across the top of his head several times.

"Oh, boy," he mumbled, as Maya rebuttoned her shirt.

"I'm sorry, Maya, I wasn't tryin' to . . ."

"Ssh, it's all right. I was there, too, remember?" she said, placing her hand over one of his.

"Nah, but I shouldn't have taken it that far. It's just that I've got these feelin's for you and . . . this is crazy."

"I know."

"What are you, some sort of witch or somethin'?" Vic asked.

"What?" Maya laughed.

"That must be it. You done put some kinda voodoo on me, right?"

"Yeah, that's it. You're under my spell now and I can make you do anything I want you to do." Maya laughed

again as she stood up. Vic joined her, pulling her
against his still-awakened body.

"I don't have a problem with that, as long as whatever you make me do keeps me feeling like this," Vic
said.

Chapter Twelve

Like Father, Like Son

"Cut it out, Victor, before somebody sees us," Maya whispered. She adjusted the scarf displaced by Vic's efforts to find his favorite spot at the base of Maya's neck. They were standing in front of the home of Victor Smalls, Sr., a gorgeous brownstone on 138th and Adam Clayton Powell, Jr. Blvd., also known as Striver's Row in Harlem. This area was an elegant stretch of old, refurbished brownstones, mercilessly clean sidewalks and streets lined with varying luxury vehicles. This strip of neighborhood screamed old-school restored by new-school money. A multicultural potpourri of professionals had reclaimed a part of history, coming in on the ground floor of a real estate boom that had taken the market by surprise.

Victor Sr. was one of quite a few who had never left Harlem. He'd purchased the brownstone for next to nothing after moving out of a nearby housing project in the late sixties. Vic, who was born and raised on Strivers Row, had witnessed firsthand the rebirth of the legendary enclave.

"Aw, babe, my dad knows how I get down. He wouldn't be surprised to find me havin' my way with you right here on his front steps!" Vic laughed.

"Oh, really? Well, I'll tell you what, why don't you find one of your previous girlfriends to 'get down' with you on your father's steps?" Maya snapped.

As she attempted to descend the steps, Vic gripped her by the waist.

"Stop it. You know I'm just kiddin'. Babe, relax. There's nothin' to be nervous about," Vic said, reading Maya's anxiety.

"Who said I was nervous?" Maya asked. In response to Vic's smirk, she added, "Well, it's not every day I get to meet a real-life superhero. The way you tell it, your dad is the best thing since indoor plumbing. What if he doesn't like me?"

"Then I'm just gonna have to drop you. I can't date anybody who Pops ain't cool with."

"You know what? You are really getting on my last nerve," Maya said, punching Vic in the arm.

"Oh, see, now I'm gonna have to tell Dad that you beat on me, too." Vic laughed as he opened the front door with his key, leading Maya through the vestibule and up a short flight of steps.

"Yo, Dad, we're here," he yelled from the top of the stairs.

"Yo, son, why the hell are you yelling? I'm sitting right here," said Victor's father, who was seated in a worn brown leather recliner in the living room, to the right of the front door. He stood up from his chair and father and son embraced.

"Well, well, well. So you're the woman who's got my son so tied up that he doesn't have time to get together with his old man anymore. I can't say that I blame him. You, sweetheart, are breathtaking," he said, taking Maya's hands in his.

"Why, thank you, Mr. Smalls," Maya answered, blushing.

"What's this 'Mr. Smalls' stuff? Call me Victor."

"Okay, Victor." Maya smiled, feeling funny because

up until then she'd only used the name Victor when Vic got on her nerves.

The resemblance between the Sr. and Jr. was uncanny. They shared the same height and build, with Victor Sr. carrying a little extra weight around his middle. The only difference being that Vic's complexion was a noticeable two or three shades lighter than his father. As the night wore on, Maya would notice that the two men also shared similar mannerisms and sardonic humor.

Vic once bragged to Maya that his father was an excellent cook, but that was an understatement. Victor Sr. had prepared a meal of shrimp creole and yellow rice that tasted like he'd had it flown up from Louisiana. The shrimp were fresh enough to jump off the plate and the spicy sauce sent her taste buds into a frenzy.

"Victor, this is the best creole I have ever eaten in my life. Where'd you learn to make creole like this?"

"Well, now, Miss Maya, there was this woman, see. A big ole, high yellow, thick-legged thang. Finest gal ever come out of Louisiana. Now, we were seeing each other for a few months, you know, still feeling each other out—"

"Pops," Vic interrupted.

"Hush, boy, when grown folks are talking. Anyway, Miss Maya, I 'call myself trying to, you know, push the relationship on ahead, over that feeling-out stage. So I went out to the market, picked up some red snapper, fresh peppers, you know. I cooked up a storm, you hear me? Now, my stewed fish was good and I knew that. I also knew that you can score big points with a woman when you feed her right. Anyway, we're eating and I'm sitting there, waiting for her to say something about the meal. You know what she finally says?"

"What?" Maya asked in anticipation. In a short time she'd come to realize that Victor Sr. could spin a tale like nobody she'd ever known, besides her own daddy.

"She said, 'Victor, this is good. But next time try marinating the snapper in a little soybean oil for about a half hour before you cook it. It won't be so dry.' "

Maya gasped. "No, she didn't?"

"Yes, she did. Now at first I was miffed. I mean, that takes a whole heap of nerves. But being the player that I was back in the day, I kept cool. The next night she invited me over to her house and made this-here creole. I tell you, I realized that I could cook from now until Little Richard wins an award and I would never have nothing on this woman. You heard the saying 'Put your foot in it'? Well, Miss Maya, homegirl put her foot, my foot and half the state of Louisiana in that creole. And the next time I made stewed fish, I did what she'd suggested and found out she was right.

"Needless to say, that's why I had to let her go," Victor continued as he helped himself to a second plate of food and then spooned another serving onto Maya's plate, who didn't refuse it. "Can't have nobody cooking better than me, now, can I? Do you burn in the kitchen, Maya?"

"Yeah—she burns the kitchen up." Vic laughed sarcastically.

"Shut up, Vic." Maya glared at Vic. "No, Victor, I don't really cook. I mean, I can make a nice lasagna and a fair omelette, but I don't really get into the kitchen much."

"Well, you need to come on over here sometimes—I'll give you some lessons. A woman needs to know how to cook."

"Why, so I can be a good wife to some man?" Maya teased.

"Hell, no! So you can eat. See, like I said before, women love to eat good. You'll get a little older and you'll get tired of eating fast food and salads and whatnot. See, a man . . . man'll eat a dry ham sandwich and be happy, especially if it's fixed by a woman he's hot for. But a woman, no sir. A woman wants to be able to lick her fingers after a meal and go back for seconds. So you see, you've got two choices: you can either find you a man who can cook some or you're gonna have to learn to cook yourself."

"Well, I know you can't cook, Vic. I've never even seen you boil water." Maya laughed.

"I can too cook, right, Pops?"

"I taught him a little something, when I could keep him in the kitchen long enough."

"So how come you've never cooked for me?" Maya asked.

" 'Cause I don't know you like that, girl, to be slavin' away at a hot stove for you."

"You want me to go upside his head for you, Miss Maya?" Victor Sr. asked as he jumped up from the table and grabbed Vic into a headlock.

"Don't worry, Victor, I'll get him later." Maya laughed. She was having the time of her life. She couldn't remember when she'd felt more comfortable. The three of them spent the next couple of hours playing poker using Nilla Wafers for chips. Maya, who'd learned to play poker at her father's knee when she was still in grade school, cleaned them both out. By the time the evening was over, Maya truly felt like she'd gained a second home.

"You remember what I said. You come on over anytime and I'll let you in on a few of my special secret recipes."

"Thank you, Victor. It was really nice to finally meet you," Maya said from inside the tight squeeze he'd thrown on her. Maya walked down the stairs, giggling softly as she pretended not to hear Vic's father whisper to him.

"Now, this one is a keeper. Mess it up, and it'll be me and you!"

Chapter Thirteen

All Work and No Play

Maya pushed her seat back from the conference room table and stood. She needed to take a break from what had already proven to be an exhausting night. She walked listlessly around the table to the large picture windows on the room's west wall. From this, the thirty-seventh floor, she could look out across Manhattan. It was approaching midnight, yet the city that never sleeps was still bustling below her.

Maya rotated her neck slowly from left to right in an effort to work out the kinks that had settled in her upper body. She thought briefly about Vic, a slow smile turning the corners of her mouth upward. Lately, it was all she could do not to think about him and remain focused on her work. His easy laughter was contagious and his sexy walk could make any girl grow weak in the knees. She was greedy for more time to spend with him, but she knew that was asking for too much. The little time she did manage to steal away from her obligations at work was all that she could hope for right now. While he said he understood, she genuinely hoped Vic would remain patient.

It was nights like this one that were the hardest on

her. She was stuck at the office, buried under mounds of paperwork, but wanting so much to be with him. She knew her career depended on the groundwork she laid today, and she believed that, eventually, it would all pay off.

So instead of getting her kinks worked out by Vic, she'd spend tonight poring over boxes of corporate documents produced by the other side in a huge patent infringement case she was working on with Richard Griesler. She would have to bring him up to speed in the morning, no excuses. She had to push all thoughts of Vic out of her mind for tonight, along with the nagging doubts she had over the Haynes case, and get to work.

A sudden knock at the door surprised her. She didn't think there was anyone else left on the floor at this hour.

"Yes," she called.

Vic pushed the door open cautiously.

"Hey, you," he said.

"Vic, I was just thinking about you." Maya blushed. "What are you doing here?"

"Well, I was downtown in the studio workin' tonight and I didn't get an answer when I called your apartment. So, I figured you must still be here. Pullin' an all-nighter?" he asked as he entered the room completely, shutting the door behind him. He removed his rust leather jacket, hanging it on the back of a chair.

"Something like that. I'm optimistic, though, maybe another couple of hours. What's that?" Maya asked, noticing for the first time the white plastic bag in Vic's hand.

"Dinner. I know you haven't eat yet," he said. He pushed a few papers to the side and laid the bag on the table. "I've got two chef's salads, some iced tea—raspberry, right?"

"Ooh, cool. That was so sweet of you. Thanks," Maya said.

"So what were you up to when I came in? Contemplatin' takin' a dive?" he asked, motioning to the windows Maya stood in front of.

He crossed the room and joined her. They both looked through the glass, the dazzling lights of the hundred-plus buildings in front of them momentarily mesmerizing. Maya glanced at Vic, his profile as alluring as a full-frontal view. He turned to face her, their eyes meeting and holding one another's gaze.

"Would you miss me?" Maya asked.

Vic's answer was clear as he cupped the back of Maya's neck, slowly drawing her face to his. He paused, his lips less than an inch from hers, a magnetic pull already connecting them. Her breathing became ragged as she took in his face, feasting on each one of his striking features. His eyes told her what she needed to hear.

Finally, his lips found hers and the contact was explosive, sending shivers up and down her spine. Maya ran her hands along his muscled back, his toned arms encircling her and pulling her even closer.

He massaged her behind, a mental picture of the way it swayed when she walked imprinted on his memory. His free hand untied her hair from the band which held it in place. Once released, her thick mane hung gloriously to her shoulders. Vic buried his face in her hair, wanting to memorize the scent of her, before moving to her graceful neck. His lips on her neck, her "spot," sent tiny bolts of electricity throughout her body, making her cling to him even tighter.

Suddenly and forcefully, she pushed him far enough away to remove the fleece pullover he wore. She needed to feel his skin against hers.

His eyes never left hers as he searched for a sign that she was at all uncomfortable. He wanted her more than he'd ever wanted another woman, but he had to be sure that she was ready. He wouldn't risk moving too fast and scaring her off. He wanted to be certain that she knew this would not just be a sexual encounter for him. It was much more.

Her eyes told him that her desire for him was as strong as his, and that they had reached the point where further conversation was unnecessary. He moved his hand slowly down her right leg until he found the hem of her skirt, pulling it upward and out of the way. Positioning herself against the edge of the table, she raised one stockinged thigh as he settled into the space between her legs.

As Vic undid Maya's blouse, the tiny buttons lost in between his large fingers, her excitement was heightened. The possibility of getting caught entered her mind, momentarily giving her pause.

"What if someone comes in?" she asked in a husky voice, aware of where their interlude was headed, yet powerless to stop it. Having never felt a desire this strong for anyone before, she was surprised at how compelled she felt to be with him. Reckless abandon had never clouded her thoughts as it did now.

"There's no one here but us," Vic said, his tone equally as urgent.

"The windows," Maya said between kisses, but her concerns were silenced when Vic freed her throbbing breasts from her black lace bra. He stared at the two perfectly rounded mounds, their mocha-colored nipples large and erect, waiting for his touch. He delicately kissed each nipple in turn as she rubbed the back of his smooth, cleanly shaven head.

"Do you have protection?" Maya whispered, her excitement changing her voice to deep and throaty tone.

Vic pulled his wallet from his back pocket and removed a condom from one of the compartments.

Maya leaned forward, brushing her lips softly against

the fine layer of hair that covered Vic's solid chest. She kissed his collarbone, sliding her tongue upward to his throat and around his neck. He moaned audibly when she inserted her tongue into his ear, egging her on.

Their movements were filled with the clumsiness of first-time lovers, so enamored by the newness of one another, yet embarrassed by the rapture that consumed them.

Maya slid her stockings down, tossing them to the carpet beneath her while Vic undid his belt buckle. His pants dropped to his knees, exposing his throbbing manhood, which strained against the fitted Jockey shorts he wore. He leaned her backward onto the conference table, oblivious to the paperwork beneath her, and sought the sweetness of her mouth again. Deftly, he shoved her panties aside, his fingers meeting with the flowing waters escaping her. She gasped as he inserted first one, then two fingers, and she arched her body in demand. When neither of them could wait any longer, he quickly slid the condom on and entered her, the joining of their bodies sending instantaneous waves of pleasure through them both. She bit the back of her hand in an effort to stifle her pleasure-filled screams, ecstasy claiming every fiber of her being. She climaxed quickly and completely, holding on to Vic tightly as he followed her to the mountaintop.

Neither could speak for several minutes afterward, each momentarily lost in their own thoughts.

"Are you okay?" Vic asked.

"Mmm-hmm," Maya responded, gazing into his sparkling eyes. "You?"

"Oh, I'm good." He laughed. "Seriously, though, are you okay with this?" Genuine concern colored his eyes.

"This was perfect. Not what I imagined for our first time, but perfect just the same."

They lingered for several more minutes, unwilling

to break the spell which had been cast over them. Finally, reality beckoned and the conference room table became just that again—and extremely uncomfortable. They rose and found their respective clothing. Maya giggled at the thought that they could have been discovered, either by someone from the next building looking into the conference room's large picture windows or from a janitor entering the unlocked room to clean it.

As Maya buttoned her blouse, Vic grabbed her, eagerly seeking out her mouth again. He kissed her deeply, feeling himself becoming aroused again. Maya disengaged and leaned against Vic, closing her eyes. He wrapped his arms tightly around her.

"Mmm, this feels so good," she said.

"Yep. But you know what I was thinkin'? We should go back to your place and maybe make each other feel even better."

"As appealing as that sounds, lover, I can't go anywhere just yet." Maya playfully smacked his roaming hands. "And if you don't leave, I'll never get any work done."

"I'll tell you what: I'll go downstairs to the mailroom and get a jump on some of tomorrow's work. You come down when you're ready, and I'll share a cab uptown with you."

"Fair enough. Now get out of here."

Neither could resist one more lingering kiss before they parted. Maya happily reviewed the remainder of the documents, basking in an energizing afterglow. She hurriedly cleaned up her mess. She had a cab to catch.

Chapter Fourteen

Trouble in Paradise

"Julia Becker's having a get-together Friday night at her place," Maya said. She and Vic were playing Scrabble on the floor of her living room on a rainy Tuesday night.

"Are you going?"

"Yeah . . . Julia's pretty cool," Maya answered. "Okay, my word is K-E-N."

"Get that outta here, that's not a word," Vic said.

"Yes, it is. It means . . . no, wait. Are you challenging me?" Maya quipped, waving a Webster's dictionary in Vic's face.

"Nah, I'm not gonna challenge you. But I know it's not a word," he said.

"Punk."

"So I guess you were one of those brainy, studious kids, huh?" Vic asked.

"Ha! Now that's a good one," Maya answered, remembering how hard she'd struggled in school as a child. "It was pretty rough for me, especially early on. By the time I got to the third grade, I could barely read and no one knew why."

"What was wrong?" Vic asked, surprised.

"Turns out I'm dyslexic. Ever heard of it?"

"Yes, but I've never known anyone with it. How did you get over it?"

"I still have it—it's not something that you cure." Maya sighed. "Dyslexia causes organizational difficulties in processing information. I had to learn how to process things differently than the average joe. Unfortunately, people hear the term and right away assume you're retarded and can't succeed."

"Well, you, Ms. Lawyer, certainly shoot holes in that assumption," Vic said admiringly.

"Yeah, I was one of the lucky ones. Growing up with a learning disability can sometimes make you feel defeated and make you retreat inside yourself. On the other hand, it can make you determined to succeed despite the odds. I think a part of me wanted to give up. I felt so stupid and the other kids in school would tease me when I couldn't read aloud or spell," Maya said, reminded of the shame she'd lived with during that period in her life.

"But my parents wouldn't let me give up. After the teachers had written me off as mentally retarded and tried to stick me in special education, my mother contacted the National Institutes of Health. Because so little was known about dyslexia at the time, it was trial and error with me. Long story short, I worked hard to find ways to modify how I processed written material since I couldn't learn in the traditional ways."

"So you kicked dyslexia's butt and here you are, beating the crap out of me in Scrabble."

Unequipped to form a new word, Vic tossed his unused letters back into the box and picked fresh ones.

"Basically. But you know, the sad part is that some people just stay locked out of learning and they never find a way out of the darkness. . . . But, on a brighter note, you're going with me, right?" Maya asked. She wanted to show Vic that the attorney-dating-a-staff-member issue was no longer a problem for her.

"Going where?" Vic asked.

Maya looked at Vic like he had three heads.

"Oh . . . nah, I don't want to go." Vic laid three tiles onto the Scrabble board. "My word is L-Y-R-E and that's a triple-word score, so that gives me—"

"Why don't you want to go to Julia's party?" Maya asked, miffed.

" 'Cause I wasn't invited."

"I just invited you. Besides, these are our colleagues."

"Wrong. They're your colleagues, not mine. Look, you go and have a good time. I have better things to do than spend a Friday night with a bunch of boring, snobby lawyers," Vic snapped.

"Am I included in that?"

"Come on, don't act stupid."

"Oh, so now I'm stupid? You know what I don't get? Why you would want to spend any time at all with somebody who's boring, snobby and stupid," Maya spat, dumping the tiles off their little bench and back into the Scrabble box. She headed to the kitchen, where she snatched open the refrigerator in search of a beer.

"Tsk." She sucked her teeth. What kind of relationship could they build if he wouldn't at least try to integrate into her social life as she had into his? Not that she was counting, but she'd already had dinner with his father a couple of times and had also gone out with Vic and his friend Malik.

Maya plopped down in one of the armchairs, angrily slurping the beer. Its cold, bitter taste sizzled as it slid down her hot throat. She hoped the alcohol would mellow her out a bit, take the edge off before the situation got any uglier. Unfortunately, its affect was the direct opposite; the more she drank, the more annoyed she got. When Vic attempted to speak to her, she ignored him. Finally, after repacking the game, Vic stood.

"I think this is a really stupid thing for us to be arguin' over," he said. "I'm not going to stand here all night and be ignored."

Maya stared blankly ahead, refusing to make eye contact with Vic. She couldn't put into words why his attitude had made her so angry, but it had.

"You know what, Maya, for a grown woman you sure know how to act like a kid when you want to." Vic's disappointment evident in his tone. "I'm outta here."

He unlocked the door and paused before turning the knob, hoping that Maya would stop him. The last thing he wanted to do was leave this way. In fact, he didn't fully comprehend what had happened to turn a pleasant evening into World War III. He glanced over his shoulder, looking for some sign from her that would make a difference. She folded her arms across her chest and looked the other way.

"By the way, thanks for a bangin' night." He sighed, opening the door.

Maya sat in the chair for a long time after the apartment door slammed. Once she'd emptied the beer bottle, she headed for bed with one of her dependable Chocolate dolls in hand to comfort her.

Chapter Fifteen

Fitting In

"You've got a really nice place, Julia." Maya was standing in front of a large oil painting of a burning farmhouse, the orange flames languidly dining on the faded red wood. The backdrop, a brilliant blue sky, was just beginning to become blackened from the fire's thick smoke. "This is eerily beautiful."

"Thanks. My dad commissioned a street artist he found in London a couple of years ago. He basically discovered the guy and made him famous. Come, why don't I introduce you to a few people."

The living room was filled with people chatting in groups of two, three or more. A waiter, whose navy-blue shorts and crisp white T-shirt made him look like a Gap ad, was making his way around the crowded room with a tray of hors d'oeuvres. Maya's stomach growled as she got a whiff of something that smelled like pizza. She followed Julia around the room, shaking hands and flashing a toothy, so-glad-to-meet-ya smile. In the kitchen was a group of people seated at the marble-topped table, playing Parcheesi.

"Mark, I hope you're not cheating as usual," Julia said.

"You know me, J," replied the rather attractive man with jet-black wavy hair and green eyes set deep into an olive-complexioned face.

"Everybody meet Maya. She's the new kid on the block at the firm. Maya, this is Mark. He's in securities and is our resident pain in the ass. Jewel, here, is a producer at NBC. She gets us tickets to all the best tapings. Over there are Jana and Barry, the newlyweds. They're both first-years at Mt. Sinai."

"Hello, everyone," Maya said in response to a chorus of hellos. She slid a stool closer to the table to watch the game. Gap ad came in and loaded her up with a napkinful of sausage- and cheese-covered bagel bites and fried zucchini.

"I'm going for a refill. Anybody?" Mark said, standing up from the table, waving an empty Corona bottle in the air.

"Yeah, get me one, would you?" Jewel answered.

"How about you, Maya? What are you drinking?"

"Nothing yet. Umm, is there any Harvey's?"

"I'll check it out. Hey, Julia, where's the good stuff?" Mark yelled as he left the kitchen.

Maya watched the game for the next half hour, chatting with the players and introducing herself to other guests who migrated intermittently into the kitchen. At one point she returned to the living room to find a bunch of people dancing wildly to Avril Lavigne's "Losing Grip." Although Maya refused an invitation to dance from a dorky-looking guy who seemed to be dancing more to the words than to the beat, Avril's smooth groove caused her head to bop as she kept time to the music.

"So, securities? That's a whole lot of money to have under your thumb every day," Maya said. She and Mark were seated on the sofa. The room had thinned out in the last hour. Maya was waiting for Julia to return from dropping off some out-of-towners at Penn Station before calling it a night herself.

"Hmm, sometimes. Then you remember that not one red cent is yours." Mark smirked. "So what about you? What's a nice girl like you doing hanging out with a bunch of lawyers?"

"Ouch!" Maya said.

"Well, Maya, you've got to admit, lawyers are a strange club."

"Yeah, but where would the world be without us?"

"Touché."

Maya's easy laughter warmed Mark, giving him a buzz as if he'd just consumed a shot of tequila straight up. Suddenly, he was glad he'd changed his mind and come to Julia's party. He'd been thinking how he wouldn't be able to sit through another one of her *I'm better than you* get-togethers, where the same people sat around talking shop for hours on end. He felt no attraction to the numerous women Julia was constantly introducing him to. They were all carbon copies of her.

Not that Julia wasn't attractive or a nice person. He was just tired of dating the same woman in a different dress over and over again. He wanted to spend time with someone who wasn't obsessed with playing the who's-who game. For once he wanted to date someone who wasn't a blue-blooded socialite like his mother.

Mark's mother was old-money rich, the only daughter born to a wealthy investment banker. His dad, whose Middle Eastern ancestry would have been frowned upon by his mother's people, had it not been for his sizable Middle Eastern bank account, was equally stiff. Mark inherited his father's swarthy skin and brooding manner. What he didn't inherit was his father's attraction to fair-haired maidens.

To his parents dismay, he was thirty-three years old and had yet to find a wife amongst the daughters of their many friends and colleagues. He wasn't certain who he'd end up marrying, but he felt sure that it wouldn't be someone his parents picked out for him.

By the time Julia returned and Maya prepared to leave, Mark found himself wishing the night wouldn't end just yet. He tried to round up a few people to go out to one of the nearby watering holes for a nightcap, but when Maya declined, the idea lost its shine. Mark walked Maya to the corner and hailed a taxi for her, openly staring at her. He was intrigued by the round, delicate nose, and found her thick lips inviting. Her doelike eyes had held him captive all night and he wanted to stay locked in their line of vision.

All too quickly, a livery cab pulled up to the curb. Maya hopped in, waved and was gone. Mark stared after her until the red taillights merged its way into the dim collage of retreating colors. He headed home, opting to walk the fifteen blocks as thoughts of his sensuous new acquaintance wreaked havoc on his imagination. Self-assured and used to always getting the things he went after, Mark was certain it wouldn't be long before he and Maya were an item. His parents would flip out, but he was used to that. After just one meeting, one conversation, he was certain that this woman was the answer to so many of his desires. He planned to pull out all the stops to woo Ms. Wilkins and to see those desires fulfilled. To hell with whomever had a problem with it.

Chapter Sixteen

If It Walks Like a Duck . . .

Maya stretched out across the floor of her living room, her mind traveling from the stacks of papers strewn before her to Vic. It was Saturday night, four days since Vic had stormed out of her apartment. It was starting to look like he'd never call. She was still pissed about having had to attend Julia's party alone the night before, and his words still stung, but she was more than willing to talk it out—if he'd just call her. Come Monday, he would be out of the office on a planned vacation from the firm to work on his music.

The lack of communication from him led her to assume that their plans to kick around the city, take in some shows and see some local talent at various open-mike venues were off. She worried that the budding romance had sizzled and unceremoniously fizzled all in one fell swoop. While their failure was not quite unexpected in Maya's estimation, she still felt a great deal let down, as though some part of her had almost believed she and Vic would attain permanency. But she knew all too well that there were no constants in her life and she had come to accept that. Why she had allowed herself to consider another possibility was beyond her rationale.

To add to the stress of her relationship with Vic, or lack thereof, she was facing a brick wall on the Haynes case. After interviewing three of the company's six brokers, it was clear that not only were some of the government's allegations on the mark, but at least two of the brokers were aware of what was going on during the period in question. While no one else at that company besides Haynes had been implicated, it wouldn't surprise Maya if the government widened the investigation to include others. No settlement had officially been inked.

The most puzzling aspect of all this was that there was no trace of where the profits had gone. The company's banking accounts and investments were all in order, there were no red flags in Haynes's personal accounts, nor were there any traces of money being held in offshore or foreign accounts by anyone in the company or their relatives. Unless Haynes had a suitcase full of cash buried in his backyard, it didn't make sense. This was obviously why the government was taking so long to charge Haynes—they were trying to find the money first.

And Haynes's story? Since neither Roger nor Maya had been granted an opportunity to interview Haynes, Maya was relying on Peter Fusco's recitation of what Haynes had to say. Allen Haynes's explanation was that while there may have been some "mistakes" in the processing of transactions, no stocks were intentionally sold short. He believed that the government's informant was either a competitor or a disgruntled client who lost money in some risky trades or something. According to Fusco, Haynes would be willing to make nonadmission restitution to clients and to implement new safeguards to avoid such future *mistakes*. Peter Fusco was awaiting the government's move before offering this version of events to them, and he seemed to honestly believe that it was going to fly.

Having flipped the scenario around for days, Maya's head was spinning. Lying on the living room floor now, staring at the ceiling and trying not to think about Vic, Maya's skin began to prickle as she gave more thought to Peter Fusco's demeanor. While he never directly instructed her to stay away from Haynes, his exact words were quite clear in their meaning.

"Don't concern yourself with speaking to Allen. I talk to him regularly."

"But—"

"I'm sure there is nothing else to say on the matter." Peter's exasperation with Maya's persistence was evident in his tone.

When she commented that they needed to conduct a mock interview with Haynes to prepare him for being deposed by the government, a task which was as important as it was eminent, Peter's answer was, "Again, don't concern yourself with speaking to him. I'll handle it." With that he'd returned to reviewing the papers on his desk, summarily dismissing Maya without another word or thought.

While Peter Fusco was known to be an excellent attorney with a long list of happy clients, to Maya the man was as oily as the English settlers when they stole Manhattan. He was a flashy dresser and fast talker with a quick smile that beamed at about a hundred megawatts. Maya never forgot her dad's advice—never trust a person with a quick smile, especially in New York City.

As Maya leafed through the manila file folder Roger Perkins had given her, a folded piece of ivory-colored paper she had not noticed before fell out. It was an invoice for services printed on Madison Pritchard letterhead, addressed to Wexton & Haynes. The invoice was for legal services rendered for the month of May of last year and the amount invoiced was a quarter of a million dollars. The amount caught Maya's attention instantly because it was an extremely high sum of money for one month of services to a small company like Wexton & Haynes. Maya searched through the piles of documents on her floor until she came upon a folder marked BILLING. It contained all the invoices Madison Pritchard had ever generated to Haynes's company.

She had retrieved this billing folder from one of the boxes of mislabeled and disorganized documents at the Wexton & Haynes offices in Boston. Maya tabulated the invoiced amounts on a scrap of paper and was astounded when the figure reached three million dollars. There was no way in the world Wexton & Haynes could have afforded to pay Madison Pritchard three million dollars over a period of only six years. Their bottom line was a far cry from three million dollars, even when the economy had a good year. Unless this number wasn't part of Haynes's bottom line.

Maya jumped up as an almost electric jolt shot through her brain, landing like a punch in her gut. What if Allen Haynes was more than just a "close personal friend" of Peter Fusco's? Peter was entirely too confident that the government wouldn't find enough to bury Haynes. He was so sure that the most they would be able to charge him with would be failure to comply with various securities reform acts and that Haynes would fare okay. And how come Haynes would only talk with Peter? Even the most eccentric clients realized that a partner at a law firm didn't handle a case entirely on his own. He had a team and, in order to provide the best representation possible, the client had to be willing to deal with the entire team.

Maya's mind was racing wildly as she tried to figure out if she was merely grasping at straws. But no matter how she tried to dismiss her suspicions, they kept coming back to her, nagging at her. The firm's business was great. They had a lot of big-money clients, high cash intake. But Peter Fusco was the partner at the firm who by far most looked like money. He had an apartment located at Central Park West, another down in SoHo. His primary residence was a four-acre home in Larchmont, New York, and he had summer homes in both Maui and Europe. He drove, or rather was driven in, a shiny new Cadillac Seville, said to be upgraded yearly. He had a son at Harvard and a daughter at Yale. According to the associate mill, his wife did not come from money, had never worked a day in her life and had had every kind of cosmetic improvement surgically possible. Rumor also had it that he had a twentysomething college student stashed at one of his New York apartments.

Maybe the other partners were just low-key with their money, Maya acquiesced. Or maybe they didn't have quite as much to flash as Peter Fusco.

Chapter Seventeen

Up All Night

"I suggest you leave it alone. Why risk your neck?" Katrina's rhetorical question was slightly muffled by a mouthful of lettuce.

"But don't I have a duty to tell the truth?" Maya asked.

"Get real, Maya, you're a defense attorney. Where's the truth in that?"

"Katrina, I took an oath to respect and uphold the law. What kind of attorney would I be if I just turned my head and allowed this mess to go down?"

"An employed one, that's what kind. I mean, think about it, Maya. You work for the man. He's a very senior partner of one of the most prestigious law firms in the city. He's got connections coming out the ass and he's calling all the shots."

"So? So what does that make him—above the law?"

"In some ways, yes. Because it's those with the money who made the law in the first place," Katrina surmised.

Maya sprayed more lemon-scented Pledge onto Katrina's cherry-wood coffee table, revisiting the spot she'd already polished twice. She watched the foamy chemical dissolve slowly until only a thin residue remained, but no answers were to be found in the clearing. She worked furiously for a moment, thinking about what Katrina had just said; she knew Katrina had a valid point. On the other hand, what did that mean for society as a whole? She sighed as she thought about it all, feeling as if the world with all its gloom and doom were resting on her shoulders.

"What about the client? No matter what magic Peter Fusco thinks he's got up his sleeve, this guy is looking at substantial jail time plus the loss for life of his license to deal in securities. Now I understand that he did in fact do the crime and he's got to face the music. But he wasn't in it alone. I'm almost one hundred and five percent sure that Peter is the missing link—he's where the money went. My duty is to represent the client to the best of my ability, Katrina, and how can I honestly say I'm doing that if I turn a blind eye?"

Katrina chewed methodically for a minute, brown wire-rimmed glasses perched on the edge of her diminutive nose. As she studiously gazed upon Maya, contemplating the question, she looked every bit the schoolteacher she'd become. Finally, she swallowed, balanced her bowl on her stomach and used her index finger to theatrically write on the wall above her.

"Maya, grow up and read the writing on the wall. This has nothing to do with truth, justice and the American way. It's about the dollar bill, and them that's got it got the game sewed."

Maya fumed. "I guess I'm supposed to be okay with that?"

"Look, I know you are a highly ethical, morally evolved person. That's one reason why I love you so much. But sooner or later you've got to accept that not everyone shares your values. And you've definitely got to stop letting this mess bother you to the point where you're driving down here to D.C. on a Sunday morning in the middle of a hurricane, arriving on my doorstep, unannounced, to spend the entire day cleaning my apartment . . . not that it couldn't use the attention."

Maya had to acknowledge that it was a little ill-advised for her to have rented a car, albeit a cute little red Corsica, and driven down to D.C. during what turned out to be a severe thunderstorm complete with torrential rains and high speed winds. But after she stayed up, the night before, tossing around her suspicions about Peter Fusco being Haynes's cohort, she was in a tailspin.

Her first reaction was to march into his office Monday morning and put it on the table. If she told him what she suspected and told him she planned to go to the other partners, maybe that would force him to come clean. But then again, it was possible that the other partners, at least some of them, already knew and were even in on it. For all she knew, they could be funneling all sorts of ill-gotten gains through the firm. The more she thought about it, the bigger the conspiracy theory grew in her mind.

By the time she woke up Sunday morning, she was confused, tired and ready to run away. That's when she decided she needed to talk to someone who kept a cooler, more methodical head than she. Before she even had a chance to call ahead, she'd rented the car from Enterprise a block away from her apartment and was on Katrina's doorstep. Now, here was Katrina, saying all the right things—things that made more sense than anything Maya had been able to come up with all night. However, she could definitely do without the sarcasm.

"Shut up, you old wench." Maya laughed, tossing the dust rag at Katrina, who lay on the sofa. It landed on top of the bowl of salad.

"Maya! Ooh," she said as she tossed it back at her friend, hitting her on the side of her face. "Now my salad's gonna taste like furniture polish."

"And you're going to eat it anyway, Miss Piggy."

"You damned skippy!" Katrina laughed.

"Oh, man, Kat." Maya sighed. "I just feel like no matter what I do or don't do, this whole thing is going to blow up in somebody's face, possibly mine."

"Stop worrying. When and if the shit hits the fan, just duck."

Maya looked at her friend for a minute, knowing that in all the years they'd known one another, Katrina had never steered her wrong. Katrina's guidance was always good, solid advice she could depend on. Maybe this time was no different.

"Yeah, Kat, I think you're right. I'm not going to worry about this."

"That's my girl. Moving right along . . . tell me about this dude you've been messing around with."

"Which one?"

The tomato Katrina was about to bite into slipped from her lips as her mouth gaped open and her eyes lit up.

"What do you mean, which one? I know you haven't been holding out on me." Katrina pointed an accusing finger at Maya.

"Maybe I have," Maya said coyly. She returned to polishing the table. She was merely pulling Katrina's leg. It didn't take a rocket scientist to pick up on the fact that the guy she'd met at Julia's party, Mark Mantale, had been flirting with her, and, quiet as it's kept, she might have been playing the game a little bit herself.

Not that she was interested in him in that way, because she wasn't, even though he'd seemed to be a very nice guy and a gentleman. But, as every woman knows, it's precisely the moment when you're pissed off with your guy that other men seem to find you most desirable, and you tend to latch on to that attention a little, just because you're angry. Letting another man buy you **a** drink or throw compliments at you, or even take you to lunch—no matter how platonic the situation—is a woman's way of letting her man know he messed up, even if he never finds out about it.

That said, Maya was, in fact, only joking. She had no real interest in Mark and, more importantly, had no intentions of kicking Vic to the curb over this—provided he called her sooner rather than later. However, the look of utter surprise now plastered on Katrina's face was priceless.

Chapter Eighteen

Don't Call Me, I'll Call You

"Well, well, well, Ms. Wilkins. You seem to have made quite an impression on a certain someone at my party Saturday night. Do tell." Julia plopped down in one of the chairs in front of Maya's desk, propping her elbows on the edge and resting her chin in upturned palms.

"What in the world are you talking about, Julia?" Maya asked, confusion wrinkling her brows. She stuck a ballpoint pen in between the pages she had been reading in the *Securities & Futures Trading Index* and closed the voluminous book.

"Oh, don't play innocent with me. I noticed the two of you chatting it up Friday night but I didn't really think anything of it. But I was awakened Saturday morning—okay, Saturday afternoon, really—by his telephone call. And the purpose of that call was to drill me about you."

There was no mistaking the hungry look in Julia's eyes. She was a junkie desperate for a heavy hit of the gossip pipe. Maya donned her most unreadable mask and deadpan tone.

"Are you talking about Mark?"

"As if you didn't know. Yes, I'm talking about Mark. He wanted to play twenty questions about you." Julia seemed to be salivating as she waited eagerly for Maya's response.

"What did he ask you?"

"The regular stuff: are you seeing anyone, what's your favorite color, where'd you go to school."

"And what exactly did you tell him?" Maya said, her skin bristling.

"I told him that as far as I knew, you were not dating. You spend all of your time working. You graduated from Albany University—"

"I did my undergraduate studies at Howard University, then I went to Albany School of Law," Maya interjected. She hated when the other associates glossed over the fact that she'd gone to Howard like that didn't mean anything. When they were speaking of themselves, they always made sure to mention both undergraduate and graduate school—the two names going together like peanut butter and jelly. Columbia and Yale, Harvard U and Harvard Law. Maybe Howard didn't fit the bill as one of *their* top schools, but she was damned proud to be a Howard University alumni and she wanted to make sure they knew it.

"Right, right," Julia continued. "Anyway, I basically told him that I didn't know anything about your favorite anything—you know, you not having been here very long and all. I also told him that he should ask you all these questions himself."

"And?"

"Well, he said he would but he didn't want to call you here at the office, since that was the only way he knew to reach you. He asked me for your home phone number, but I don't have it. Besides, I wouldn't give it to him unless you told me to." Julia's vain attempt at passing herself off as a confidante was wasted on Maya.

"Well, thanks a lot, Julia."

"So?" she asked, leaning back in her seat with an expectant glisten in her eyes.

"So, what?" Maya asked.

"So what's the story? Are you attracted to him? He's obviously way interested in you. You two seem to have made a definite connection."

"He's really a nice guy and all, but we just shared friendly 'party' conversation. There really wasn't anything going on," Maya answered in as matter-of-fact a tone as she could muster. There was no way she was going to sit there talking boy talk and giggling with Julia. She didn't know a lot about the woman, but she knew enough to know the story would be all over the office before lunch. She felt herself get a little heated again when she realized that if Vic had attended the party with her, this conversation wouldn't be taking place.

"Okay, well," Julia began, sensing that Maya had no intentions of discussing the issue further, "here's his telephone number, just in case you want to talk to him." She picked up Maya's notepad, pulled a pen from the penholder between them and scratched down a telephone number.

"Thank you, Julia. Oh, by the way, it really was a nice party," Maya answered, not looking at the notepad at all.

"Thanks, Maya. I'm glad you enjoyed yourself. I'll see you later on," Julia said as she left the office. Maya got up from her desk and went around to the door, shutting it softly.

"Hmm." She sighed as she returned to the desk and picked up the notepad.

"What next?" she said aloud. Here she was with a job smack in the middle of white America that she was struggling to digest, living in a city where she had no friends, no ties, dating a guy who according to the societal rules about status and dating she shouldn't be dealing with and who she was dying to see again. On top of it all, a friend of a co-worker—both of whom happened to fall outside her race—was interested in her. She had never imagined herself dating outside her race, not even when she was growing up in Tarrytown, New York, where her classmates and neighbors were predominately white or Asian. Truth be told, she had never really felt comfortable around them.

As for the occasional show of interest from white men, she was never sure if they were genuine or merely making an attempt at experimenting, so she kept her distance. It always felt as though they were watching her every move, sizing her up. Relationships were difficult enough without having to crab crawl across the interracial minefield. She'd leave all that multiculturalism to Katrina, who had dated men from every color in the Crayola box.

Maya tore the page off the pad, folded it and stuck it absently in her top drawer. That done, she returned to the wonderful world of securities.

Chapter Nineteen

Lonely Heart

"Come on, man, play ball," Malik said, his eyes shooting daggers in Vic's direction.

"All right. Let's go," Vic answered, wiping the sweat from his forehead with the bottom of his T-shirt. He shook his head from side to side in an effort to clear his mind.

The men were playing a game of three-on-three at the Harlem YMCA, and Vic's team was getting stomped. Malik, Vic's closest friend since third grade, was growing steadily more impatient with Vic's poor performance as the game wore on. Vic's brother-in-law Andre, the final member of their team, attempted to cover Vic where he could, scoring five of their nine points. Malik had scored the other four, making Vic a serious handicap.

The other side reached fifteen in a seemingly effortless showing. Andre, Vic and Malik left the court and headed for the showers, promising the other side a rematch the following week.

"What's up with you, man? My grandmama could have beat you out there today," Malik said.

"Hey, now, take it easy on the brother," Andre defended.

Vic stepped into the shower stall, the hot water pelting his skin with force. "Whatever, Malik," he yelled over the loudness of the water. "My head just wasn't in it today."

"Yeah, well, you keep playing like that and I'm gonna have to retire this little trio we've got going. I can't be coming down here every week and getting embarrassed just 'cause your head ain't in it." Malik twirled his towel as he spoke and then snapped it in Vic's direction, missing hitting his thigh by a hair.

"Knock it off, man," Vic hissed.

"Aww, what's the matter with the poor baby? I bet it's that girl. Man, she's got you whipped with a capital *W*," Malik joked.

"You don't know what you're talkin' about. Ain't nobody whipped over here," Vic said.

"I don't know, Vic, Malik may be on to something. You and Maya seemed to be going at it pretty hard for a minute there and now all of a sudden, nothing. You haven't mentioned her name once the last two times I've seen you. What's up?" Andre asked.

"Nothing's up. Things are a little icy right now, but I'm not stressin' it."

Wrapped from the waist down in bath towels, the men exited the showers and moved into the changing area.

"So the lovebirds had a little fight? Well, I can't say I'm mad about that. I was sick and tired of hearing you go on and on about that girl. Maya this, Maya that. Man! Maybe now you'll have time to hang again."

"Damn, that's cold, Malik." Andre laughed.

"It's the truth, though. If I've said it once, I've said it a thousand times, women ain't nothing but trouble. That's why you're supposed to hit it and quit it," Malik bellowed emphatically.

"Spoken like a true bachelor," Andre answered.

"That's right. Bachelor for life. Getting through the day is hard as it is. Then you want to add to the daily tasks of living having to deal with some woman and her numerous issues. Love 'em and leave 'em, I say," Malik said, swaying his hips from side to side.

"Vic, I hope you don't take half of what this fool has to say seriously. Listen, man, I've never met Maya so I wouldn't begin to guess if she's the right woman for you. Your sister, however, had nothing but nice things to say about her."

"Yeah, they hit it off," Vic answered as he toweled himself off.

Vic listened intently to Andre, hoping he could help clear up the mixed emotions he had been experiencing since the argument with Maya. He had come to look at Andre as a big brother of sorts. Andre and Victor's sister Phyllis had met when Vic was a sophomore in high school. At that time, Vic had been hanging with a pretty rough crowd, getting into fights and cutting classes, among other things. The more time Phyllis and Andre spent together, the more they tried to include Vic in their outings.

Phyllis was worried about Vic getting into serious trouble so she asked Andre to connect with him. Andre, four years Vic's senior, had become someone Vic could talk to in addition to Pops, who wasn't always able to cross the generational divide.

It was Andre who convinced Vic to go back to college. Vic had dropped out of Morgan State after only one semester, convinced academia wasn't for him. Truth was, he was homesick. He came back to New York and landed a job at Madison Pritchard as a rounds clerk in the mailroom. He worked days and spent his nights partying. His father stayed on his back, warning him constantly about the dangers of not developing a life plan. But it was primarily Vic's conversations with

Andre that prompted him to reconsider furthering his education.

"All I know is, when you do find the right woman, well, that's when life gets easier," Andre concluded.

"I don't know about that, Andre. I thought Maya and I were headed towards somethin', but then just like that—"

"See, that's what I'm talking about. Women have too many issues," Malik said.

"Man, everybody's got issues. So what? Vic, listen, if you're feelin' this girl, then don't let her slip away. You don't want to have to spend the rest of your days kicking it with this idiot and talking about would've-could've."

"Shut up, Dre. You've been married to Phyllis all of two minutes and you act like you're Bill Cosby or somebody, giving advice," Malik said.

"Phyllis and I have been married for more than three years and together a lot longer. Believe me, I know what I'm talking about."

As Vic headed home alone, Andre's words rang in his ears. The thought that he could be right and that Maya could be "the one" scared Vic. At the same time, he was strangely comforted by the possibility of it. He spent the remainder of the day doing some serious soul-searching as he tried to figure out what to do.

Vic paced around the brownstone like a hungry lion. The past two weeks had been agonizing, but they were nothing compared to tonight. Finally, he decided he needed to talk to Maya, to work things out. He couldn't stand not being able to see her and talk to her. He realized how stupid their argument had been, and while he believed it was she who turned a molehill into a mountain, he didn't care. His intention was to just apologize if he had to in order to get back into the routine they'd created.

This willingness to apologize for having done nothing wrong was an incredible feat for Vic. He would sooner walk away from a relationship than be made to feel like a punk. But Maya was different. Try as he might, he could not get her out of his head. He thought about her at work, hoping to bump into her, but at the same time praying he didn't. The torment of seeing her and having her turn up her nose at him would be too much for him to bear.

He replayed their kisses a thousand times. Explored her body in his mind a million times. Every time he was with her, he wanted to take her in his arms and make love to her until she begged him to stop. He wanted to talk to her all day and all night, eager to exchange ideas with her or hear her opinions on every topic imaginable.

Tonight, driven by thoughts of her sexy smile and soft body, Vic had decided that enough was enough. The desire to hear her laughter and to smell her perfume was unbearable. Across the street and about a quarter of a block from her building, Vic parked his bike in the only available spot. He was shutting off the ignition when he saw her exit the building. She had on a cream dress that dangerously hugged every curve and stopped midthigh. The tall, matching leather boots gave her a couple of inches and fit her shapely calves like a glove. She sashayed down the steps and slid into the passenger's seat of a waiting silver BMW. The tinted windows and the distance from which he stood prevented him from getting a look at the driver. The car took off, leaving him standing there in its dust.

By the time Vic regained his senses and became inclined to follow them, the car had long since turned the corner. He fought the urge to race around Manhattan after the car like a madman until he tracked them down and tore his woman from whatever man's embrace he found her in. Instead, he went home and wore a new groove into the hardwood floors, his Jordans making a squeaking sound as they slapped against the floor's polyurethane surface. The muscles in his neck and back were taut with tension, rendering him unable to relax.

"Hey, son," Victor Sr. said as he came in the house some time later.

"Hey, Pops." Vic was now sprawled across the brown leather sofa with his head thrown back and a forearm covering his eyes. Exhaustion had finally brought his body to rest, his mind still racing full speed. R&B crooner Carl Thomas's latest ballad blared from the oversize TEAC speakers situated on either side of the room. Save for the glow cast by a large jasmine-scented candle-in-a-jar on the coffee table, the room was dark.

"Uh-oh," Victor Sr. said as he made his way to the stereo. He lowered the volume, took another look at his son and sat down in the recliner across from the sofa. "What did you do?"

"I don't know what you're talkin' about," Vic replied.

He was too weary with anger and disappointment to get into it with his father. Unfortunately, Victor Sr. wasn't about to drop the subject.

"Yeah, I think you do. You've been sulking around here for the past couple of weeks, barely speaking, barely eating. And now you're laid up on the sofa looking like Who Shot Johnny and listening to love songs. Einstein I'm not, but I'll bet my last penny that you and that gal are fighting. And since I know you like I know the back of my hand, I know you did something. So what did you do?"

Vic sighed. There was no use trying not to have this conversation. Vic knew his dad wouldn't let it go.

"We had a fight . . . over somethin' stupid."

"So apologize and move on."

"Yeah, well, that's what I was plannin' to do. Until I saw her steppin' out with the next dude."

"Whoa."

"Yeah, whoa is right." Vic again felt the anger at seeing Maya, looking fine as hell, on her way out with God knew who to do God knew what, Vic obviously having been diminished to a distant memory.

"Does she know you saw her?"

"Nah, she was too busy slippin' into the dude's car."

"Do you know the guy? Maybe he's a co-worker, a cousin," Victor Sr. ventured.

"Please. As dressed up as she was, he definitely wasn't a co-worker. I didn't see him, but I didn't have to."

"Wait. Hold the phone. You didn't see him? You didn't see the person in the car at all?"

"Nah, but—"

" 'Nah, but' nothing. How dare you make assumptions about that girl before you know what's what. It could have been a female, or a bear for that matter." Victor Sr. threw his hands into the air. "Boy, do you have anything in that head besides straw? You know what, you keep on actin' the fool and I guarantee you're gonna lose her. And you'll have nobody to blame but yourself."

Victor Sr. shook his head a couple of times before heading to the kitchen. He secretly wished there was some way to pass his years of experience and heartache on to his son so as to spare him from making some of the same mistakes. He knew Vic was too young to understand that sometimes you had to fight for your woman. You had to be strong enough to slay any dragon, be it physical or psychological. Sometimes a woman wanted you to prove that you were willing to go to the mat for her.

Victor Sr.'s biggest regret was not fighting for his wife. When she walked out, he let his wounded ego stop him from going after her, even though he knew where she was staying for the first couple of months. Hindsight was definitely twenty-twenty and, given the opportunity to do it all over again, he would have done things differently. Watching his son wallowing in self-pity because of damaged pride, possibly allowing the best thing that had ever happened to him to slip through his fingers, was too much like looking into a mirror. Victor Sr. had met a lot of women in his day—enough to know a good one when he saw one. As he'd said before, Maya was a keeper. He just hoped Vic would realize that before it was too late.

"I'm gonna make us some burgers," he called over his shoulder.

Vic didn't bother to tell his father that he still didn't think he could eat. He just hung his head, thinking about what his father had said. Maybe it wasn't a guy. But did it matter? She still was obviously not the least bit upset about their separation. He tried to get mad all over again, but the only emotion he could muster up was wanting. He wanted Maya so bad that it was starting to hurt. Maybe it was time for him to cut his losses before this thing started costing him too much.

"Damn," Vic said aloud, knowing that no matter which way he went, he was caught out there.

Chapter Twenty

Out on the Town

"Girl, I'm about to burst. Let's go to the ladies' room," Maya said, gathering her wrap around her bare shoulders as she stood. Katrina followed her as she headed out of the center seats of row D and up the aisle toward the main lobby. It was Friday night, two weeks after Julia's party and even longer since she'd spoken to Vic. She was still pissed off at his attitude, but that didn't stop her from missing him like crazy. She was prepared to forgive his behavior and move on. However, he hadn't called her.

She'd been so busy at work lately that she'd barely seen more than a passing glimpse of him at the office. She'd been getting home after midnight almost every night that week, and the first thing she did when she entered the apartment was check the answering machine. Each time she was disappointed to find that there were no messages from him, not even a call and hang-up. In her opinion, the disagreement they'd had was hardly serious enough to warrant a permanent split. She figured they'd both take a couple of days to cool off and then he'd come by her office or call her and say something silly. Things would go back to normal. It never occurred to her to call him because he was the one who'd walked out angry, so it was up to him to walk back in. That was what the rule book said, everybody knew that. A no-brainer, as far as she was concerned. But obviously Vic didn't know about "The Rules."

So here it was, two weeks later and nothing. She was grateful when Katrina called Thursday night to say she had gotten last-minute tickets from a colleague for Friday's eight o'clock performance of *Aida*. Katrina drove up the next afternoon and Maya cut out of the office shortly after three. They'd had time to get dressed up and enjoy dinner at L'Impero, a French restaurant in Tudor City, where Katrina exchanged telephone numbers with some guy she claimed was recently featured on the cover of *Black Enterprise* magazine. During dinner Katrina only mentioned Vic's name once, to which Maya's resounding response warned Katrina to let that sleeping dog lie.

The ladies came out of the restroom still laughing about the bourgeoisie woman who'd been so busy primping and putting on airs that she didn't realize she had toilet tissue stuck to the bottom of her shoe. Maya would have told her if not for the fact that the woman had slapped Maya in the face with a toss of her mangled weave and then looked at Maya as if it were her fault. Between the blue eye contacts, the fake claws and the nasal, valley-girl speech, the woman looked like a Barbie doll dipped in coffee and come to life.

"PB in full effect." Katrina laughed. PB stood for Pretentious Bitch, a term Katrina used to describe all the wanna-be–white black women who had bought into the myth that beauty equaled long hair, light skin and blue eyes. There was nothing worse than a black woman who went to great lengths to look like something out of *Vogue* magazine and ended up looking like a blow-up doll with a bad weave.

Maya was laughing so hard, she didn't hear her name being called at first. It was Katrina who tapped her and nodded in the direction the voice was coming from. Maya turned around just as Mark Mantale reached her, her final snicker catching in her throat.

"Maya," Mark said, "I thought that was you. How are you?"

Mark smiled, his eyes twinkling, looking truly thrilled to have bumped into her. This "chance" meeting was just the opportunity he needed. He made a mental note to send flowers to Julia, who had run into Maya as the latter left the office that afternoon, learned of her plans for the evening and then given Mark the heads-up.

"I'm fine . . ."

"Mark," he filled in, trying to brush off the fact that she couldn't remember his name. He was certain he had made a good impression on her. Granted, she hadn't called him, although Julia swore she'd given Maya the number, but that was a small thing. It was obvious to him that he'd have to work a little harder than usual to bait this fish, but he'd never been a quitter.

"Yes, Mark," Maya finished, noting the effect her intentional memory lapse had on him. "And you?"

"Good. I'm here with a co-worker, Wendell. His sister plays the lead."

"Oh, really. She's very talented."

"Mmm-hmm," Mark said. There was a moment of silence in which Maya became lost in her thoughts. Julia had told her of Mark's interest and, certainly, had reported back to Mark. The fact that Maya had not acted on it made this encounter awkward. Maya hoped he wasn't offended, but if he was like most guys, he had taken it personally. Guys never seemed to understand that there were times in a woman's life when she just wasn't interested and it didn't matter if she was seeing someone or not. Even if you were the finest thing on two legs, the most educated, worldly or whatever, she was unmoved.

As the silence grew more pronounced, Mark smiled down at Maya as if waiting for her to apologize for not calling. Maya was trying to think of something to say when she felt Katrina nudge her thigh with her evening bag.

"Oh, where are my manners? Katrina Brewster, this is Mark Mantale. Mark, this is my best friend Katrina."

"Hi, there," Katrina said, slipping the tips of her fingers into his outstretched hand.

He shook her hand warmly.

"So, don't tell me you two beautiful ladies are out alone this evening?"

Maya coughed uncomfortably, but Katrina quickly responded.

"We're not alone—we're together." She smiled as Mark nodded, laughing at her cleverness. Good answer.

"Well, do you two together ladies have plans after the show? Wendell and I were thinking about going for a drink or something."

"Well," Maya said slowly, looking at Katrina sternly, "Katrina kinda raced up here from D.C. this afternoon and she does have to get back early tomorrow, so we really didn't plan on—"

"Nonsense, Maya," Katrina interrupted, "I won't turn into a pumpkin at midnight."

Maya stood there, wondering what had happened after all these years of friendship to make Katrina slip up like that. They had always been able to read each other's minds, follow the other's leads without so much as making eye contact.

"Good. Why don't we meet out front after the show?" Mark said as the lights began to flicker.

Maya kept a pained smile pasted to her lips as she and Katrina made their way back to their seats.

"What'd you do that for?" she hissed the minute they were seated.

"Do what?"

"That . . . back there," Maya said, nodding her head toward the lobby area.

"What 'that'?"

"Katrina, don't even play with me. Why'd you agree to go out with Mark and his friend?"

"Why not? I thought he was a friend of yours."

"Acquaintance, that's all. We met at a party last week," Maya informed Katrina.

"So what's the big deal?"

"The big deal is that he's the friend of a co-worker who is extremely nosy and the creator, owner and chief executive officer of the gossip mill at the office. Top that off with the fact that she told me he was interested in me and gave me his telephone number, but I never called. I really don't think going out with them tonight is a good idea."

"Because you didn't call him, right?" Katrina asked dubiously.

"Right, I didn't call him, and I had no intentions of calling him."

"Because he's a friend of a co-worker?"

"Right, a nosy co-worker."

"Bullshit," Katrina snapped.

"Bullshit?"

"Yes, bullshit. You didn't call him because he's a white guy who's interested in your black ass."

"Katrina! That is so not true."

Maya stomped her foot testily, her tone having gone up a notch. This outburst prompted a glare from the woman seated in front of them.

"Yes, it is," Katrina whispered. "When's the last time you dated a white guy?"

"Katrina, that really has nothing to do with—"

"Mmm-hmm. Like I thought: never."

A look of complete satisfaction spread across Katrina's face as she watched Maya squirm uncomfortably in her seat.

"Look, I'm not about to argue with you over my dating history. I just really don't think that I want to risk having my business spread all over the office."

"Okay, now you're reaching. You don't want your business all over the office, yet you're dating—or were dating—a guy who actually works there."

"That's different," Maya defended.

"Why?"

Since Maya didn't have an answer to that question, she sat silently sulking for the next twenty minutes.

"Look, Maya. Mark seems like a nice guy and I really need to hang out and have some fun. I've been cooped up with those damned college kids for way too long. And with Dominic acting like . . . Look, if it's going to make you uncomfortable, I'll come down with a headache or something."

"He won't believe that now, after you were all cheerleader peppy!"

"Uh-huh. Yes, he will. I'll even faint at his feet for effect," Katrina said, throwing her head back against the seat and fanning herself dramatically.

"Oh, stop it, would you? You are definitely not Oscar material. It's all right, we can go."

As a grin broke out on Katrina's face, Maya added sternly, "For a little while."

"Yes, mother," Katrina said.

"And what's going on with you and Dominic, anyway?"

"Drama, girl, but I really don't want to talk about it right now."

"What hap—" Maya began, but broke off after reading the smoldering glare in Katrina's eyes. Maya would wait either until Katrina wanted to talk about it or until she was forced to shake it out of her.

At the end of the play, they headed up the aisle, Maya still certain that this was something she could live without doing. She ran her hand down the back of her dress, smoothing out the wrinkles courtesy of the seat she'd occupied for the last two hours. She thought about Vic for a minute, wondering if he'd ever call and considering further how she would feel if he didn't. Before she could come up with an answer, Katrina interrupted her thoughts.

"So, have you ever met Mark's friend Wendell?"

"Nope," Maya answered.

"Oh, great, so I could end up with the son of Godzilla or something for a date," Katrina said as she sprayed Cinnamon Burst breath spray in her mouth.

"First of all, this is not a date. It's just four people going out for drinks," Maya said, just as they reached the main exit door. "And secondly, this was your bright idea, remember?"

Katrina didn't get a chance to answer because they spotted Mark waving at them from the curb. He was standing alone.

"Maybe Godzuki got caught by the zookeeper," Katrina whispered through clenched teeth as they walked over to where Mark stood.

"Stop it," Maya whispered back. "Mark, hi."

"Ladies," he responded. "Wendell decided to go and get the car. He should be pulling up any minute."

"Okay," Katrina answered, shooting a quick look at Maya, who remained expressionless.

The three of them stood chatting for a minute about the play until a silver-gray Jaguar pulled up next to them. Wendell, a tall, slim, freshly tanned, R&B singer Jon B look-alike got out of the car and came around to the sidewalk where they stood.

"Wendell, this is Maya Wilkins, the savvy female bloodhound I told you about, and this is her partner in crime, Katrina Brewster." Maya couldn't help but smile at Mark's introduction. He certainly wasn't kidding when he said that lawyers usually left a bad taste in his mouth.

"It's better than pushing around other people's money all day," Maya directed at Mark jokingly. She shook Wendell's hand and sneered at Mark, who clutched his chest as if mortally wounded.

"Hi, Wendell. Nice to meet you," Katrina said as she took her turn shaking Wendell's hand, smiling in a way Maya was certain meant she was pleased that Wendell bore no resemblance to any monsters.

Wendell opened the front passenger door and Katrina slid into the seat. Before Mark could do the same with the back door, Maya opened it, sat down and closed it behind her. She was determined to do everything she could, subtly, to drive home the point that this was not a date and that she and Mark were, and would remain, merely acquaintances.

Chapter Twenty-One

Poor Substitute

The evening turned out better than Maya expected. They ended up at an after-hours spot on the lower east side. Trunie's was a storefront watering hole that was nothing to look at from the outside. It was in the middle of a nondescript block and the frosted windows restricted the view from the street. Inside, however, it was like a tropical paradise. There were large, lush potted trees and plants in every available space from the floor to the ceiling. Interspersed between the greenery were small four-seater tables, each adorned with two tapered, floral-scented candles.

In the center of the room a small platform had been constructed to serve as a stage. A band played in the far right corner of the room while an assortment of talents took the stage one after the other. There were poets, blues singers, Bohemian rappers, you name it. Some of the talent was incredibly good. In particular there was a guy who recited a poem called "Vagina Servitude" whom Maya found herself intrigued by. The fact that he bared a strong resemblance to Vic was most likely the reason for the attraction; thinking about Vic then brought a melancholy mood over Maya, but Mark worked diligently to lift it.

"I wonder what the prettiest girl in the room is thinking about that's got her looking so forlorn right now?" he asked.

"Smooth," Maya said. "At least you didn't offer me a penny for my thoughts."

"I'm certain your thoughts would be worth much more than a penny."

"That's right. Inflation." Maya laughed.

She glanced at Katrina, who was openly flirting with Wendell. It amazed Maya the way Katrina could hold a person in rapture with the tiniest iota of effort. Her smile was as sweet as it was seductive, and Wendell looked as if he'd fallen in love at first sight. She giggled softly at his jokes, never taking her eyes off him. He leaned in so closely toward Katrina, it appeared he would fall off the edge of his seat at any moment.

Maya had every intention of chewing Katrina out later about being such a tease, especially given the fact that Dominic had been her steady boyfriend for the past three years. Those two were most assuredly headed for the altar and had even been voted Best Couple in law school. Secretly, however, Maya wished she could be a little more like Katrina. Here she was, sitting in a sensuous setting across the table from a very handsome man who obviously was interested in her, and Maya was thinking about another man who thought she was "a stupid snob," to paraphrase.

She turned her attention to Mark, making every effort not to think about Vic anymore that evening. They talked about music, books, places they'd each visited. Maya admired the fact that Mark was so well traveled. It reminded her of her father, who loved to regale her with stories of places he'd visited, both far and near, a memory she shared with Mark. When Mark began to ask more questions about her father, Maya changed the subject, steering the conversation to safer waters where the pleasant mood of the evening could remain unhindered. Under Mark's gentle probing, Maya informed him that she was seeing someone.

"You don't sound too sure about that," Mark said intuitively.

"Well, we've hit a little bump in the road . . . nothing serious," Maya responded.

"Mmm, that's too bad," Mark lamented sarcastically.

Maya decided to let that little dig slide and direct the conversation in a different direction.

"So, Mark, tell me more about yourself. How'd you get involved in securities?"

"My dad always told me I needed to focus on a career in finance. He's a banker—heads one of the internationals. Anyway, he said the best way to ensure you'll always make money is to surround yourself with it."

"Come on, don't tell me you're just in it to get rich? Don't you enjoy what you do?" Maya asked.

"Yes and no. I mean, I get a rush sometimes, trying to determine what's going up, what's going down in the market. But sometimes I wish I could do something else."

"Then why don't you?"

"Short answer? My father."

Maya considered Mark's words, contemplating that no matter how different people were, there was at least one commonality, that being the magnitude of the impact a parent's ideals had on their children's lives, in one way or another.

"What else would you do?" Maya queried.

"I don't know. I've never really thought much about it. Finance is in my blood, I guess."

"Hmm. Well, personally, I don't have a brain for

numbers. I'm dealing with this case now, a securities fraud situation, and just trying to decipher all that financial mumbo jumbo makes my head ache."

"Well, it's a good thing we met then, huh? I could give you a crash course and turn you into an expert overnight. I'm sure you'd make a terrific broker or analyst. Believe me, we could use more pretty women like you in the field."

Maya had to admit that Mark's boyish charm and flattering comments were endearing. Unfortunately for him, those characteristics paled in comparison to Vic's attributes.

"Thanks, Mark, but I think I'll stick with the job I already have."

"Are you sure? It'd give me an excuse to spend more time with you."

Maya laughed Mark's flirting off, realizing it was time to bring the evening to a close. Wendell drove the ladies back to the parking garage at the theater, where they retrieved Katrina's car. The ladies politely turned down Mark's offer to follow them home to make sure they were safe.

Later, Katrina informed Maya that there would be no connection between her and Wendell.

"I was just enjoying the night, that's all. What about you and Mark? Now *he's* got it going on."

"Yeah, well, he can keep it going on with someone else. He's not my type."

"Ah-ha. Well, I'm hoping to find out what your 'type' is, provided your mysterious, gorgeous mailroom man really does exist. I'm starting to wonder."

Me too, Maya thought.

Chapter Twenty-Two

Reunited and It Feels So Good

"I'm sayin', Maya, what do you want from me?" Vic asked.

Vic was tired of going around in circles with Maya, which was what they'd been doing since he'd arrived at her apartment an hour ago. While he was grateful for his father's encouraging words that prompted him to go there, he was uncomfortable in the emotionally charged confines of Maya's living room. Like most men, he was more concerned with the end rather than the means. He just wanted everything to be all right between them without having to rehash the whole ordeal.

He fiddled with the FSU fitted cap in his hands, tracing the red and gold lettering, preoccupied by the butterflies in his stomach.

"You say that like I'm asking you for the moon or something. All I want is to know where we stand. I mean, is it too much to expect not to have to go to parties alone? Too much to know that if I have a business function or something else to attend, you'll put on a damn suit, tux or whatever and go with me, willingly?"

Maya paced back in forth in front of Vic, too nervous to sit down. She had waited for weeks for him to make the first move, having run different scenarios through her mind of how their conversation would go. Now that he was finally seated in front of her, all she wanted to do was kiss and make up. Suddenly, she realized the disagreement wasn't so important to her anymore. Yet there was still that small part of her that wanted to prove her point.

"Maya, you and I do things all the time. But just because I'm not interested in goin' to some party with the people whose faces I gotta be in all day long doesn't mean I don't want to be with you," Vic answered.

"But to me, if you're seeing someone, you shouldn't show up at functions alone. That must mean then that you're not really seeing someone."

"You know what? I'm confused now. Sounds to me like you need an escort service, not a man," Vic said.

"Cute," Maya responded.

"Look, Maya, I don't want to argue about this anymore."

Vic walked toward her, eager to erase both the mental and physical distance between them.

Maya sighed. "Me neither."

"So, let's call a truce."

"Are we meeting on middle ground or something?" Maya smiled. The close proximity of Vic had weakened all her defenses.

"Somethin' like that. Let's agree to figure these things out as they come up, without all the fussin'.'"

"Sounds good to me. Shake on it." Maya extended her hand to Vic, who took it and pulled her closer to him.

"Kiss on it," he said, and planted warm lips over hers. "I missed that," he admitted when they separated.

"Hard to tell," Maya said, laughing.

"What's that supposed to mean? Oh, I get it. You was just sittin' back, waitin' to see how long it would be before I punked out and called you. Since I didn't jump on the phone the first day—"

"That's right. It took you more than two weeks to call me."

"Well, what's up with your phone, huh? What, it don't dial out?"

Vic snatched the cordless phone from the coffee table and pretended to dial various numbers.

"Anyway . . ." Maya laughed, heading for the kitchen, where she retrieved a small bowl of sliced fruit from the refrigerator.

"Yeah, anyway," Vic said.

"Come on, let's do something," Maya said as she slipped a piece of watermelon into her mouth.

"I'm with it," Vic said, a devilish grin playing at his lips as he looked at Maya's mouth, wet from the fruit she'd eaten.

"Cut it out." It wasn't difficult to figure out where Vic's mind had gone in that instant, his raging hormones rendering him transparent.

"I mean, let's go out somewhere. Do something outdoors."

"Now?"

"Yes, now. I want to get out of here."

"It's cold outside!" Vic complained.

"It's not that cold, Vic."

"Do you know what time it is?" he asked.

"So what? Come on."

"You're buggin'. Nothin's open at this time of night."

"Come on, we'll find something. Give me two minutes to get ready," Maya said, jubilantly zipping into her bedroom. Vic's amused protests trailed behind her.

Two minutes turned into twenty, but by the time Maya came out of her bedroom, she'd lost her ponytail, having hot-curled her hair and tied a black scarf around her hairline, and was wearing a tangerine bodysuit under black denim jeans and black patent leather boots.

"Damn, baby," Vic said approvingly, coming up behind her, wrapping his arms around her waist. "You sure we gotta go out?"

When he started nibbling her neck and tickling the inner part of her ear with his tongue, Maya almost dropped her jacket on the floor and agreed to stay in. For some inexplicable reason, however, the urge to get out and paint the town red with him was pressing.

"Come on, Vic, I really want to go out." Maya reluctantly pulled herself from Vic's embrace, slipped earmuffs onto her head and moved toward the door. Turning around as she opened it, she realized Vic hadn't budged.

"Don't stand there looking like a lost puppy."

She walked back to him and pressed a slow kiss on his lips, ending it with a firm but short suck on his lower lip.

"There'll be plenty of time for indoor activities later."

"Promise?" Vic asked as he followed her out the door.

"Mmm-hmm."

Thirty minutes later they were climbing the subway stairs and stepping into a dark clear night.

"I can't believe you've got me down here," Vic said as they passed the basketball court on the corner of West Fourth Street in Greenwich Village. The court was empty with the exception of two guys in basketball shorts and T-shirts playing one on one, apparently oblivious to the fact that it was November in New York.

"What's wrong with the Village? Don't tell me you're homophobic?"

"I'm not homophobic. I just don't see what the big deal is about hangin' out down here. Everybody's always like 'The Village this, the Village that.' I don't get it," Vic said, sweeping his arms around in front of him as he surveyed the shops and people they passed.

"Are you kidding? The ambience alone is reason enough to come down here. I mean, where else can you go and see people performing in the street, a good game of street basketball, a movie, have a delicious meal at an outdoor café, sit in on some poetry readings and then pick up some freaky lingerie and erotic literature all in one day, within a ten-block radius?"

"You're crazy!! Who says I'd wanna do all that in one day anyway?" Vic shouted as he covered Maya's hand with his. "I don't care what you say," he continued, "I still ain't impressed."

"And you're telling me it doesn't have anything to do with the many same-sex couples who hang out down here?"

"Nope, not at all. I don't worry about stuff like that."

"Because?"

" 'Cause if some dude makes a pass at me, I'm gonna have to knock him out, no hostility, no drama. Just a straight two-piece, Roy Jones Jr. style, right to the grill!"

"Oh, no, you're not at all homophobic." Maya laughed. "Come on, Vic. Chill out and have some fun with me tonight. Besides, you're with me and nobody's gonna make a pass at my man while I'm with him."

"Your man?"

"Yeah, did I say something out of turn?"

"Nah, not at all. *I* know I'm your man, but I just didn't know if *you* knew it."

They walked in silence, reveling in each other's company, then stopped at a Starbucks on University Place, where Maya ordered flavored hot coffee for both of them and Vic conversed with a couple of ABC daytime soap opera actors. They sipped their coffees as they continued walking, hand in hand like high school kids. When they came upon a street vendor selling cotton candy, Maya couldn't resist. She bought a huge multicolored bag of it and tried in vain to get Vic, who thought it would cost him four teeth, to have a small piece.

Before they knew it, they'd walked to the Westside Highway. They stood for a while, watching the lights gleam off the black water of the Hudson River. Maya finished her cotton candy, its gummy residue sticking to every finger on her left hand and around her mouth.

Vic laughed. "You're a slob."

"Takes one to know one," Maya answered.

She retrieved a napkin from her purse and attempted to wipe the sugar from her fingers, but Vic stopped her by taking her hand and sticking each one of her fingers, one at a time, into his mouth, sucking them until they were all sugar-free.

Maya watched him, amazed at the sensuousness with which his mouth moved as he dined on each finger, and wondered what his mouth would look like in other places. A tingling sensation started at the center of her belly, right below her navel. Then he cleaned her mouth in the same way and the tingling curled up into a knot in the center of her gut. By the time one of his hands reached her breasts, her nipples were already erect and straining against her bodysuit. When he squeezed one nipple between his thumb and forefinger, Maya heard herself moan from that same spot below her belly button and it sounded like it had come from clear across the river.

"Let's go," she managed to say as she struggled to breath between his kisses.

"Nah," he whispered against her cheek, "you're the one who wanted to come outside."

He pressed her back against the railing and she moaned again as his mouth traveled down her neck and collarbone, his lips finally coming to rest on her left nipple. He began caressing it with his tongue right through the bodysuit and brassiere she wore. Two strollers passed by. From a distance Maya heard their footsteps but she didn't care. She gripped the back of Vic's neck and closed her eyes as the knot in her stomach turned into a fireball.

"Damn," he whispered through lips held tightly with desire. "We'd better go, baby."

This time it was Maya who wouldn't stop. She teased his earlobe with her tongue, her breath hot and sweet, and just before Vic got caught up in the heat of the moment again, he moved away from her.

"If we don't stop right now, we're gonna get arrested."

Maya laughed. "This is the Village. They expect people to get their freak on down here."

Vic, disinterested in the voyeur scene and eager to get her alone, took her hand and they began walking. Maya pulled her jacket across her body to cover the wet spot on her bodysuit. It was three o'clock in the morning as they stood on the empty subway platform at West Fourth Street, waiting for the A train. They continued holding hands, unwilling to break the electric current flowing between them. As the train pulled into the station, Maya could no longer resist the urge she'd had earlier, so she stood in front of Vic, slid her hand down between his legs and felt the bulge in his jeans, hard as stone. Vic arousal was apparent as he looked at her.

They got into an empty car, took a seat in the corner, and, as the train pulled out of the station, Vic's mouth found its place on her breast again. Maya, feeling like she was out of her body, watching this whole scene, freed Vic's bulge from his pants and lay her head down in his lap. When her lips first touched the tip of his erection, he moaned loud enough to rival the grinding metallic sound as the train sped through the tunnel.

She lowered her mouth slowly over him, opening and closing her lips, the train rocking them to and fro. She felt like she was watching a movie.

"Shit," Vic wailed, his head thrown back against the wall. "Stop, baby, stop. Oh . . . wait, I'm gonna . . . stop," he begged as he pulled Maya's head away from him.

Maya quickly grabbed a handful of napkins from her purse and covered him as he released, moaning. When he was finished, he wiped himself and closed his pants. Maya leaned her head against his chest and closed her eyes for the rest of the ride, a comfortable solitude enveloping them.

Inside Maya's apartment, Vic asked if he could take a shower. While Maya could hear the shower water running from the bathroom, she paced around the living room. Although it was quickly approaching a new day, a nervous energy flowed through her, giving her fuel. She was as intrigued by what had happened between her and Vic as she was confused and apprehensive. She'd never been compelled to engage in any sort of sexual activity in public before—no man had ever moved her to that point the way Vic had. Maya was so wrapped up in her thoughts, she did not hear the water stop running, nor did she notice when Vic came out of the bathroom.

"That was amazing," he said as he rubbed Maya's Dewberry lotion on his face, neck and arms.

He was standing in the doorway of the bathroom with a plain white towel wrapped around his waist that barely covered him, water still dripping from his chest and back.

"What, the shower?" Maya asked nervously.

"No, definitely not the shower."

"I can't believe I did that," Maya said, feeling embarrassed.

"Why?"

"Because," she began, "I don't make a habit of doing stuff like that, you know. In public, no less."

She didn't want him thinking she was some kind of freak or something, which was exactly what she would have thought of a person who'd behave like that in a subway car—up until she actually became that person.

"I know you don't," Vic said reassuringly as he walked over to her.

He put his arms around her and lifted her chin so he could look into her eyes. "That's why it was so amazin'. I have never felt so overwhelmed by somebody like that. I wanted to make love to you right there on the train. It was like . . . like . . ."

"Passion," Maya filled in for him.

Vic was quiet for a moment as he studied Maya, seeing much more than he'd ever seen reflected in her eyes at any other time. For the first time he saw himself not in the moment, but later, in the future. Or at least he saw what he wanted for himself down the road. Maya was the first woman who had ever made him consider whether his future held marriage, children or anything along those lines. And now that he was looking at those possibilities head on, he felt like the lights had come on in a room he hadn't been aware was even dark.

"Yeah, passion," he agreed. "I always imagine stuff like that and I write about people who are overwhelmed by emotions . . . cats whose noses are wide open over their girl. But that was . . . I was . . . gone, out of my mind. I mean, lust is one thing, I've felt that . . . anybody can have that. But this was . . . I was so into you I didn't give a damn about nothin', nobody."

"Was?"

"Is. Am. Whatever," Vic said, undoing the towel around his waist and letting it fall to the floor. He pulled at the shoulders of Maya's bodysuit until her arms were free, then removed her brassiere so her breasts and belly were exposed. But before they got started again, she stopped.

"Wait, Vic, let's talk a minute."

"Now?" he whined, pressing himself against her.

"Yep, now." Maya backed away, led Vic to one of the armchairs and sat down on the edge of the coffee table in front of him, careful not to let her eyes fall below chin level.

"I know we talked about our argument earlier—"

"And it's over now."

"I realize that, Vic, but look, I understand that we're not going to always agree on everything and I know we'll have to work through things. But I don't think it's cool for us to go for two whole weeks not speaking to one another. It's silly and childish."

"I agree."

"Good." Relief flooded her, allowing her to relax a bit.

"So does that mean next time we fight you won't sit back like a spoiled princess waitin' for me to make the first move?" Vic asked.

"I am not spoiled. But I do admit that I could have called you."

"And I'll admit that I should have called you sooner," Vic said as he reached out to stroke Maya's face.

"I wanted to call you."

"So why didn't you?" he asked.

"Pride, I guess," Maya shamefully admitted.

"Pride is a poor substitute for lovin', you know."

"I know."

"So are we cool now?"

"Yes, very. I'm gonna take a shower," Maya said, rising.

"Can I come with you?"

"You've already bathed." Maya laughed as she walked backward, toward the bathroom.

She slowly undid the button on her jeans and then the zipper. By the time she'd stepped into the bathroom and was sliding the jeans down her thighs, Vic was standing in the doorway. She turned both faucets on, setting the shower nozzle so that it emitted a full blast of warm water.

Maya caught sight of Vic in the vanity, wild desire unmistakably recognizable in his eyes. She was certain she bore the same expression. Her need to feel, taste and smell him was causing her soul to strain against her flesh in eagerness. As the steam rose, coating the mirror and dimming her view of Vic, she turned to face him. Not trusting her voice, she let her aching body do the talking.

Clad in a black lace thong only, she stepped into the shower and felt along the shelves of the shower caddy until she found a can of scented bath foam. She shook the can and sprayed its contents into her palms. Slowly, she rubbed all over her body. A sudsy layer of soap coated her and the bathroom filled with the scent of bergamot coriander.

Vic was mesmerized by her every movement and the cocoa-colored skin which glistened under the cascading water. He stared as she glided her hands slowly across her breasts, belly and thighs, teasing him but at the same time showing him what she liked; his mounting passion boiled within. He moved slowly toward her, unable to resist her beckoning any longer. His hands replaced hers, exploring first her face and the delicate lips which parted slightly to receive his thumb. The heat her mouth released on his digit was almost feverish. He slid downward, silky skin egging him on in his exploration. Her full breasts weighed heavily in his hands and in his mouth. Her tight belly quivered when he blew hot breath against her belly button.

She backed against the wall as he lifted her left leg and rested her foot on the edge of the tub. He slid the soaked thong down around her hips and thighs and Maya stepped out of them. His nose touched her center first as he inhaled her womanly scent. He kissed her opening tenderly, over and over again until the screams which had been caught in her throat began to escape, echoing across the tiny bathroom. His tongue introduced itself and received a warm and grateful greeting as her body arched against him. He dined on her with vigor, artfully meeting her body's demands with increased pressure as needed. Each time Maya climaxed, she reached a higher level of craving, desire making her beg for more.

Vic rose and stepped out of the shower, reaching to open the medicine cabinet. From the top shelf he retrieved a bright blue packet. Maya took the condom package from him and tore it open. She kissed him deeply as he stepped back in the shower and she took hold of his steely manhood, rolling the condom slowly down its length. With one hand Vic raised both of Maya's arms above her head, pinning them against the wall. With the other, he guided himself into her. As the tip entered her waiting nest, she gasped. He stayed there, unmoving and barely breathing as she arched her body forward, wanting to take him completely inside.

"Don't tease me," she begged. "I want all of you."

At her words, Vic leaned against her, allowing himself to fully enter her body. He moaned uncontrollably as her tightness closed around him. Her eyes were aflame and with each thrust he stared into them, memorizing the desire they held for him and only him. She called his name over and over, until her voice was weak from the effort. This time, when she climaxed, he drew all the fire from her body, leaving her totally spent and near collapsing. He held on to her, as he, too, released his juices into the condom which separated them.

Dazed and amazed, they braced each other as they left the steamy shower and found the welcoming coolness of Maya's bedsheets. Drained, they lay in a tangled mess of arms and legs, both satisfied beyond words. They lingered in and out of sleep, until the sheer memory of the heights of pleasure earlier reached awakened them. As the sun rose over the city, their lovemaking continued, each time filling their souls with wonderment.

Chapter Twenty-Three

Look, But Don't Touch

"Maya Wilkins."

"Maya, how are you? It's Mark Mantale."

"Fine, Mark, and you?"

The intoxicating effects of the past few days she'd spent with Vic had yet to wear off. Maya, happy as a lark, had practically danced all the way to work and had yet to come down from the love high she was on. She was flying higher than a 747 and had no intention of landing any time soon. It was late Monday afternoon, and all she could think about was seeing Vic again after work. The cheerful tone with which she answered the telephone was indisputable evidence of her blissful mood. Mark was thrilled to have caught her at what appeared to be a good time.

"Just great, although I could use some of whatever it is you're having," Mark joked.

"Unh-unh, not sharing." Maya laughed. "So, Mark, what can I do for you?"

"Just thinking about you."

Although she had already told Mark she was involved with someone, Maya wasn't surprised he was calling her. It was obvious that Mark was a man who was not easily discouraged. She would have to impress upon him that friendship was all she was offering, with firm subtlety, of course.

"Oh, really?"

"Yeah. I was wondering how you're making out on that case of yours. The securities thing?"

"Well, nothing's changed. I'm still trying to sort some things out."

"I meant what I said, Maya. If I can help at all, please let me know. Confidentiality is my middle name."

"Doesn't quite fit well with Mark, but . . ."

"I set myself up for that one, didn't I?"

"Yeah, you did. Listen, Mark, I really do appreciate the offer, but—"

Maya stopped midsentence. Maybe she could, in fact, use Mark's help. Obviously she couldn't mention names or other identifying information, but there were certain issues surrounding the case that she could definitely use an expert's opinion on. She wasn't getting anywhere with the client, nor with Peter Fusco, for that matter. She thought that if she could just understand the situation a little better, fit the pieces of the puzzle together, her mind could be at ease and she could put to rest the nagging suspicions that had been plaguing her since she was first assigned to the case. Maybe she was wrong about Peter. Maybe the government was wrong about Haynes. There were way too many maybes, and they left Maya feeling unsettled, a state of being she despised.

"On second thought, Mark, there are a few things I'd like to run by you."

"Sure, shoot."

"I've got a meeting to get to just now. How about I take you to lunch tomorrow? Are you free—say, twelve-thirty?" Maya asked.

"Works for me."

Mark was elated by Maya's change of heart. Ever

since the night they'd spent with Wendell and Katrina, all he could think about was seeing her again.

"Great, let's meet at Hamburger Harry's on 46th and Madison."

"It's a date," Mark quipped, a not-so-innocent comment Maya decided to ignore.

Mark mulled the conversation over for some time. The boyfriend thing was a definite monkey wrench in the wheels of progress, albeit a minor one. The fact that she had not actually referred to the guy as her boyfriend, but merely someone she was seeing, was not lost on him. Maya struck him as a one-man type of woman, so he would definitely have to act fast before some sort of permanency was established with this other guy. First he'd have to find out who he was.

Measuring up the competition early in the game was a business tactic his father had taught him, and it was one that could also be applied to most other areas of life. It was important to know not only who the other team was, but their strengths and weaknesses as well. With that aim in mind, he called Julia. She'd know something—he'd bet a week's pay on that.

"Julia, doll, how are you?"

"Just dandy, Mark, and you?"

"Can't complain, and if I did, who'd listen?" Mark joked.

"So to what do I owe this pleasure? Oh, wait, let me guess. You're calling about Maya again, aren't you?"

"Julia, babe, is that a hint of irritation I'm detecting in your tone?"

"Not necessarily irritation, Mark. Let's call it curiosity. I have never seen you pursue anyone with such ardor. What's this girl got that's got you so fired up? I mean, don't get me wrong, she's a nice enough person, I guess. Well, not that one could really tell. She's a bit secretive, if you ask me. But I suppose I can see the attraction. But, Markie, is she really worth the trouble?"

Julia asked.

Julia found Mark's dogged interest in Maya extremely uncharacteristic of him. If she didn't know better, she'd swear he was in love with the woman.

"Well, I guess that's precisely what I'm trying to find out. She's got something special, I'll say that. And I don't think the admiration is one-sided. I just need a little more time to break through that shell of hers. And that's where you come in."

Julia leaned backward in her chair, shaking her head. In all the years she'd known Mark, she wondered what kind of woman would eventually snag his interest. He was, after all, the proverbial good catch who had yet to be caught. Not for lack of trying, mind you. Many an eligible young woman in their circle, Julia acknowledged, had tried to get Mark's attention for more than a nanosecond, but to no avail.

Even now it was difficult for her to believe that he was truly all that serious about Maya Wilkins. It was more probable, in her mind, that the idea of the forbidden was what had so ferociously piqued Mark's interest. There was no way Maya would fit into Mark's family's social alliances. His mother, for certain, would not have it. Both she and Mark came from families whose mandates were as traditionally rigid as they were impenetrable. Obviously something about Maya had caused Mark to temporarily lose sight of that fact.

Julia stole a glance at herself in the cosmetics mirror situated on the corner of her desk. She wished her eyes weren't quite so close together and her nose less pronounced. But other than those things, she felt she was pleasing to the eye. She supposed Maya could be considered attractive, and for a fleeting moment felt a tinge of jealousy as she thought of Mark preferring someone like Maya over someone like herself.

She quickly recovered, however, when she concluded that this attraction was most assuredly just a passing fancy on Mark's part. He and Julia had been friends for a long time, and eventually that friendship, coupled with the dictates of their common family traditions and social circles, would draw them closer when the time was right. And if, in fact, she was still available, she would receive him with open arms.

"What do you want to know, Mark?" Julia asked.

"I need to know who she's seeing. She's mentioned some guy, not by name and not with any defined terms. Do you know who he is?" Mark questioned.

"Well, there was some talk of her seeing a guy in the mailroom, but I—"

"The mailroom? There, at Madison Pritchard? You can't be serious," Mark scoffed.

"Like I said, there was some talk. I don't know how true it is. He's the supervisor, Vic something. Wait, let me look him up. There it is. Victor Smalls, Jr. Nice guy."

"Is he black?"

"Yes, why?"

"Just curious. All right, Julia, thanks for your help."

"Anytime, Mark. And I hope the payoff is worth the chase." Julia smirked.

"Aah, why don't you just let me worry about that."

Mark hung up, his pulse racing. A sardonic smile spread across his face as he thought about Maya's boyfriend. A clerk in the mailroom was certainly no competition for him.

Seated at a booth at the rear of Hamburger Harry's dining area the next day, Maya began second-guessing herself. From the moment she'd met Mark outside the eatery, she'd been immensely aware of his attraction to her. He'd greeted her with a kiss on the cheek and a too-familiar hug. His dark eyes seemed to smolder as he gazed intently at her from across the table. Even now, as they sat, Mark devouring a burger deluxe and fries, Maya enjoying a California Cobb salad with grilled shrimp, he was quite obviously enamored.

"All right, Mark, help me out with these," Maya said, handing Mark copies of some of Wexton & Haynes's trade records and pages from their bookkeeping ledgers. They spent the next half hour looking at the questionable transactions. To ensure confidentiality, Maya had blacked out all names, addresses and dates on the copies. Mark explained how the trading was supposed to have worked and then pointed out how Haynes was able to predict which transactions to manipulate. It was really quite a simple scam for someone who had access to a lot of other people's money to gamble with.

By the time they'd finished, Mark had given Maya a crash course in stocks, futures and trading. All she needed now was to determine precisely who the key players were and to find the money trail. She never mentioned her suspicions of Peter Fusco to Mark. His association with Julia Becker afforded the possibility that he'd break their confidences. Maya was certain she'd find herself tossed out of Madison Pritchard faster than she could pack her briefcase.

"So, Mark, what do you do in your spare time? You know, when you're not playing with people's money?"

"Try to get a beautiful woman to give me the time of day," he answered soberly.

"Look, Mark—"

"Seriously, Maya, I really like you. I know you're seeing someone, but why not give me a shot? Dinner sometime, a movie?" Mark took Maya's hand, holding it in both of his.

"Mark, you're a really great guy and maybe if we'd met at a different time . . . who knows? But it won't work. Not right now. I'm in a relationship with someone special."

"Oh, so it's been upgraded to a relationship, has it?"

"Yes, it has. I'm sorry if I led you to believe otherwise."

"No, no, not at all. I guess I was just hoping," Mark said, releasing her hand and slumping in his chair.

"And I'm hoping that this doesn't mean you and I can't be friends. I really appreciate your insight and, like I said, I like you."

"I'm mortally wounded, my beautiful lady, but friends it is." Mark laughed. "So who is this guy? Another lawyer? Don't tell me I'm getting beat out by an ambulance chaser."

"No, he's not a lawyer." Maya laughed. "But, Mark, I meant what I said. I really hope we can be friends. I don't know many people in New York and, well, you're a good guy."

Not used to being shot down, Mark made a quick exit, assuring Maya that they'd remain in touch.

Chapter Twenty-Four

Two Plus Two Equals Five?

It was pretty much a safe bet that Edna Tully, the firm's bookkeeper, knew nothing about what was going on between Peter, Haynes and the firm's wallet. She and Peter didn't appear to have any personal relationship; she was, after all, nowhere near being a sexy twenty-year-old.

She owned a small house in Bayside, Queens, with her husband, had a grown son who'd attended Fordham University on a partial scholarship and seemed to live a modest lifestyle. Having been with Madison Pritchard for twenty-six of the company's thirty years, however, made her one of the oldest employees. If she was like every other competent bookkeeper in the world, she would have recorded every penny. Peter would have had to give her some bogus explanation for every deposit, and if she was unaware of any cover-up, there'd be a paper trail.

Maya arrived at the office before eight o'clock one morning, hoping to catch Edna alone in the financial department before the assistants came in. The less people who knew she was asking questions, the better.

"Hi, Edna, how are you?" Maya said as she tapped on the door, which was ajar.

Edna looked up from the *Daily News* and took a sip from a coffee mug which read *What Do I Have to Do to Make You Go Away?*

"Hi, Maya. Can't complain. What can I do for you?"

Edna's thick, round spectacles were held by a chain and perched at the end of her nose as she looked over the top of them at Maya.

"Well," Maya began, hoping her speech didn't sound too prepared, "we've received an audit request on Wexton & Haynes, one of Peter Fusco's clients."

"Oh, another one of those. I hate those things."

"I know what you mean. They're so bothersome. But anyway, do you think you can help me?"

"Sure. Do you need detailed invoices or just statements?" Edna asked as she typed the Haynes client and matter numbers into her computer.

"Uh, I guess you might as well give me detailed. That way I don't have to bother you anymore."

"No bother at all, kiddo. Okay . . . there. Detailed invoices. For what period?"

"Why don't you give me everything you've got . . . since the first invoice?"

"What? You can't be serious?" Edna asked incredulously.

Maya froze, afraid she had underestimated Edna's adroitness. She quickly tried to think up a proper rationale that wouldn't raise Edna's curiosity any further for why she needed to get all the invoices ever issued to Haynes.

"Boy, those auditors don't care how much trouble they put us through. So now they can't just go back to the previous backup we've sent them. No, they want it all over again. So we have to reprint every damned thing. . . . Just kill all the trees on the planet, why don't we."

"I know that's right," Maya agreed.

Edna typed a few more keystrokes and her printer began to whir. Five minutes later, Maya had in her hands every invoice and the accompanying pro forma statements that showed each time entry and disbursement ever charged to the Haynes client file number. She thanked Edna again and made a beeline for her office.

With the door securely locked, Maya retrieved the invoices she'd found in the client files and began comparing them to those obtained from Edna. It was no surprise to her that they didn't match.

"Ladies and gentlemen, may I have your attention." Peter Fusco tapped his fork three times against the side of the champagne flute he held in his massive right hand. "Well, that usually works in the movies." He laughed along with the crowd.

Slowly the room grew silent as everyone gave Peter their attention. He gazed around the massive ballroom filled with his peers and their spouses or significant others, his hypnotic blue eyes making contact with several of his colleagues. He spied his wife standing near the bar, working on what was probably her third or fourth glass of vodka. He'd have his driver take her home right after his speech, before she did something to embarrass him.

Peter straightened the knot of his Brooks Brothers tie and smoothed the lapel of his charcoal-gray Valentino suit for emphasis. He spoke at long last.

"As you know, we're all gathered here tonight for two reasons. Firstly, with Richard Griesler and Marjorie Chapman at the helm of the Markson case, this firm has just experienced one of its greatest successes. Winning this case has both immediate and long-reaching consequences for the firm. This victory propels Madison, Pritchard & Fusco ahead of the pack."

"Here, here!" someone yelled as the crowd erupted into thunderous applause. After several moments, the room grew quiet again and Peter continued.

"Secondly, this year marks the firm's thirtieth anniversary of practice. We're stronger than ever, we've got the best group of practitioners on the East Coast . . . hell, worldwide! We have shot to number one with a bullet."

Once again the crowd followed Peter's words with a loud cheer. Maya joined the rest of her co-workers in their enthusiastic commendation.

"So eat up, folks, and drink to your hearts' content. We're here to celebrate tonight. Tomorrow's another day, and you young soldiers will need to get your game faces on. I hope that each of you will return to the ring ready to do battle. Cheers," he said, raising his glass in salute.

Maya watched Peter from a distance, her disdain for the man hidden behind the tight smile pasted on her lips. Vic ran his hand lightly across her back, instantly drawing the tension from her with his touch. They were seated at a table toward the back of the room, having just arrived moments before Peter took center stage.

"Maya, you made it." Julia approached with Michelle Morrison, Allison Curtis and Vanjee Silverman in tow. These three female associates were the Charlie's Angels of the firm—beautiful, cultured women whom everyone wanted to know or know about. If people weren't talking about them, they made it their business to find out what it was people were talking about.

"Ladies, good evening," Maya quipped. She had yet to get used to the unabashed nosiness of this crew. Despite all their blue-blooded upbringing, they thought nothing of sticking their pretty little noses into everyone else's business.

"Vic, surprised to see you here. I've always wondered why the partners never invite *staff* to these func-

tions. You guys would certainly liven things up."
Allison smiled at Vic.

"So, what, are you guys, like, together?" Julia asked.

Maya suppressed the angst building within and
smiled back at Julia. She reached for Vic's hand, who
squeezed hers back.

"As a matter of fact, we are," Maya answered.

The open-mouthed looks exchanged between the
trio were priceless. Maya almost burst out laughing at
their ridiculousness. Vic rose suddenly from his chair
and nodded slightly to the women.

"Babe, let's dance," he said to Maya. "Excuse us,"
he added as he smiled at the group. He took Maya's
hand while he deftly pulled her seat away from the
table as she rose. Vic's stride was Billy Dee debonair as
he led her to the center of the dance floor. Maya was
equally striking, her Dolce & Gabbana gown fitting her
like a glove and hugging every curve. With her head
held high, she followed Vic's lead, giggling inside all
the way.

Sliding one arm around Maya's waist, Vic pulled her
to him. He took her hand in his and moved to the beat
with masculine agility. The couple danced smoothly to
the band's rendition of "Forever in Love" by instru-
mentalist Kenny G.

"All eyes on are you, Ms. Wilkins," Vic whispered,
his lips brushing her ear.

"No, Mr. Smalls, I do believe all eyes are on you,
with your fine self." Maya laughed.

"Aah, the price of being a sex god," Vic joked.

"Well, how about we blow this joint and find someplace private where I can properly worship you?"

"Now that's what I'm talking about." Vic laughed
devilishly as he led Maya from the dance floor. The
stares they received from those who'd noticed them
were duly noted by the pair, but neither of them cared
in the least.

Chapter Twenty-Five

Secrets

"Vic, can you grab the mail for me? Oooh, I gotta go!" Maya had opened the mailbox in the vestibule, but was now racing against nature up the stairs to get to the bathroom.

Vic laughed. "I told you to slow down on the Slurpees."

He reached inside the box, retrieving half a dozen envelopes and a couple of magazines. As he closed the box, a few pieces of mail fell from his grasp. Picking them up, Vic innocently read the return address on the fattest envelope. It was from a correctional facility. The prison stamp and inmate identification number were easily identifiable. The name Andrew Payne, however, was not recognizable to Vic.

As he walked upstairs to Maya's apartment, he stared at the envelope. Who could be writing Maya from jail? It certainly couldn't be a client—why would she give out her home address? She'd never mentioned a friend or relative being incarcerated.

By the time he reached the apartment door, his stomach was churning. In spite of himself, a twinge of jealousy was building in his brain as he tried to conceive why Maya would be playing pen pals with a brother behind bars.

"Whoo, that was close," Maya said as Vic entered the apartment. "Did my *Essence* come?"

"Yeah," Vic replied. "And you got some other letters and stuff." Vic handed the mail to Maya, purposely placing the prison letter on top of the pile.

"Ah, probably just junk," Maya said, tossing the envelopes onto the counter without looking at them. "Oooh," she continued as she spied the cover of the latest edition of *Essence.* "Doesn't my girl Latifah look good?!"

Vic didn't respond as Maya thumbed through the magazine, sharing bits and pieces of information with him.

"What's wrong with you?" Maya finally asked.

"Nothin'," Vic said.

"Oh, I bet you're starving. Okay, okay, I promised you some spicy hot chili and you're gonna get it."

Maya went about the business of preparing dinner from her dad's recipe. That was the only dish her father could make and he did it painstakingly, following his own father's recipe to the letter. Over the years, he and Maya had made a few modifications to it, coming up with what they thought was the perfect balance of flavor. Maya worked diligently from memory, cutting up the jalapeño peppers, onions and fresh garlic.

Meanwhile, Vic stewed in the bedroom, pretending to watch an HBO movie on Maya's new television. He was glad she'd finally bought one because it gave him an excuse not to talk to her at the moment; it gave him time alone to think. By the time dinner was ready, he had convinced himself to forget about the letter for now and wait until Maya told him about it. While he managed to enjoy dinner and the remainder of the evening, thoughts of that letter lingered, giving him a nagging sensation, like an itch you couldn't reach to scratch.

A couple of days later, Vic had successfully forced the situation to the back of his mind. He worked contently all day. With two guys out, he was quite busy covering all the work that flowed in and out of the mailroom. He scarcely had time to think of anything else, save for his meeting that evening with Boss Records and one of their top recording artists. Through a contact at NYU, Vic had been able to submit a copy of one of his songs, and they apparently liked it. A label executive had eagerly arranged tonight's meetings, and Vic hoped they'd offer him the type of deal he had been waiting for—one that would set his career in motion. If things went the way he hoped, he'd have something to celebrate tonight and Maya was the one and only person he wanted to celebrate with.

As luck would have it, the moment he allowed himself to get excited about tonight, in walked Rashon with the seemingly sole purpose of bringing him down.

"So how long are you gonna be little Miss Attorney's backroom piece?" Rashon said to Vic as she sashayed into the mailroom.

"What's that supposed to mean, Rashon?" Vic snapped.

He had been in the process of trying to readjust the fan bolted into the ceiling, which served to cool off the two xerox and three fax machines in the room. At Rashon's statement, he jumped off the stepladder and landed squarely in her face. Rashon seemed undaunted by his explosive response.

"I'm saying, I know you're seeing her twenty-four–seven, but she sure ain't publicizing that fact. So while you seemed to be digging this girl, I bet you none of her little lawyer friends know," Rashon answered snidely.

She had convinced herself that she was really only looking out for Vic's interests. He was a nice brother who didn't deserve to get played. But had Rashon been honest with herself, she would have acknowledged that she was quite envious of Maya. In the years they'd worked together, Vic had never approached Rashon in more than a friendly way, even when she had "put it out there," so to speak. Then in walked Maya Wilkins and he was drawn like ants to a picnic.

"First of all, why you all in my business? What's the matter? Don't you have nothin' to do with yourself but get in my face? For your information, Maya and I are both professionals, so whether or not we have somethin', it ain't somethin' that needs to be shouted out all over the office. That ain't got nothin' to do with nobody being a backroom anythin'."

"Damn, you're a little defensive," Rashon replied.

"That's 'cause I don't like how you came at me and I damn sure don't appreciate it."

At that point, Rashon decided to back off a bit, not wanting to do serious damage to a friendship she'd been hoping would one day become more.

"I'm sorry, you're right, Vic, it's really none of my business. But," she added, because she couldn't stop herself, "I just don't see what you see in her, besides the paycheck."

"See what I'm talkin' about? Now why it got to be all that? Yo, check this: in addition to being an attractive woman, Maya is kind, considerate, intelligent and fun to be with. Don't none of that got anythin' to do with how much money she makes. That's what's wrong with black women now—always dissin' the next sistah." Vic scoffed.

"Oh, no. Don't even start trying to tell me about being a black woman," Rashon cried.

"Somebody should. Maya came up in here just as nice and tried to make friends with you. Unlike you, she ain't all caught up over status and shit. She saw a sistah and figured ya'll would be cool automatically. And what do you do? Act all shady with her, for no reason."

"Whatever, Victor, I ain't even tryin' to hear all that."

" 'Whatever' is right," Vic said as he turned his back on Rashon and climbed up the stepladder again.

He didn't look back when he heard Rashon stomp out of the room, leaving her sour mood behind to ruin the rest of his day.

Rashon was apparently oblivious to the splash Vic and Maya had made the night before at the Marriott. He assumed the rumor mill hadn't reached her yet, but didn't see the point in bringing her up to speed. No matter what he said or didn't say to her, it was obvious Rashon would think want she wanted to think.

Vic shook his head, as much disappointed in Rashon's behavior as he was saddened by it. Rashon could be a good woman to someone if she spent more time working on herself, developing some goals and using her brain for good instead of evil. He knew she was interested in him, she'd made that much obvious long ago. He also knew he could never be interested in a woman like Rashon. She, like many people with whom he'd grown up, saw life with tunnel vision. There was only what was already done and what had been laid out in front of her—nothing more. She didn't see that life was a myriad of color, a maze of possibilities to be explored and investigated. And, so, people like Rashon remained in the box designed for them, never reaching the potential that lay dormant inside.

He didn't want that kind of life. His father had taught him to aspire to greater things and to surround himself with people of a like mind. Maya was the kind of woman with whom he would continue to grow, of this he was certain. The big question was, did she feel the same way about him?

He had spent the remainder of Saturday and all day Sunday with Maya, and as far as he knew, she never looked through her mail. It was torture not saying anything about the letter, but he'd resisted. He knew he had no business looking through her mail and even less business questioning her. However, he couldn't completely shake the green-eyed monster who had grabbed hold of his imagination and was working it double-overtime.

Rashon throwing salt into the wound didn't help matters. He was hoping Maya would bring up the subject and tell him about her little pen pal, but he knew if she didn't do it soon, it would only be a matter of time before he lost control of himself and confronted her.

Once again Vic was faced with the unsettling feeling that he had fallen too hard and too fast for Maya. He worried that on some level, Rashon was right. Maybe this *was* a game to her, or an experiment of sorts. She said she cared for him. She acted like she cared for him. But it was evident that she still had secrets from him, parts of her life he knew nothing about. How did she expect them to move forward if she didn't confide in him?

By the time his workday ended, Vic was wound up tighter than ever. He hurried off to his meeting, anxious and out of sorts. Two hours later he arrived at the brownstone and immediately dialed Maya at the office.

"Hey, you."

"Hey, yourself," Maya responded. "Where are you?"

"At home, where *you* should be."

"Yeah, well, unlike you I don't live the charmed life of a songwriter. Speaking of which, how'd your meeting go?" Maya inquired.

"I sold the song," Vic said breathlessly.

"You sold the song? Get outta here! Congratulations, baby. I'm so happy for you."

"Thank you. Cool, huh? My first sale."

Vic did a quick two-step. He was so hyped up over his success, he couldn't keep still.

"Which song did he go with? 'Wings'?"

"Nah, he wanted something a little more up-tempo. Remember the one I had Steve Mills do the beat for? 'Another Lover'?"

"Oh, yeah. I love that one. But I thought for sure 'Wings' was more his style. But whatever," Maya quipped. "Did you get the ka-ching?"

"Listen to you. You know I did, girl. I haven't even called Steve yet. He's gonna go bananas. I wanna celebrate. What time are you gettin' out of there?"

"As soon as you come and get me," Maya answered.

She had a ton of revisions to do on a sentencing memorandum, but there was no way she wasn't going to be with Vic tonight of all nights. She'd just get cracking on it early in the morning and have it on Marjorie's desk by close of business as requested.

"Cool. I'll be there in thirty minutes."

Chapter Twenty-Six

Ghosts of the Past

"Why can't you just let it go?"

"Why should I?"

"Because, Maya. You said yourself, if Peter Fusco is as deeply involved in this mess as you suspect, he went through a lot of trouble to cover up his involvement. Now, you go fishin' around, you might end up runnin' home to Kansas like Roger did."

"I'm not from Kansas," Maya reminded Vic.

He was brushing her hair as she sat in the V of his legs, reviewing the list of trades for Wexton & Haynes for the years 1996 through 1998. Vic loved the way her soft, thick hair felt in his hands, the strawberry scent which rose from her freshly shampooed head intoxicating him. Maya had once told him that his hands on her head felt better and served to relax her more than a massage at one of those high-priced uptown salons. Since then, he sat her down and played with her hair as often as she'd allow. He wanted her to always feel mellow when they were together, especially when he wanted to talk to her about something important.

"My point exactly."

"But, Vic, this stuff really stinks to high heaven and it's going to come out. You know it will."

"Maybe. Maybe not. People do get away with crimes every day, you know. And he's been gettin' away with this one for a while now. From what you say, the government seems to think this case is already sewn up and Haynes is their man. Why would they go diggin' around for more dirt?"

"Because there's always some overambitious ADA who wants to land the big fish," Maya informed.

"And there's always some ambitious little black girl trying to prove herself," Vic said, putting the brush down and shoving the papers away from Maya.

He reached up and turned off the halogen lamp above their heads. The only light now coming into the room was from the orange sunset outside. Maya couldn't say anything because she knew Vic was right. On some level she was trying to prove something, mostly to herself.

"I just keep asking myself, 'What would Daddy do?' Would he turn his back, tuck his tail between his legs and pretend nothing is going on? I think . . . no, I *know* he'd find a way to make things right. That's just how he was."

Vic quietly traced the line down Maya's forearm that divided the lighter underside from the slightly darker outer part. He wanted to explain to Maya that it wasn't her responsibility to make the whole world a better place. But he knew that wasn't the type of woman she was.

She was righteously indignant. She believed in goodness and mercy, and who was he to tell her that these things were elusive and most people were hard-pressed to live that way? In fact, with any luck at all, he hoped some of her idealism would rub off on him. Not that he was pessimistic. No, he considered himself more cautiously optimistic. Suddenly, Vic peered down in front of Maya.

"What?"

"I'm just lookin' for the *S* I'm sure is branded on your chest."

"Stop it." Maya laughed, turning so that her lips found Vic's. Dusk fell around them as they settled into one another.

"Where do you see yourself in ten years?" Maya asked Vic as they lay wrapped in a quilt on the living room floor in the hour of the night when the stars were at their brightest. This was their favorite time of night. For Maya, because it was quiet. For Vic, because he liked to watch the shadows created by street lamps and moving vehicles as they danced across the walls and ceiling. Since they'd been together, it was the time when they found themselves able to talk most freely, both too sleepy for their conversations to be guarded, but still awake enough to understand the importance of the secrets being shared.

"Ten years? Alive, I hope," Vic responded.

"Seriously, Vic. I mean, what do you think life has in store for you?"

"I don't know," Vic answered slowly. "I try not to think about it."

"Why not?"

"Because if you start thinkin' too far ahead and plannin' too far ahead, then you end up livin' only for the future. I want to live for today. I want to enjoy the now 'cause tomorrow is not promised, that's for damn sure."

"You sound a little jaded."

"Yeah, maybe. I guess you could say that. But I do know one thing."

"What's that?"

"I'm enjoyin' this *now* immensely."

"Me, too," Maya whispered.

She watched the shadow of a car as it zipped across

the ceiling, moving too fast to enjoy the beauty of this twilight.

"Don't you ever feel like talking about your mother?"

"What's there to talk about?" Vic asked.

"I mean, you've told me she walked out on you guys when you were a kid and that you never heard from her again. But what about before that . . . before she left?"

Vic was quiet for a while, and just when Maya figured he'd fallen off to sleep, he said quietly, "Before she left . . . things were good. I mean, I was just a little kid, so I guess I didn't know the real deal."

"Were you happy?"

"Yeah, like most kids, you know. And we did a lot of things together . . . all of us. My mother had a beautiful singing voice," Vic said softly.

"Really?"

"Yeah. Pops used to say she sang like an angel. She would sing all the time, too. Her voice had a jazzy sound to it. Kind of like Nancy Wilson, but softer."

"Did she ever sing professionally?" Maya asked.

"She was singin' in a nightclub when her and Pops met. He used to love to tell the story of how he went into this smoke-filled joint in Brooklyn and saw her up onstage. Before she'd finished her first song, he'd swore to his buddies that he would marry her. She said she almost forgot the words to the song she was singin' when he walked in."

"That's beautiful."

"Yeah, it was. Love at first sight, I guess. Anyhow, somebody made the introductions and the rest is history."

"Did she continue singing after they married?" Maya pressed.

"Some, but as time wore on it became harder for her to get gigs that wouldn't take her away from home for too long. I remember them arguin' about it sometimes, when they thought my sister Phyllis and I were asleep. She wanted to keep singin'."

"And your father wanted her to stay at home?"

"He just didn't want her to get her hopes up. There were so many people out there takin' advantage of young women in those clubs and on the road. He wanted her to do somethin' safe like become a music teacher or give private vocal lessons. She wanted more.

"Sometimes at night, when she would tuck me in, she would sing to me, you know, tryin' to get me to go to sleep. After the last note my eyes would still be wide open. I just couldn't get enough of lookin' at her . . . hearin' her voice. I would beg for another song. Only after I'd promised that I would go to sleep would she sing again. This time, I would close my eyes and let the satiny rhythm of her words carry me away. Her voice would sail through my dreams, makin' me feel like the luckiest little boy in the world."

"That's a wonderful memory to have," Maya said softly, memories of her own mother's loving touch coming to mind.

"But," Vic sighed, "all little boys have to grow up eventually."

"That doesn't make it any easier."

Vic grew silent again, his emotions bittersweet.

"What do you think went wrong for her?" Maya asked as she stroked the back of Vic's neck, wanting him to keep talking.

"I don't know. I used to think about it a lot, but now it doesn't matter."

"It always matters," Maya said to Vic, and to herself.

"You were tossin' and turnin' last night. Was it about that case again?"

Vic threw a handful of peppers, onions and zucchini

into a sizzling pan of oil. He had been hesitant to mention it, but when he'd found one of Maya's Chocolate dolls buried beneath her pillow the next morning, it was a sure sign that she was very upset about something. By the time he sat up in bed, she was headed out the door, yelling a quick good-bye over her shoulder.

"No." Maya sat in the living room, applying a coat of nail strengthener to her fingernails and avoiding Vic's eyes.

"What's wrong?"

"Nothing. I just have trouble sleeping sometimes is all."

"It seemed like you were havin' more than trouble sleepin'. You cried out a couple of times, too."

Vic added a dozen jumbo shrimp into the skillet and continued stirring the contents of the pan.

"What did I say?"

"I don't know, couldn't make it out. You quieted down after I put my arms around you."

"Well, then, that's the solution. You'll have to sleep with your arms around me every night."

Vic had been spending more and more time at Maya's. On the occasions that he stayed all night, he derived immense pleasure from waking up next to Maya.

"That's cool. But seriously, Maya. What's wrong? Is it somethin' I can help you with?"

Vic walked into the living room, carrying steaming plates. The shrimp and vegetables lay on a fluffy bed of yellow rice.

Maya sighed. "Ever since my parents died, I have nightmares . . . not every night . . . just sometimes."

"You want to talk about it?"

"There's nothing to talk about."

"Come on, Maya."

But she couldn't talk. She sat staring at the wall, so Vic waited patiently. He walked over to the framed pic-

ture of her parents on the shelf and looked at them as
he had many times before. He could tell that they were
in love, just by the way their bodies sort of leaned into
one another, Mrs. Wilkins's shoulder fitting directly
into the groove of Mr. Wilkins's armpit, his arm draped
across her, his hand dangling over her shoulder and her
hand lightly clasping his fingers. They looked comfortable in their embrace, not stiff and posed. Then Vic
looked at Maya, who was still staring forlornly at the
wall, and he could tell that her parents had loved her
and cared for her a million times over.

It was clear to him that everything beautiful she'd
become was because of those two people and that it
hurt her deeply not to have them anymore. This knowledge made him miss them, too, made him wish they
were still alive so that there would be no place in
Maya's heart he couldn't reach. Nothing that would
make her toss and turn in her sleep, or make her mouth
turn downward sometimes, not frowning but melancholy just the same.

He returned the photo to its place and walked over
to Maya, dropping to his knees in front of her.

"After my mother left us, Dad did his thing, you
know. He raised us well. But . . . well, I kinda know
what you're goin' through, havin' somebody you love
leave you without warnin'."

"Yeah, Vic, I know you do." Maya sighed.

She wanted not to feel the grief she still felt over her
parents. She wanted desperately to just enjoy the moment, enjoy the newness of the feelings that were growing for Vic. But it seemed like every time she tried to
forget and allow herself to get caught up in the happiness of the moment, something made her hit the brakes.
It made her remember that when you love, you lose.

"But, Maya," Vic was saying, "your story is different than mine. You had really lovin' parents who didn't
choose to leave you, who wouldn't have left you for the

world if they could have helped it. They were always there for you, and look at you now: you're successful, intelligent . . ."

"Beautiful," Maya added, a smile sneaking its way onto her face.

"No doubt!" Vic laughed. "Look, all I'm sayin' is that maybe you should try rememberin' everythin' that you've got goin' for you, everythin' your parents gave you. You know, instead of focusin' on them not bein' around anymore."

"I know you're right, up here." She tapped her temple. "I just get lonely sometimes, you know?"

"I know," Vic answered. He wanted to tell her he hadn't felt too many of those lonely moments since he'd met her, but decided against it. He still hadn't gotten used to his feelings himself, so there was no way he was going to thrust them on her. Not just yet. So he put his arms around her instead.

"You really don't know how great you are, do you?" he asked.

"Vic, there's some things you don't know about me. Things that would make you think twice."

Vic stiffened, his thoughts flashing momentarily to the prison lover, or whatever Dear John was to her.

"I doubt that anythin' you say could change my mind about you," he said as wholeheartedly as his doubts would allow.

"When my mother got sick, I don't think I fully appreciated the seriousness of it. I guess I didn't want to come to terms with it. I never for one instant thought she would die. I figured she was so strong, so beautiful, that with the right treatment, the cancer would be cured and she'd be okay."

"You couldn't have known."

"I think she knew. I think that's why she and my father insisted that I return to school. Maybe she didn't want me to be around for the really bad times. Maybe they wanted to spend her last days alone. I don't know. But I went back to school even though I wanted to stay home with her. I went back and did well. I even managed to have some fun. My mother was home dying and I was partying," Maya said, the intolerable memory causing her to hang her head in shame.

"Stop it, Maya," Vic demanded. He refused to allow her to beat herself up any longer. "You did what your parents wanted you to do: live. Finish your schoolin', enjoy your life. You can't feel guilty over that."

"But I should have been there. If I had been there, he wouldn't have . . . he'd be . . ." Maya trailed off, unable to continue. Tiny beads of sweat broke out across her hairline as she pressed her lips together. Her lungs grew tighter—they seemed to be pushing the inhaled air back toward her throat before it could infiltrate her body. She shook her head once, then again, trying to fight off the waves of nausea that twisted her stomach into a knot. Vic pulled her closer to him and began stroking her damp head.

"It's okay, baby. Shh."

"It's my fault. It's all my fault. He worked so hard taking care of her. He fed her, bathed her, gave her her medications. He was there around the clock. He didn't have anyone to help him. I should have helped him."

"Shhh," Vic whispered as he smoothed her hair.

"He couldn't take care of her and his business, too. Besides, there was Andrew Payne."

Vic bristled at the mention of the name.

"He and my father had been friends for twenty years, business partners for almost as long. He was my godfather. We trusted Andrew."

"What happened?"

"During the time my father was nursing my mother, Payne rented space at the company's warehouse to a big-time drug dealer. They apparently housed thousands of dollars in drugs and weapons there. And he helped this crook transport his crap across state lines along with regular client shipments. DEA agents received a tip from someone and raided the warehouse. Payne was arrested and eventually convicted. But in the meantime, the company's license to do business was suspended and customers whose shipments were delayed or confiscated filed lawsuits naming the company and both Andrew Payne and my dad, individually."

"Damn," Vic said.

"My dad was ruined." Maya continued sniffling. "He fought hard to come back and to restore his good name. By the time the government released his license and warehouse, most of his major customers had made other arrangements, and it was like starting from scratch. He was so stressed out and still grieving over my mother."

"That's when he had the stroke?"

"Yeah. It happened late one night while he was up working on the company's books. It wasn't long after my mother's funeral. He was so thin and worn. I held his hand in the ambulance and I begged him not to leave me. He just looked at me with the most tired-looking eyes I'd ever seen. He squeezed my hand one time, closed his eyes and that was it. I lost my daddy before we even reached the hospital."

Maya sat numbly, motionless except for the intermittent blinking of her wet eyes.

"Babe, you can't blame yourself. None of that was your fault."

"I should have been there."

"Maya, look at me, baby." Vic placed a finger beneath Maya's chin. Slowly she lifted her head, meeting his eyes. "I know you think you're a superwoman, but you're not. You were a kid. A kid who followed her parents' instructions because that's how you were raised.

You respected and loved your parents and you did nothin' wrong."

"I just feel like things could have turned out differently," Maya whispered.

"I doubt that. Your father stood by your mother because that's what he was supposed to do. And you did as you were told and your parents were proud of you. Payne is the one who screwed up. He betrayed your father at a time when he needed him most. I don't know what the man's reasons were, but the end result is the same."

"What kind of reasons could he have had for destroying the business he and my father had taken years to build?"

"I don't know, Maya. Sometimes people do things they wouldn't ordinarily do. Sometimes their backs are against the wall and they don't know what else to do. Or maybe he was just a greedy bastard. I don't know," Vic said, shaking his head.

Maya rose and walked to the kitchen. She retrieved an envelope from the top of the refrigerator and returned, handing it to Vic. It was the letter from Andrew Payne, currently a resident of the Federal Correctional Institute in Otisville, New York.

"You haven't opened this," Vic said, turning the envelope over in his hands.

"I'm afraid to read it. Would you do it for me?"

Vic slid his finger beneath the top flap of the envelope, slitting it open slowly. He removed two sheets of white lined paper and unfolded them. The entire time he did this, he kicked himself for his stupidity. He had spent the last couple of days feeling jealous and suspicious when Maya was being tormented by memories of her past. Now he was ashamed at his ridiculous assumptions and thankful he had not confronted her.

"Dearest Maya," Vic began. He glanced at Maya,

wanting to gauge her reaction. She nodded and he continued.

"Words cannot express how heartbroken I am to know that my deeds have caused me to lose you. You were like the daughter I never had, and for years I shared in the pride and joy you continuously brought to your parents' lives. My deepest regret is that I shattered our relationship and that I will never again hear you call me 'Uncle Andy' in that sweet little voice of yours. I get down on my hands and knees and pray daily that you will one day know I never meant to hurt you. If I could, I would take back all the pain I caused you and suffer a thousand times over so that you would not have had to.

"I am writing this letter to you after all this time because I cannot bear the thought of you never understanding why I did the things I did. I am not the monster I am sure you believe me to be. Your father was my best friend, and I loved him like a brother. To this day I do not understand why God saw fit to spare me and took your father's life, but I do truly believe he has gone on to a better place. He is with your mother and their souls are in God's heavenly care now, a blessed thing indeed.

"I apologize for the intrusion of this letter into your life. I tracked you down to New York City because I felt it was time to contact you and to explain certain things. I am certain this letter will find you leading a happy and successful life. You were always destined for great things. If by chance you are gracious enough to in fact read this letter, maybe you can find it in your heart to pay me a visit so that I may express myself to you in person. I have taken the liberty of adding your name to my visitors' list, just in case. But believe me, if you don't come, I will understand. I know I don't have the right to ask anything of you. But please, Maya, think about it. I really need to see you and there are some things you need to hear. Remorsefully yours, Uncle Andy."

"Unbelievable," Maya snapped. "He has the nerve to ask for my forgiveness. What the hell could I possibly want or need to hear from him? He must think I'm stupid or something. Oh, so now that he wants to clear his guilty conscience, I should just run up there and let him pour his heart out? I don't think so."

Vic sat quietly, rereading Payne's letter. When he finished, he refolded the letter and returned it to the envelope. He went to the kitchen and poured a glass of soda. Returning to Maya, he offered her a taste, and when she refused, tipped the glass to his lips and drank heartily.

"What are you thinking?" Maya asked.

"Nothing. I mean, well, I was just thinkin' that maybe he's not askin' for too much."

"Are you crazy? Not asking for too much? He doesn't have the right to ask anything of me. He ruined my life!" Maya yelled. She couldn't believe what Vic was saying.

"Hold on a minute, before you get all pissed at me. I'm not sayin' Payne deserves anythin'. You don't owe him a damn thing. All I'm sayin' is that *he* owes *you* somethin' and it may be about time you collected."

"I don't want anything from that man."

"Not even an explanation? An apology?"

Maya stewed silently, chewing on Vic's words.

"Listen, Maya. Just hear me out. You've been walking around for years blamin' yourself for somethin' you had no control over. You've shut yourself off from a lot of things, and even now, with me, it's like you're holding somethin' back. You're scared to take a real chance on me."

"Vic, I don't mean to make you feel like that. You're the best thing that's happened to me in a long time."

Vic scratched his head, racking his brains to think of

a way to get Maya to understand where he was coming from.

"Baby, I'm not blamin' you, and I don't want any more from you than you're ready to give. All I'm sayin' is that you're carryin' so much baggage, you don't have room for anythin' else. Maybe it's time for you to put those heavy bags down for good. Seein' Payne, hearin' him out and lettin' him know exactly what you think of him might be just the release you need."

"I don't know, Vic. Seeing him might make it hurt all over again. I don't know if I'm strong enough for that."

"Oh, you're definitely strong enough," Vic said, pulling Maya into his arms. "And I'll be with you, if you want me to."

Maya smiled. "What did I do to deserve a guy like you?"

"It must be your lovin', 'cause it sure ain't your cookin'," Vic joked.

"Shut up and kiss me, you jerk."

Chapter Twenty-Seven

Showdown

The hour-and-a-half drive to Otisville was spent in quiet reflection. Maya's stylish outfit—jeans, turtle-neck and blazer, coifed hair and flawless makeup—belied the turmoil raging within. Vic drove, making casual conversation and the occasional joke in an effort to ease her anxiety.

When they arrived at the prison they remained in the car parked at the far end of the parking lot. Vic held Maya in his arms, neither of them speaking until she felt strong enough to remove herself from the car. He walked her to the main gate of the prison's entrance, which was as far as those without a visitor's pass were allowed to go.

"I'll be right out here," Vic said.

"I know. I'll be okay."

Maya kissed Vic deeply and approached the gate, which the outpost guard swung open to allow her to enter. She followed another guard down a long concrete walkway, past a courtyard and a cluster of empty picnic tables. When they approached the brown brick building that housed the inmates, Maya walked through a metal detector and was turned over to a female guard, who escorted her to a small room.

After showing identification and signing in, she was asked to empty her purse and remove her jacket and shoes. Each item was searched meticulously. The guard then patted Maya down from shoulders to ankles and passed a handheld metal detector across her body, front and back. She accompanied Maya to a locker area, where she was allowed to secure her personal items. Two long corridors and several locked gates later, Maya took a seat in the visiting room.

"The prisoner will be brought in shortly," the corrections officer said.

Maya looked around the room, surprised to find it not quite as dismal as she had expected. The pastel walls were decorated with framed paintings of landscapes and oceans. There were four other tables besides Maya's, a vending machine containing soft drinks and another filled with various snack items.

Maya surveyed the handful of other people scattered about the room, talking quietly to one another. Two unsmiling armed guards leaned against the walls, one at each of the two doors leading into the room. The inmates and their guests seemed equally happy to see one another as they were saddened by the circumstances that separated them. The animosity she carried toward Payne made Maya feel like she didn't belong there amongst these other people, as though she were an interloper to their misery.

The buzz as the room's back door opened drew Maya's attention just as Payne walked through it. Maya sucked in a deep breath when she saw him; he looked almost the same as he had the last time she'd laid eyes on him at his sentencing. He was dressed in prison-issued khaki pants and shirt. His bright smile waned as he approached her stoic figure.

"Maya, I'm so glad you came. I . . . I don't know what to say. You look wonderful." Payne hesitated, and took a seat across the table from Maya, watching her intently, waiting for a sign that some small part of what they'd had before had survived.

"Thanks," she said.

"How was the drive up here? It's actually some beautiful country."

"Look—don't. Let's not waste your time or mine on idle chitchat. You wanted to see me and I'm here."

"Cut to the chase, huh? Okay, Maya, any way you want it."

Payne sighed, realizing this was going to be harder than he had imagined. He stroked his graying beard thoughtfully as he searched for the right words.

"What I did was reprehensible, no doubt about it. I took your father's trust and friendship and trashed them. At a time when your father needed me most, when he was going through the greatest trial in his life . . . I wasn't there for him."

Payne's words were a sickle stabbing right through Maya's heart. She bit her bottom lip as she willed away the almost physical pain his words caused.

"There are some things about me you don't know. Things your father didn't even know. It started back in college. I met some guys, guys I should have steered clear of, and they got me into playing the numbers and the ponies and stuff. It was a great high for me and I got pretty good at it. I didn't bet on anything major at first, didn't spend a lot of money. But I guess that's why gambling is such a sweet addiction. It begins so slowly, so innocently. . . .

"Eventually, I was betting on games, horses, anything. Over the years I'd get in pretty deep, and it would scare me. I'd quit . . . for a while . . . promise myself that I was done. But it never lasted. I could never manage to stay away. I lost my wife, Natalie, because of it. I don't think you'd remember Natalie. You were a little girl when she left me."

"My father didn't know about this?" Maya asked.

"He helped me out from time to time, when I couldn't cover my losses. But he believed me when I said those were isolated incidents. He never really knew how deeply I'd dug myself. . . . I hid it well from him. But the truth is, I was broke. No savings, no assets, nothing.

"Up until that last time, I had been doing better. Hadn't so much as played the lottery in almost two years. Things were going well with the business. I don't know what happened . . . I guess I just had something missing in me . . . so many holes that needed filling."

Payne searched Maya's eyes again, wanting to find some understanding there, but failing.

"Anyway, by the time your mother got sick, I was in way over my head. I was dealing with some pretty tough guys . . . scary people, and I'd run out of time and excuses. They were going to kill me, of that I have no doubts. And you know, I was probably ready to die at that point. I felt so worthless."

"But then you thought of a way out? How convenient." Maya rolled her eyes in disgust.

"No, no, it wasn't like that. They knew I didn't have any family, no kids. They knew that you guys, you and your parents, were the closest thing to family I had, and they threatened you all. They told me if I didn't help them, if I didn't do what they wanted, they'd come after you. Don't you see, Maya? I couldn't let that happen. Not after all Milton had done for me. I couldn't let anything happen to him or his family. I'd die first," Payne said emphatically.

"You honestly expect me to believe all that?" Maya asked incredulously.

"It's the truth, Maya, as God is my witness. They told me it would just be for a short period of time. With Milton away, I figured I could control the situation and get them off my back. I knew it was a risk, but what choice did I have?"

Maya was silent as she contemplated his words. The small room had become very stuffy; its walls seemed to have closed in around her. She wanted to get up and leave, just run away until her legs could no longer carry her. She didn't know whether or not she believed what Payne was saying. What was more, she didn't know if it mattered. As Vic had said, the end result remained the same.

Payne stared at Maya, unable to read her thoughts. In a moment of desperation, he reached across the table and took her hand. Maya snatched it away as if he were a flame.

"I'm sorry. I just—"

"Stop," Maya said, shaking her head from side to side. "I've heard enough. Do you think any of this makes a difference? Do you think that somehow this excuses what you did?"

"I just wanted you to understand why," Payne pleaded.

"Understand? No, you don't understand. Don't you see that in the end they killed him anyway? And you helped them. He died trying to save the business he'd spent all those years building!" Maya yelled.

"I helped him build that business."

"And so did my mother. He lost her, and all he had left was what they'd built together, and you sabotaged that!" Maya's voice had risen to a level that began to attract the attention of the other inmates and visitors in the room. The guard nearest to their table glanced at them, his face issuing a silent word of caution.

"You're right, Maya. Everything you've said is right. But I just want you to try to understand how I felt. I was between a rock and a hard place, and I know now that I made the wrong decision. If I could take it all back, I would."

"But you can't, can you?"

"No, I can't," said Payne, resting his head in the palms of his hands.

"I will never, ever forgive what you've done. Never. It is something we'll both have to live with forever. But as my dad used to say, God is the only judge, so I won't sit here and judge you anymore. I have to let it go. That's what my parents would want me to do."

Maya rose from her seat and looked down at Payne, feeling pounds lighter than she had when she'd first sat down.

"Please don't ever contact me again," she said before turning her back. She walked away from the table, out the door. Several locked gates and two long corridors later, she was back outside. With each step toward Vic and away from Otisville, she let go a little bit more of the pain.

Maya walked along the winding path slowly, the chilly March morning prompting her to pull in her jacket a little bit closer to her body. Whitmore Cemetery consisted of more than fifty acres of sprawling grass, old hanging trees and headstones of varying shapes and sizes. She found her parents' headstones easily, without looking at the names, because when her mother died, she and her father had chosen the plot nearest a large honey-locust tree. Maya stooped to place half a bunch of calla lilies in front of her mother's headstone, the other half in front of her father's.

Looking around the cemetery, she noticed another group of people gathered around a grave a few yards from where she stood. Their mound of earth was freshly laid, the headstone still shiny, and their grief was clearly freshly formed. Maya wondered if grief could ever become stale, if it could get so old that it became flat and distant instead of the festering wound it remained for her, even though almost four years had passed.

"Mom, Dad, I'm sorry I haven't been here in a while." Maya sighed. "I've been so busy at work, working eighty-hour weeks, you know."

She pulled her jacket closer and hugged herself. She felt sure her parents knew she was lying. They, of all people, would know that the real reason she hadn't been there in several months was that, even after all this time, it was still too painful for her to come and face their graves—the place where she'd watched their bodies lowered into the ground and sealed up, never to be seen, touched or heard again.

When her mother died, her father had been a rock. He'd held her up, made the arrangements and gotten her through the funeral and the days that followed. Their nightly talks were the pick-me-ups she'd needed to look forward to the future. When he died, Mrs. Armstrong helped as best as she could, but Maya took care of everything on her own. She remembered how desperate she was to have just one more conversation with her father.

She hated coming to the cemetery, hated talking to the cold granite headstones as if they were her parents. But Maya also knew it was her obligation to her parents to pay her respects every now and again, so despite her discomfort, she came.

"My apartment is pretty run-down, Mom, but I'm working on it. And, Dad, I made a nice piece of change on those securities you transferred to me. Mr. Ryder at Charles Schwab treats me like he and I were old college buddies instead of you and him." Maya laughed.

Maya talked to her parents' headstones for a while longer, catching them up on the goings-on in her life. She told them about Vic, wanting them to know how special he was becoming to her, even if she was still unsure what the future held for them. She told her mother she'd been right on the mark—having someone to talk to in the twilight hours did bring peace to your soul.

She brushed away the pollen that had settled on top of the headstones, thinking.

"I wish there was something I could have done for you guys. I wish I could have helped more somehow, but I understand now that sometimes things are outside of our control. I'm trying to make you guys proud of me. Trying to do the things that I know you'd want me to do, even when it's not the easiest thing to do."

The gentle breeze that caressed her face seemed also to clear the confusion in her mind.

"You don't have to worry about me anymore. No more sulking around. Believe it or not, with a little effort, I think things are going to be all right again."

Maya stayed by her parents' graves for a long time that morning, letting the memories of them serve as balm on wounds too long nursed. By the time she left the cemetery, promising not to stay away so long again, Maya was glad she had gone. For the brief time she was there, it was as if her parents were not dead but right in front of her, listening, laughing and advising like always.

Chapter Twenty-Eight

That's What Friends Are For

Seated on the end of the third row of bleachers in McHenry Park in Queens, Maya and Katrina had a good view of Vic and the other players as they ran up and down the court. His light blue shorts hung low; his matching T-shirt with the SPONSORED BY RICKY'S BARBER SHOP logo embossed on the front and the number forty-four on the rear stuck to his upper body. During a short time-out, he stopped for a swig of Gatorade at a nearby table, winking at Maya as he passed by to rejoin his team on the court. She giggled like a high school girl cheering for her man from the sidelines of the school's gymnasium.

The game was part of a tournament sponsored by local businesses from the five boroughs. It was designed to raise funds for various worthy charities, most notably those aimed at providing aid to low-income families. It was a warm Saturday afternoon in April and for the first time in weeks, Maya had decided to leave her work—and her troubles—at the office and spend the day outdoors with her two favorite people.

Vic and Katrina had met face to face for the first time today, and seemed to hit it off. The park was filled with guys and girls, some teenage and some Maya's age or older, all of whom gladly paid the five-dollar admission price in the spirit of giving. There was a deejay who played the latest hip-hop cuts.

Vic's team, the Vikings, were part of the second set in the tournament to play. The three of them had watched the first game together. Now Katrina and Maya were rooting Vic's team on, listening to the beats and sharing occasional comments with the girls seated on the bench next to them.

"So, looks to me like this thing with Mr. Songwriter is getting serious," Katrina remarked.

"You think so, huh?" Maya fought to keep a straight face, eyes on the court. When she finally turned to Katrina, the corners of Katrina's mouth were twisted into a sarcastic grimace and her eyes held her signature *cut the crap* glare.

Maya pushed it. "What?"

"Maya Wilkins, don't even play with me. What's up with you two?"

"We're just kicking it, you know. It's not that serious."

"Uh-huh, and I'm Eartha Kitt's mama."

"You do that *purrrr* thing really well."

When Katrina looked like she was ready to punch Maya, Maya stopped giggling.

"All right, all right. Yes. Yes, I really like him a lot and yes, we've been spending a lot of time together and . . . well, it's good. It's a really, really good thing."

"Thank you. Was that so difficult? You always have the hardest time admitting how you feel about somebody. I mean, it's like, just say it already, Maya. Nothing's gonna happen if you do."

"I'm not too sure about that, Kat. Seems like whenever I get comfortable with somebody . . . loving somebody . . . something happens."

Katrina wound an arm around Maya's shoulder, pulling her close.

"Don't think like that, Maya . . . you can't. I know you've been through enough crap to last a lifetime, but you can't stop believing in forever. That's no way to live."

"I'm trying, Kat, I am. Vic's got me wide open . . . like a tenth-grader when the captain of the varsity football team asks to walk her home from school."

"Mmm! Now that's open."

"Yep."

"Girl, enjoy it. Run with it. Play with it. You really deserve some happiness. I mean that. And he seems like a nice guy . . . cute, polite. If I'm wrong, and he turns out to be a jackass, then I'll be all over him like a rash!"

"Thank you, Kat. Thanks for being my girl." Maya squeezed Katrina for a minute, blinking away the tear that had formed in the corner of her eye.

Maya knew if she lived to be one hundred and met a million people, she'd never find anyone as special as Katrina. The kind of sister-love Katrina had given Maya almost from the day they met was what helped ease the pain caused by her parents' deaths and her breakup with Gerald. Although she had lost a lot in a short time, she'd also gained a lot, as though God had sent Katrina to her as retribution. And now there was Vic. Only time would tell if God was still paying his tab.

"What about you, Kat? Are you happy?" Maya asked. She brushed a crinkled curl from Katrina's eye.

"Me? Happy as a pig in mud," Katrina remarked.

The hollowness in Katrina's tone might have been lost on anyone else, but Maya picked up on it right away.

"Is everything all right between you and Dominic? School?"

"Of course. Why wouldn't it be?"

"I don't know . . . just . . . Well, if there's something you need to talk about, you know I'm here, Kat."

"I know, baby girl." Katrina paused, then opened her mouth again, as if to speak.

"What?" Maya asked.

"Whoo-hoo!" Katrina clapped loudly. "Stop grilling me and look at your man, girl! He just shot a three from down low."

Katrina hopped to her feet, pulling Maya up with her and joining the rest of the crowd in congratulating Vic's NBA-style performance. For the rest of the afternoon, Katrina avoided the subject, but Maya's radar was now turned all the way on. She decided she'd give Katrina some time, but the conversation would definitely resume at a later date.

"Let it ring, baby," Vic whispered, his face buried in Maya's neck.

The slow dance his tongue was grooving across her collarbone turned Maya into a prisoner, unable to break free in spite of the telephone's insistent ring. Maxwell moaned from somewhere in the living room, his *Fortunate* album on replay in the stereo.

"Leave a message." *Beep.*

"Maya?" said a sobbing Katrina over the answering machine.

Maya jumped up, nearly shoving Vic to the floor. The tone of the single word uttered by Katrina was one of desperation and immediately triggered alarm in Maya. She snatched up the phone.

"Kat? Kat, is that you? What's wrong?" Maya swallowed the taste of fear that had risen in her throat.

"Maya." Katrina continued sobbing. "I—I—oh, God, Maya."

"Katrina!" Maya yelled. "Kat, you've got to tell me

what's wrong. Are you hurt? Is somebody hurting you?
Vic, get my cell. Call the police—"

Vic sprang from the bed in search of Maya's purse.

"No, no, Maya. Don't call the police."

"Then tell me what's wrong, Kat," Maya said as she
reached out, touching Vic's arm to stop his search.

"I can't believe this is happening to me. Why me?"
Katrina wailed.

For the first time since she'd picked up the phone,
Maya realized Katrina's speech was slurred.

"Katrina, have you been drinking?"

"Yeah. So what? Why shouldn't I? I'm gonna die,
Maya. Do you hear me?" she screamed. "I'm—I'm
dying."

"Katrina, look, I don't know what's going on, but
I'm on my way. Okay? I'm on my way."

Maya tried to keep her voice calm, although panic
had already accelerated her pulse. She had never heard
or seen Katrina lose control like this, and the fear of
not knowing what was wrong was agonizing. A blanket
of dread covered Maya, causing goose bumps to rise
on her naked body. Vic slipped into his jeans and
T-shirt, then threw a pair of Maya's sweats on the bed
next to her without saying a word. Maya met the questions in his eyes with a raised hand and slipped into her
sweats; all the while, Katrina moaned and sobbed into
the telephone.

"No, Maya, don't come. Don't come."

"Yes, I'm coming. I'll be there in a few hours. Is
your mother still in Paris? I'm calling her."

"No!" Katrina shrieked. "Don't tell her. Please,
Maya, don't tell her. Oh, God, she'll die if she knows."

"Okay, okay. Calm down, Katrina. I won't call her.
But I'm on my way. Please, Kat, tell me you'll be okay
till I get there."

"Okay."

Vic watched Maya intently, trying to figure out what

was going on from her end of the conversation. He stuffed some of Maya's clothing and other personal items into a duffel bag in preparation for whatever the situation turned out to be.

"You sit right there and wait for me. Okay?" Maya pleaded. "Katrina, do you hear me? You sit right there and wait for me!" Maya was yelling now, unable to suppress the mounting anxiety.

"Okay, Maya. Hurry up." The line went dead and for a moment Maya was torn between dialing Katrina back and just racing down to D.C. She was momentarily frozen in a state of indecision.

"Babe, come on," Vic insisted, handing Maya her purse. "Come on," he said again when Maya didn't move. "We'll go pick up my dad's car."

Maya snapped out of her daze and followed Vic out of the apartment. They rode his bike uptown and, after having hastily explained the situation as best they could to a sleeping Victor Sr., made their way to Interstate 95. Uncertain as to what they were driving into, but knowing it was imperative that they get there without delay, Vic broke every speed limit on every stretch of road, and Maya did not protest. All the scenarios of what could be wrong with Katrina stampeded through Maya's mind, her thoughts a jumbled mass of concocted theories.

The sickening sensation in the pit of her stomach brought her back to the day she'd found out her mother's cancer was inoperable and terminal. Maya was gripping the edges of her seat so tightly, the veins in her hands strained against her skin. Vic reached out to her, rubbing her shoulder, trying to assure her that everything would be all right. Somewhere between New Jersey and Pennsylvania, the burning sensation in the pit of Maya's stomach caused her to become physically ill. Vic pulled over to the shoulder while Maya doubled over and lost her dinner in the darkness.

They arrived at Katrina's place in record time. The housing complex was quiet, save for the sound of Vic and Maya trying to get into the apartment.

"Kat, open up!" Maya yelled as she banged on Katrina's apartment door. It was after two o'clock in the morning, but Maya didn't give a damn about waking the neighbors. They stood on the second-floor hallway veranda, Vic peering through the open blinds next to Katrina's door, unable to see anything but darkness within.

"Maybe we should call the cops," Vic said.

Maya continued banging for what seemed like hours, and just as she was about to tell Vic to make the call, she heard movement inside. The locks turned and the door opened an inch. Maya pushed the door open and found Katrina sitting on the floor beside it, her head in her hands. Maya slid to the floor beside Katrina and gathered her in her arms. Vic shut the door behind them and began searching the apartment. Finding no threat, he retreated to the bedroom to give Maya space to find out what had happened.

It was a long time before Katrina began talking. Maya held her gently, rubbing her back and telling her over and over again that she wasn't alone anymore.

"I didn't tell you this before, I couldn't. Dominic is such an asshole. I didn't want you to know."

"Katrina, you could have told me. You can tell me anything. Tell me now."

"No, no. You would just worry. You always worry about everything. I didn't want you to know . . . I was so unhappy. That bastard. That spineless coward."

"What did he do, Kat?"

"He was cheating on me, Maya. Some chick on his job. Then some other chick at the club. The bitch was in my step class. Can you believe that? She was probably giving me dirty looks and shit behind my back, and me, like a fool, didn't even know."

"How long?"

"How long has he been cheating on me? I don't know. Probably since the first day I met his sorry ass."

"No, how long have you known?"

"I'm so stupid, Maya. I knew since . . . I knew for a long time. I confronted him and he swore it wasn't true. And even though I knew better . . . I'm so incredibly stupid."

"Shh, honey. Stop it. You're not stupid. You just loved him."

"To death." Katrina grimaced.

"Where is he, Kat?"

"I don't know. The bastard didn't even have the guts to tell me in person. He waited until he knew I was at school, came by, took all his shit and left me a note. Can you believe that?"

"What did he say? Is he leaving you for someone else?"

"Leaving me for . . . leaving me . . . for . . . someone . . . Jesus, Maya, haven't you been listening to me? He's leaving me because I'm dying . . . he's dying."

"Katrina, you're not making any sense. What do you mean, he's dying, you're—"

"That son of a bitch is HIV positive!" Katrina screamed. "God, I want to kill him!"

Suddenly, the room got a little bit smaller, and the thickness of the air began choking Maya. Now it all made sense. Katrina was absolutely hysterical, a condition foreign to her, at least in the years Maya had known her. No wonder. Maya's temperature began to rise as she, too, wanted to kill Dominic. Katrina had begun to wail again, her body shaking uncontrollably. Maya knew she had to somehow remain calm and get control of the situation.

"Kat, sweetie, calm down. Are you sure?"

"Yeah, I'm sure. He spelled it all out for me. Got a call from one of those . . . those whores he was dealing

with a year or so ago, and she told him she'd tested posi
. . . posi . . ."

"Tested positive?" Maya asked.

"Yeah. Thinks she got it from her husband, no less.
Dominic claims he got tested a few months back and
he's got it, too. The little degenerate didn't even have
the guts to tell me to my face."

Katrina reached for the bottle of Hypnotic on the
sofa and was immediately angered by its emptiness.
She pulled away from Maya and crawled across the
floor to the entertainment center. Snatching a bottle of
Remy Red from the lower tempered-glass shelf, she
turned the near-empty bottle up to her lips and drained
it. Disgusted, she hurled it across the room. It shattered
against the terrace door, sending shards of glass everywhere. The sound brought Vic from the bedroom, but
he halted at the door.

"It's okay, babe. An accident," Maya told him.
"Okay, okay, come on, Kat, calm down."

"I don't have anything else to drink. Victor, you
gotta go get me sumtin to drinkkkk," Katrina whimpered.

"No, sweetie, you've had enough already," Maya
cooed.

"Don't tell me when I hada . . . hada . . . a . . nough!"
Katrina attempted to stand, but only made it to her
knees. Maya grabbed her from beneath both arms and
pulled her back to the floor.

"Shhh. Shhh." She rocked the whimpering Katrina
in her arms. "It's gonna be all right. We're gonna make
it all right."

"No, it's not, Maya. What if I have it? What if I'm
sick? This is gonna kill my mom. She's not strong. She
won't be able to take it if I . . . if I die."

"Shhh. Nobody's dying. Hush now. You don't even
know if you're infected. One thing at a time, sweetie.
We'll call your doctor tomorrow and take the test. Then

we'll find out what all the options are. It's gonna be all right."

"Please, Maya, make it all right. Please don't let me die."

"Hush. I'm right here, and I'm not gonna let anything happen to you."

Even as Maya said the words, the weight of them pressed down on her chest, making it difficult to breathe. Maya held on to Katrina, who eventually fell asleep. Maya continued holding her friend's sleeping form, praying fervently like she'd prayed over her mother in those last days. This time God had better answer her prayers or she didn't know what she'd do.

"Look, Katrina, you've got to eat something. I got you some egg-drop soup. Even got those greasy crunchy noodles you like. Here." Maya sat a bowl of Chinese soup in front of Katrina, who didn't budge.

"I'm not hungry."

"Katrina, you haven't eaten much of anything since I got here. Now either you're gonna pick up that spoon and eat some damn soup or I'm gonna sit on your chest and pour it down your throat."

"Damn, you're a little violent," Katrina said. She met Maya's demanding gaze for a moment, before taking a small spoonful of soup. "Happy?"

Maya smiled. "It's a start." She pulled out a chair at the small glass-topped table and sat next to Katrina to watch her eat. She noticed that Katrina's frizzy hair looked dirty and limp.

"Hey, finish up. I've got an idea."

"What?" Katrina asked.

"Just finish up. We're getting out of here," Maya said, jumping up from the table.

"Come on, Maya, I really don't want to go anywhere."

"Katrina, we've been holed up in this apartment for three days. Now, I don't know about you, but I'm going a little nuts."

"So, you can leave then."

"I know I can leave, smarty-pants. But I'm not going anywhere just yet. I do, however, have to get back to New York and you have to get back to classes."

"Says who?"

"Says me. Look, Katrina, I know you feel like somebody's pulled the rug out from underneath your feet. You're angry and you're scared and you have every right to be. I am, too. But sweetie, we can't let this thing lick us. We won't know if . . . if you're infected or not for a while and you can't just lie down and die until you find out. You've got to keep on getting on. You know, my daddy used to tell me all the time that adversity separates the men from the mice."

"So?"

"So it's time to man up! Now put some clothes on and let's get out of here."

Grudgingly, Katrina did as ordered. While Maya was not ecstatic by Katrina's choice in clothes, especially the T-shirt with the SCREW YOU slogan on the front, she was content with being able to get Katrina out the door.

First stop was the local beauty salon, where Katrina's hair was washed, conditioned and styled in a neat French braid. Then they drove around for a while before taking a tour of the National Council of Negro Women Inc. Headquarters at 633 Pennsylvania Avenue. Something about walking through halls once roamed by famous black civil rights leaders and dignitaries proved soothing to even Katrina's tortured soul. They also visited the Washington Monument, the Lincoln Memorial and the Capitol Building.

By the time they arrived at the Heart & Soul Cafe in Capitol Hill for an early dinner, Katrina had actually worked up an appetite. The exquisite American Southern cuisine and welcoming aura of the small but elegant restaurant seemed to be just what the doctor ordered as Katrina devoured two orders of catfish bites and a medley of collard greens and cabbage. They ended the night on Katrina's terrace, watching the sun set as they sipped Jamaican Blue Mountain coffee.

"Why do you suppose God puts us in this rat race just to snatch us up outta here right when we think we've got it licked?" Katrina asked wistfully.

"I don't think that's his plan at all. Maybe heaven is truly the reward and when he thinks we've suffered enough down here . . . or fully served our purpose . . . he calls us home."

Katrina drained her coffee cup, grateful for the warmth the liquid provided as the night became chilly, the wind beginning to paw at her thin T-shirt. While she no longer felt like crying, the irony of her current situation had made her weary. She was not what you would call a drama queen—she did not entertain calamity. In fact, she steered clear of disasters and folks who caused them. She faced challenges head on, as they appeared, but never allowed herself to be swept up in turbid situations. She refused to provide misery with her company. Yet here she was, faced with a cheating man and the possibility of a life-threatening disease. If that wasn't drama, she didn't know what was.

"Well damnit, I ain't going anywhere. Shit . . . I'm definitely suffering right now, but I sure as hell haven't served my purpose yet," Katrina said with a smirk.

Maya smiled, glad that some of the old Katrina seemed to have returned. That enduring spirit of hers peeked its way through the ruffled exterior, readying itself to do battle, and Maya was certain her friend wouldn't go down without a fight.

"Good, 'cause I really don't think God would know what to do with you up there anyway." Maya smiled.

By Sunday, Katrina was through the worst of it and determined to resume her life. While Maya was certain there would be rough days ahead, she and Katrina both had adopted an attitude of modest optimism.

"So how is she?" Vic asked. It was one o'clock in the morning when Maya, unable to sleep, dialed him.

"She's doing much better. That's the thing about Katrina—I don't think there's anything that can keep her down for long. She'll get through this."

"And how are you?" Vic asked worriedly.

"I'm fine. Just seeing her smiling and getting back on her feet is enough to make me happy. She's looking forward to getting back to her students tomorrow. And she even called her mother."

"Really? I thought she didn't want her to know what was up?"

"When she calmed down and came to her senses, she realized she had to. Mrs. Brewster is the coolest mom on the planet and she's got that girl's back—no matter what. They had a good long talk. I really think that's what did the trick. And when Mrs. Brewster gets back from Paris next week, I'm sure she'll be right here to help Katrina get through this."

"And so will you," Vic said.

"Yep. She's giving me the boot, though. Something about her not needing a baby-sitter and me needing to get back to tending to my own business. I knew she was feeling better when she started packing my bag for me." Maya laughed. "So I'm catching an early train in the morning."

"Katrina's lucky to have a friend like you."

Even though Vic missed Maya terribly, he admired

the way she'd dropped everything and gone to be with Katrina.

"I don't know about that. I do know that she's always been there for me, and that's not an easy thing, you know."

"Tell me about it." Vic laughed.

"Hey, watch it now."

"I'm just playing, baby. I miss you," Vic said.

"Well, you'll see me tomorrow."

"Not soon enough. What are you wearin'?" Vic asked. The night was warm and he'd turned on the ceiling fan above his bed. The breeze that blew across his bare chest did little to cool him off.

"A tank top, one of yours, I think. Why?"

"I just want to have a picture of you in my mind before I go to back to sleep. What else are you wearing?"

"Panties."

"What color?"

"Red. Sheer," Maya whispered. She tossed the sheet off her body, the temperature in the room making it unnecessary.

"Yeah, I like that picture." Vic smiled.

"What about you? What are you wearing?" Maya asked.

"Nothing."

"Stop playing, Vic."

"I'm serious, girl. It's hot in here."

"Why don't you turn on the air conditioner?" Maya asked.

"Nah, I like it hot," Vic said seductively.

"I wish I were there with you," Maya answered.

"What would you do if you were?"

"I'd kiss you all over."

"And then what?" Vic pressed.

"I'd touch you."

"Where?"

"Where do you want me to touch you?"

"Touch me where I'm hardest," Vic said, touching his growing erection. He closed his eyes, Maya's sultry voice causing the blood to flow toward his pulsing groin.

"Then I'd touch you there. I'd move my hand up and down, feeling all of your hardness. I'd open and close it, squeezing you gently at first, then harder." Maya squeezed her legs together as the thought of Vic's firm body lying naked beside her caused her core to throb with wanting.

"Can I taste you?" Vic asked, as he made a fist around himself, envisioning Maya's hand in place of his own.

"Yes, please," Maya responded as she moistened two of her own fingers and then placed them where she imagined Vic's mouth to be. Slowly she moved, her fingers doing the work Vic's tongue had so expertly performed before.

"Umm, baby, you're so wet," Vic said.

"Mmm-hmm," Maya agreed.

Maya whispered Vic's name, over and over again, driving him steadily onward to the point of completion, when all the pieces seemed to come together, tightly pressing against one another until they burst apart, tiny fragments of sensation flying everywhere until his body shook uncontrollably. She cooed softly in his ear as she herself reached the sweetest moment of release. At that instance, she wrapped her own arms as tightly around herself as she could, letting her mind believe it was Vic's arms enveloping her.

"I'll meet you at Penn Station," Vic said sleepily. For the moment he was placated, but this telephone rendezvous could never do for him what she could in person.

"Noon. See you tomorrow, baby. Sweet dreams." Maya hung up and curled her arms tightly around her pillow, pretending it was Vic she was holding on to.

Chapter Twenty-Nine

Gentle Giant

"What's wrong, baby?" Maya said, dropping her packages on the bottom step of her apartment building. She was returning home from shopping and as she approached the building, saw a figure sitting on the stairs, head down. She knew instinctively that it was Vic, his muscular rounded shoulders and baseball cap on his head tilted to the side a giveaway. She quickly climbed the four stairs and put her hand on his shoulder. Vic looked up at her, his eyes red and face ashen from the tears he'd already cried. In the six months that they'd known one another, she'd never seen him in this condition and it scared her stiff.

"Oh, my God, baby, what happened? Is it your father?" She pleaded with him now to tell her what was wrong, but it was as if he'd lost his voice. He shook his head and just stared at her. Maya picked up her two Macy's shopping bags and took Vic's arm.

"Come on, let's go inside," she said, pulling a limp Vic to his feet. He followed Maya through the vestibule and up the stairs to her apartment door, where he slumped against the wall until the door was opened.

Inside, Maya dropped her bags and headed straight

to the kitchen, where she retrieved a bottle of Heineken from the fridge. Removing the top quickly, she returned to Vic in the living room. Vic was hunched over in one of the chairs when she handed him the beer, from which he took only a small sip.

From the floor in front of Vic's feet, Maya watched his face for some clue as to what had brought him to such a state. As he gripped the bottle tightly, Maya noticed that the knuckles on his left hand were blood-crusted, bruised and swollen.

"Vic, what happened to your hand?" Maya asked.

Vic looked curiously at his hand, as if for the first time noticing the damage.

"I punched a wall," he said finally.

Maya went to the bathroom in search of some first-aid tools. She was annoyed to find that the medicine cabinet contained only an almost-empty tube of Neosporin and a box with one Q-tip. She wet a washcloth with warm water, took another dry cloth from the shelf and headed to her bedroom, retrieving an Ace bandage from her sock drawer.

Maya returned to the living room and an immobile Vic. She worked silently on his damaged hand, and when she was satisfied that she'd at least made the abrasions a bit more comfortable, went to the kitchen. She lit a fire under the tea kettle, taking with her the virtually untouched Heineken bottle. She returned a couple of minutes later, two cups of herbal tea in hand, to find Vic asleep, his head thrown back against the chair.

Maya sighed before depositing the tea cups on the kitchen counter. She placed Vic's slack arm around her shoulder, hers around his waist and, supporting his weary body, moved to the bedroom, where she helped him lie down on the bed. Then she removed his shoes and curled up next to him. She wrapped her arms as fully around his body as she could, wanting to comfort him so completely that he'd be able to finally share with her what tragedy had hit him so hard.

She listened to his breathing as he slept, a heavy sound like a man who had not slept for days. It was as if his body were devouring the slumber hungrily, each weighty breath running rhythmically into the next. Maya pulled herself up on an elbow and stroked the side of Vic's sleeping face, worried about this man whom she herself had looked to for strength and comfort. It was his turn now, and she knew she would be there for him, talkative or silent, for as long as he needed.

Her gut lay in a knot in her belly as she wondered what could have been so terrible that it had made Vic punch a wall and then literally sent him into shock. Whatever it was, it was obviously big.

Maya awoke with a start, uncertain as to when she had dozed off. Vic was still sleeping soundly. She looked at her watched—an hour had passed since she and Vic had lain down. Stealthily, she removed herself from the bed. The evening had brought a little chill into the apartment, so she pulled the quilt from the foot of the bed and spread it over Vic, who didn't even stir. In the kitchen she busied herself with making dinner—lemon-baked chicken breasts, rice and a Caesar salad. Once the meal was ready and the plates were laid, right on cue, Vic emerged from the bedroom. His shirt was rumpled and his face contorted like a confused little boy.

"How long have I been asleep?" he asked, scratching his bare scalp.

"A couple of hours. Feeling better?" Maya asked.

"I guess. That smells good," Vic said, moving into the kitchen. He stood behind Maya, lacing his arms around her body and kissing the nape of her neck.

"Come on and eat a little," she said.

Vic released her as she carried their plates to the snack tables she'd set out in the living room. Vic excused himself to the bathroom. When he returned, he was minus his shirt and a damp hand towel hung around his neck. He rejoined Maya and dug into his meal with a voracious appetite.

"Thanks, baby. That was really good," Vic said when he'd finished.

He attempted a quick smile, a sign that to Maya indicated he was a lot closer to his usual self than when she'd found him on her steps that afternoon.

"You're welcome," Maya said, peering at him. She didn't want to push, but she really wanted to know what was going on. She waited patiently, but expectantly, watching Vic polish off a second glass of lemonade.

"Where you been?" he asked.

"Shopping downtown. I went to the mall at Herald Square, then Macy's and Saks."

"Oh," Vic said, noticing the shopping bags near the coatrack for the first time. He sighed then, rubbing his forehead with his good hand.

"You've got a headache?" Maya asked.

"Nah, it's all right." Vic paused. "Thanks, Maya . . . for everything."

"You're welcome . . . for everything. Do you think you're ready to talk about it?"

"No, but I guess I owe you that much."

"No, no," Maya lied, "if you don't want to talk about it, it's cool. I'm here when you're ready."

Vic was silent for a moment, staring at the Ace bandaged wound around his throbbing hand. He looked at Maya and smiled.

"Florence Nightingale?"

Maya laughed. "Something like that."

"I saw my mother last night," Vic said flatly.

Maya gasped. "Your *mother?*"

She had known the bare bones of the story of how his mother had left his family when he was about ten years old, without saying goodbye or anything. There was a short note for his father, saying something to the effect that she was suffocating and that she knew he and the kids would be fine without her. The fact was that they had done very well without his mother, but Maya knew, despite what Vic said, his mother's disappearance had hurt him deeply, so she never mentioned his mother unless he did.

"Yeah," Vic said weakly.

"Where'd you see her?"

"She came to the house . . . my dad's house."

"Last night?"

"Yeah. My dad had called me earlier in the day. Said he needed to talk to me about somethin'. I was supposed to be there at seven o'clock but I got hung up. Anyway, when I got there she was there. Sittin' in the livin' room like she'd never left."

"What did your father say?"

"He introduced us. Can you believe that? He had to introduce me to the woman who gave birth to me. And she was all smilin' and goin' on about how big I've gotten. Yo, at first I was like, this has got to be some kind of joke or somethin'."

"And then?"

"And then I looked at her and realized that it wasn't a joke. Phyllis looks just like her."

"Was Phyllis there?"

"No, she's still visiting Andre's family in California."

"Oh, that's right. Well, does she know?"

"I haven't called her. I don't know if my father has or not."

"Wow," Maya said.

She was dumbstruck. She couldn't imagine what she'd feel like if her mother had just up and walked out on her when she was a little kid. She couldn't understand how any mother could do that. It was unfathomable. Popping back in like nothing had happened was even more outrageous.

"Did she say where she'd been or why she came back?"

"She was talkin' a whole bunch of foolishness. And my dad was just kinda sittin' there, like he was a guest in his own house. Finally I said to him, 'Is that what you called me over here for?' "

"Well, Vic, I'm sure he didn't mean for you to find her there like that. I'm sure he wanted to talk to you first."

"Yeah, well, I don't know why he bothered at all. He should have just told her to take her ass back where she came from. Period."

"Come on, now, Vic—"

"Come on, nothin'. *She* left *us,* not the other way around. Why the hell would she think we'd want to see her after fifteen years? My sister was twelve years old when she left—just about to hit puberty and her mother disappears. Do you know what that did to her?"

"I can imagine it was hard for Phyllis. But what about you, Vic? You were just a little boy yourself."

"I handled it. I was all right . . . I had my dad. But a little girl needs a mother, right?"

Maya winced because she knew firsthand that a big girl needed a mother, too.

"Vic, little boys need their mothers, too," Maya said softly.

She watched Vic's face, his eyes staring into hers. All of a sudden they filled with water, the brims instantly turning red.

"I saw her leave," Vic whispered. "I saw her leave and I didn't stop her."

Confused about the meaning of Vic's words, Maya took his hand.

"Vic, you were ten years old."

"I should have stopped her. I should have woke my father up. I heard a noise and came out of my bedroom into the hallway. She was standing by the fireplace, all dressed in her hat and coat. I remember looking toward the window and wondering where she could be going in the middle of the night. She put an envelope on the mantel and walked to the door. She never turned around. Never saw me standin' there watchin' her. She picked up the big suitcase she and my dad always took on vacations, opened the front door and walked out.

"I couldn't move. I just stood there in my Spider-Man pajamas, wishin' I could shoot a web that would trap her in the doorway. I couldn't call out to her. It was like I was mute or somethin'. I knew somethin' was wrong but I couldn't do anythin' about it.

"Finally, I went back to bed and stayed there for hours, until my father came in to get me. By then I'd peed the bed. He just cleaned me up and took Phyllis and me into his room and told us that our mother had to go on a trip for a while. He called it a trip. A trip!"

Maya rushed to Vic's side, pulling his face into her bosom just as the dam broke and he began to violently cry.

"What'd she come back for, Maya? Huh? Why couldn't she just stay gone?"

Maya continued rocking Vic against her body, without answering.

"She's dead to me. She's dead." Vic kept crying.

Maya cried, too, silently brushing tears of understanding from her own eyes. She felt Vic's pain and fought hard against the mounting hatred she was beginning to feel toward the woman who had done this to him.

When his sobs quieted, Maya once again led Vic to the bedroom. This time she helped him remove his clothing and lay face down on the bed. She turned off the lights and lit three kyphi spice scented candles. Vic

waited patiently while Maya prepared for whatever she
was planning to do to him. He was too tired to question
her as she straddled his thighs. When she poured a
warm liquid on his back, he stirred, trying to turn his
head backward to see what she was doing.

"It's just almond oil. Relax," she whispered.

The sound of her voice and the feel of her hands as
she started to rub the oil into his back forced him to
surrender. Maya worked the oil into his muscular
shoulders, in between the blades and out to the backs
of his armpits. She marveled at the smoothness of his
back as she pressed the balls of her hands firmly into
him. She kept moving, kneading, pressing, rubbing for
half an hour.

While her movements made her feel sensual, she
didn't find herself turned on in a sexual way. Her heart
felt inexplicably full, like it couldn't hold another
thing. She blocked out every thought except for the
task at hand, wanting to ease every inch of pain and
confusion out of Vic's body, even if she had to pull it
into her own. She wanted to make love to his body with
just her fingers, her heart and mind. He needed that.

He moaned once or twice, softly, which prompted
her to linger in some places, knead more deeply in others. She worked her way down to his behind, smiling at
the memory of the first time she'd put her hands around
its firmness. She moved down his thighs, one at a time.
His muscular calves softened under her touch as did
the rest of his body. As she began to ascend his body,
moving just as slowly as she had on the way down, he
whispered, "Are you trying to seduce me?"

"No, baby," she answered, "I'm just tryin' to love
you."

Nothing else was said between them that night, not
even as Maya finished her massage and lay down next
to him. Vic wrapped an arm loosely around Maya's
waist and they fell asleep, both full with something

they'd each been missing for longer than they cared to remember.

"Did you mean what you said last night?" Vic asked as he sat on the bed and zipped up the back of Maya's dress.

"About what?" Maya asked.

"About lovin' me."

"That's not what I said."

Vic rose from the bed.

"Oh, no? So what did you say?"

"I said I was *trying* to love you." Maya grinned.

"Right. Uh, what's the difference?"

"The difference is the space between something that is and something that isn't yet. Get it?" Maya leaned against Vic, giggling.

"Yeah, it's like the difference between bullshit and cowshit." Vic kissed Maya, trying to unzip the zipper he'd just fastened.

"Come on, now, Vic, you know I've got to be in court this morning." Maya smacked his hand as she pulled away from him.

He watched her adjust her clothing, followed her to the bathroom and continued watching as she twisted her hair into a bun.

"What are you looking at?" she joked.

"You."

"Oh. Well, in that case, do you like what you see?"

"Very much so. In fact, I love what I see," Vic answered softly, a smile playing on his lips.

Maya understood the full meaning of his statement but did not respond. Vic decided to end the game-playing and just come out with it.

"I'm in love with you, Maya."

Maya stopped pinning her hair, turned to face him and leaned back against the sink for support. She couldn't trust her weakened knees. She looked down at the floor, up at the ceiling, anywhere she could find to look instead of Vic's face. But when she'd run out of places to focus in the tiny bathroom, she met his unwavering eyes.

"And as much as I try to ignore it, I am so in love with you, too," she finally said. Once she had, it felt as though her heart, which had been full to capacity, burst and the sweetness it held filled her whole body.

They stood, grinning at each other, neither of them knowing what to say. Finally Maya looked at her watch and realized she had no more time to linger under Vic's spell. She kissed him good-bye and flew out the door.

The panic Vic was certain would accompany this moment in time was nowhere to be found. He felt calm and assured, and no matter what lay ahead, he was determined to see this thing to the end. This time the ghosts of the past wouldn't lure him away from the treasure he'd found. Or, if they did, he'd go kicking and screaming.

Chapter Thirty

Watch Your Back

April had proven to be an exhaustive month and May wasn't looking any better. Maya was extremely busy at work and still not spending much time with her co-workers, other than an occasional lunch. She talked to Katrina daily, sometimes twice a day just to make sure she was hanging in there. After getting a negative result on the initial testing, Katrina had pretty much bounced back to her normal self, or she so had appeared on the surface. Inside, she was one step from falling apart, Maya knew. That's why she called her so often, just to remind her that they were in this together. Maya had accompanied her to the doctor for the first set of results and had every intention of being there when she got final results in a few months.

The emotional fatigue the waiting caused had Maya worn to a frazzle, but it was Vic who kept her spirits up. Lying in bed late one night, Maya reading the *American Lawyer* and Vic watching the *The Sopranos,* Vic came up with an idea he hoped would boost Maya's spirits.

"Babe, what do you say we go away for the weekend?"

Maya looked up from her reading. "Go where?" she asked.

"I don't know. Someplace warm and tropical. How about the Bahamas? Phyllis and Andre spent their wedding anniversary there, and they said it was great."

"The Bahamas? We can't just up and shoot down to the Bahamas at a moment's notice," Maya replied.

"Why not? It's the Fourth of July weekend. Even you can't be planning to work this weekend."

"No, but—"

"And your birthday is next week. We can celebrate on the beach."

"But, Vic, I'm sure it's pretty expensive to get plane tickets and hotel accommodations at such short notice," Maya reasoned.

"Why don't you let me worry about that?" Vic said, kissing her palm.

"Oh, look at you. Sell a couple of songs and now you're a baller?" Maya laughed.

"No, but I can still afford to treat my lady special from time to time. Come on, babe, you need a break. And I need to spend some quality time with you away from everything and everybody. Please?" Vic begged, working his way up her arm with a flurry of kisses.

"All right, all right. No need to beg. If you make all the arrangements, I'm there. But I can't leave before Friday evening and I have to be back on Monday."

"Aye-aye, captain," Vic teased.

He was glad to have secured the opportunity to get Maya away for at least a couple of days. Hopefully he would be able to remove some of the stress she had been carrying around. He knew that an even greater part of what weighed on her was the Haynes case and that clown, Peter Fusco.

Vic suddenly placed the television on mute and made a surprising request, given the fact that he was not the type of man who'd interfere in his woman's business affairs.

"I want you to leave the firm."

"What?" Maya asked sleepily.

"I want you to leave the firm. You're smart, talented. You could get another job in a heartbeat."

Maya folded the magazine and turned onto her elbow to get a better view of Vic. She was waiting for the punch line, something to let her know he was merely joking. It never came.

"Where did that come from?"

"Maya, you think I don't see what's going on? This case with Fusco has got you buggin'. You work around the clock, you're tense as I don't know what. And before you say it's this scare with Katrina that you're trippin' over, don't. You were stressed out before that."

"I'm scared for her," Maya commented.

"Babe, I know you are. I am, too. But how do you expect to be there for her if you're runnin' yourself ragged for a bunch of overpaid, underprincipled lawyers? Huh?" Vic smoothed Maya's hair lovingly. "Maya, this is not good for you. And besides, I don't like the idea of not being there with you."

"Look, Vic, I told you, I've let it go. I'm not doing anything but my job. You were right—whatever Peter did or didn't do is none of my business. Allen Haynes is my client and that's that," Maya argued.

"Then why are you still so stressed out? Why do you still toss and turn all night long?"

"I don't know, I'm just overtired, probably."

"Wrong answer. It's nerves, baby. Plain and simple. This case . . . the whole damn firm has gotten under your skin and it's eating you up."

"Vic, I know I've been working a lot, but that's the price you have to pay as a first-year associate. I knew that going in. But I promise, things are going to start lightening up soon, with summer coming. Judges go on vacation and whatnot. Before you know it, we'll be spending so much time together, you'll get sick of me."

"Maya, it's not just about us spending time together. Not that I wouldn't love that."

"Then what?"

Vic sighed, sitting up against the headboard. He contemplated his next move, trying to figure out how to tell Maya that two nights ago, he'd worked late and was walking past Peter's office but stopped when he heard the man speaking to someone on telephone. Vic knew Maya would tell him he was overreacting, but in his gut, he knew his mistrust of the man was justified.

"Look, I don't like Peter Fusco. Never did and I especially don't now." Vic hoped that would be enough to get Maya to see where he was coming from.

"Did something happen, Vic?" Maya sat up, every muscle in her body immediately becoming alert. "Did he say something to you? I'll go in his office first thing in the morning and tell him—"

"See? See what I'm talking about? You're so quick to come out swingin'. Relax." Vic paused, unsure if what he was about to tell Maya would prove to be more of a burden. "Look, I overheard Fusco talkin' on the phone. He was sayin' something to the effect that he'd 'make her back off.' Then he hung up."

"What does that prove, Vic? You don't even know if he was talking about me. Come on, aren't you the one always telling me to relax?"

"Nah, I just didn't like the way he said it. Man, if I knew for sure that he was talking about you, I'd have been all over him." Vic didn't go on to tell Maya that he had made his presence known to Peter by pushing his door open and dropping a piece of mail on the corner of his desk that ordinarily would have gone to the secretary. Peter looked up as Vic entered the room, but did not speak. Victor had glared at Peter for several seconds before leaving.

"All I'm sayin' is that dude is shady, real slick, and I don't like you messin' with him."

Maya surrendered. "All right, Vic, message received."

"Meaning?"

"Meaning, I'll watch my back," Maya said. "I'm not leaving my job, however, so you're just gonna have to trust me. Now, I'm sure you can think of other things to occupy me to keep me out of trouble." She giggled as she clicked the television off and tossed the remote to the floor.

Chapter Thirty-One

Forever My Lady

"Hey, Pops, what's going on?" Maya yelled as she hung her coat in the hallway closet of the brownstone.

"Nothing much, baby girl," he responded from his usual spot—the exhausted leather recliner in the living room.

Maya leaned down to kiss his bearded cheek.

"I like the new look," she said.

"Yeah, makes me look rugged, don't it?" Victor Sr. smiled, proudly stroking his newly grown facial hair.

"Is Vic here yet?" she asked, plopping down on the sofa and checking her watch. Vic had asked her to meet him at the brownstone because they were taking his father out to dinner for his birthday. Victor Sr.'s birthday was really next week, but he would be spending that time in Las Vegas with a couple of buddies. Tonight's reservations were for nine o'clock at B. Smith's, and it was already a quarter after eight. Maya hated being late for anything, a trait she inherited from her punctual-to-a-fault father.

The large Sony flat-screen television was tuned in to the Knicks/Pacers game, the surround sound reverberating throughout the room. It was the third quarter and the Pacers were up by ten. Maya was immediately swept up in the action as a Pacer rookie fed the shooter an around-the-back pass in the post. A sweet two points.

"No, he didn't get here yet. Phyllis is in the back, though," Victor Sr. said, prompting Maya to get out of her chair and head down the long hallway.

"Hey, girl," Maya said, rapping three quick times on the halfway-open bedroom door.

"Come in, Maya," Phyllis answered. "What's up? Ooh, that's a bad top you've got on."

Phyllis's dimpled smile was the first thing people noticed about her. At five-feet–one, one hundred and fifteen pounds, Phyllis was what you would call petite. Her beautiful bronze skin and wavy auburn hair gave her an exotic appearance. Without ever having seen a picture of their mom, Maya knew Phyllis had to be a dead ringer for her. While Vic was the spitting image of his father, he and Phyllis did share some characteristics that evidently came from their mother.

The first time Maya and Phyllis met, it was as if they'd already known one another for years. Phyllis possessed the same warm, teasing personality as her father. Over dinner that night, she and Maya had conversed almost exclusively, until Vic and Andre threatened to leave. Phyllis absolutely doted on Vic, making it clear that she had attempted to fill the void created when their mother left. For that, coupled with her endearing disposition, Maya liked her instantly.

Phyllis was ironing her father's shirts, which Maya guessed meant that Mrs. Velazquez, the Cuban immigrant housekeeper who had been coming in twice a week, had bit the dust like the others before her. It was Phyllis who insisted her father have someone come in to do the vacuuming, dusting, laundry and other chores because she felt that, with her father still working so hard as a loan officer at the Bank of New York, he didn't need to have to come home every day to keep house as well. Phyllis used to take care of all that for him, but with her job and husband, she couldn't get over there as much as she used to. With Vic spending so much time at Maya's or working with artists, he, too, wasn't around much to help out.

Unfortunately, every time Phyllis hired someone for her father, he found some reason to let the person go. This one didn't know how to make a bed right, that one was too busy eating up his food and using his phone. There was always some reason or another to let the help go.

"What's up with the ironing?" Maya asked.

"Mrs. Velazquez's mother is ill in Texas so she went to take care of her. She'll be back in a couple of weeks."

"Oh, I thought your dad canned her, too." Maya laughed. She took the blue cotton shirt Phyllis had just ironed, finding a hanger for it.

"No, believe it or not, I think he actually likes her. He hasn't complained once since she started."

"That's good. So what's new with you?" Maya asked.

"Same ole, same ole, girl. But I've got some good news, too. Andre got a promotion the other day—director of marketing and sales."

"Get outta here! Go, boy! That's great, Phyllis."

"I know. He worked so hard for it, but we were worried he was going to get passed over. He'll be the first African-American ever to hold that position in that company and they have more than a hundred years in the business."

"Well, all right, I guess that just makes his victory all the sweeter. So what'd you guys do to celebrate?"

"Well, it started out with a little bubbly, a couple of two-pound lobsters and some candles—"

"Watch out now!" Maya laughed.

"Watch out is right, girl. The next morning he was like, 'I'll get a promotion every day for a repeat!' "

The women whooped and hollered until Victor Sr. called from the living, wanting to know what was going on.

"I'm truly happy for you guys," Maya said.

"Thanks. So now I really feel like the ball is in my court, you know?"

"How so?"

"Well, Andre wants us to start having kids and so do I . . ."

"But?" Maya asked, sensing the conflict in Phyllis's tone.

"But . . . I was thinking about doing something else," Phyllis said excitedly.

"Something else like what?"

"I think I might want to go back to graduate school. I mean, I did almost a year toward my master's in child psychology, so I'd only have a little more than a year to go."

"Mm-hmm," Maya said.

"And, well, I like teaching, don't get me wrong. But I think I could better serve children in the capacity of counselor or psychologist. And with Andre's promotion, I could stop teaching and go take classes full time."

"Sounds like a good idea to me. What's the problem?" Maya asked.

"I haven't told Andre yet. I mean, like I said, he really wants to start having kids now and I don't want to disappoint him. We've been married for almost four years and he says now's the perfect time, while we're still young enough to keep up with them. The fact that his mother keeps calling every other day talking about how she's not getting any younger and asking when we plan on making her a grandmother has got him feeling pressed. And, Maya, I take my hat off to women who work, go to school and raise a family, but I don't want to be one of those women."

Phyllis turned the iron off, wrapping its chord around the handle. Maya collapsed the ironing board for her and walked to the closet with it. As she set it down inside, she thought about Phyllis's concerns.

"Phyllis, you know you have the right to choose when you start a family. That time should be when it's right for both of you."

"I know, but I'm not getting any younger either, you know."

"You're twenty-six years old. Hardly time to collect social security," Maya said, sitting on the edge of the bed next to Phyllis.

"I'm almost twenty-seven. I'll be pushing twenty-nine when I finish school. Then you figure I'll need at least a couple of years, maybe three or four, on the job before I even think about taking any maternity leave. I'll be damn near thirty-five before I give birth and we want at least two kids. I'll be an old mother!"

"So what? A lot of women nowadays are waiting until they're older to have kids. I think you're putting the horse before the cart."

"You sound like Daddy," Phyllis remarked.

"Then you should listen to us. Look, Phyllis, you've got to follow your dream. Just talk it over with Andre, and I'm sure you'll figure out how you can have it all."

"I guess you're right."

"I am right. Now don't worry about it. And when you do start popping out those babies, put me down for baby-sitting or whatever, 'cause Maya loves the kids," Maya joked.

As the two women hugged and made their way down the hall, Victor Sr. was pulling on a light beige sports jacket.

"I was just about to come get you two. Vic called and said we should meet him at the restaurant."

"I figured as much. He's running late as usual," Maya said lightheartedly.

"That's all right. I get to escort my two favorite ladies myself. Ladies," he said as he held the door for them.

To Maya's surprise, Vic had reserved a private room. When they arrived, Vic and Andre were already there. After the five were seated and their orders taken, a pair of violinists entered the room and began playing Luther Vandross's "Here and Now," which struck Maya as a strange selection for a birthday dedication. After the serenade, Vic rose on shaky legs.

"Okay, everyone, I guess it's show time," he said, clearing his throat. "Everyone at this table knows why we're here—except for one person, that is."

With that, Vic turned to Maya, who wore an expression that was a cross between confusion and trepidation. Maya quickly looked around the room to see Victor Sr., Andre and especially Phyllis grinning from ear to ear back at her. Then she looked back to Vic.

"Maya, I've got somethin' to ask you, and I decided that the most appropriate way for me to ask you this question would be in front of my family. You're the best thing that has ever happened to me and they all know it."

"Amen to that!" Victor Sr. testified.

"A'ight Pops," Vic warned.

"Anyhow, Maya, I know we've known each other less than a year, not very long by most standards. But I know enough to know that when somethin' is meant to be, you don't let it slip away from you. So . . ." He hesitated as he pulled something from underneath the napkin in front of his plate Maya had not noticed before. It was a small red velvet box. Opening it, he slid down on one knee, causing the breath to catch in Maya's lungs.

"Maya, will you be my lady? My wife. . . . Will you marry me?"

Maya stared from the ring to Vic then back to the ring in astonishment. She looked around the table at each face, all of which were still beaming and grinning at her.

"Vic, are you serious?" she asked; she thought for sure either this was some elaborate joke or she had fallen down somewhere, bumped her head real hard and landed in Oz.

"Dead serious, babe," he answered.

"Well, girl, you plan on answering my son tonight?" Victor Sr. said.

"Pops," Phyllis hissed.

"Yes, Pops, I most certainly do plan on answering your son." Maya laughed. To Vic she said, "Like you said, we've only known each other for a short while, but in that time, well . . . as Katrina would say, you've got me sprung."

Andre laughed out loud at that, until Phyllis punched him in the arm.

"And," Maya continued, "since you've got the best family in the world and I couldn't imagine not being around to eat more of your dad's shrimp Creole . . ." Maya laughed.

Vic jumped in. "Oh, you're enjoyin' this, aren't you?"

The laughter in the room was mounting and Vic was starting to sweat. Maya decided to let him off the hook.

"I also couldn't imagine my life without you. Yes, Vic, I will marry you."

"Well, I'll drink to that," Victor Sr. bellowed, summoning a waiter.

Vic deftly slid a pear-shaped one-and-a-half-karat

diamond set in platinum onto Maya's ring finger. The beauty of the ring was indescribable, but paled in comparison to the beauty of the man kneeling before her. She kissed him tenderly, wishing immediately that they were alone.

"All right, you two. Break it up and let's get this party started," Victor Sr. ordered.

The violinists had returned and, on Victor Sr.'s cue, resumed playing. The waiter popped the cork on a bottle of Cristal champagne and the group partied until closing time.

Later that night, after hours of delicious lovemaking, Vic slept peacefully while Maya tossed and turned, the romantic excitement of the night preventing her from resting. She slid from beneath the arm Vic had tossed across her nude body and padded to the living room. Acknowledging that it was after two o'clock in the morning, Maya hesitated, but only briefly, before picking up the phone and dialing Katrina's number.

"Aaaah!" Katrina screamed into the telephone when Maya shared the news. The grogginess with which Katrina had first answered evaporated as she began jumping up and down on her canopy bed. After whacking her head on the rails, she plopped down and crossed her legs Indian-style.

"Girl, I just know you are lying to me!"

"Am not," Maya said. "See." Maya shoved her ring finger against the mouthpiece of the telephone. "Honey, this ring is blinding me right now! I just know you can see it through the wires."

"Aaaaaah!" Katrina screamed again. "I knew the boy had you strung out, but damn, ya'll move fast!"

"Well, like my daddy used to say, when that luxury ride comes sailing down the block, you either jump in or get left behind sucking exhaust fumes," Maya said confidently.

"I know that's right. But, Maya, are you sure? I mean, it wasn't that long ago that you thought Gerald was the one."

Katrina hated to bring up the Gerald thing, but Maya was her girl, and she had to be sure she knew what she was doing. Vic seemed like a great guy and all, but Katrina also knew that Maya, like most women, had handpicked a few losers in her day, too.

"Katrina, I never thought Gerald was the one. I just wanted a family again. I wanted somebody to belong to after I lost my parents."

"I can dig that. But I'm saying, how do you know you're not doing the same thing again?"

The last thing Katrina wanted to be was a wet blanket, but she also didn't want to see her best friend make a big mistake.

" 'Cause with Vic it's so different. I mean, yes, I love his family and they've welcomed me with open arms. But more important than that, I see myself growing with him, not just being with him for right now." Maya paused, trying to put the right words together to convey what she was feeling. "He's supportive of me and what I want and he's driven. He wants to live life, not just exist in it. Ooh, Kat! Sometimes I get hot just thinking about him!"

"For real?" Katrina oozed dreamily.

"Mmm-hmm. It's that good, girl. And we talk, Kat. Talk about anything and everything. One night we talked all night long, and when the sun came up we still had stuff to talk about. He's so talented. The way he writes, it's like . . . it's poetry, and he means what he says and it means something to him, you know? And he's considerate, Kat, down-home considerate. He's opening-doors, pulling-out-chairs, foot-massage kind of considerate. He really cares about how his actions affect other people. He reminds me so much of my daddy." Maya smiled.

"So I guess it's true when they say that we do eventually wind up marrying our parents. Now, that is a scary thought!" Katrina laughed. "All right, girl! I'm sold. Let's do this! So what are we talking about, next spring? Summer? I think June is nice for weddings. How about—"

"Uh, Kat? What do you think about this Labor Day weekend? Do you think you can handle that?"

This Labor Day weekend? Labor Day weekend as in September? Are you crazy? It's July now. There is no way in hell we can pull off a wedding in two months," Katrina snapped.

"Yes, we can, Katrina. People elope on a dime every day. How hard can it be to plan a little wedding in two months?"

"First of all, if you even think about eloping, I'll kill you." When Maya laughed devilishly, Katrina added, "No, first I'll tell everyone who will listen about the time we went to Lake Echo and you—"

"All right, all right, say no more! No eloping. But come on, Katrina, we can do this."

When Katrina found herself even considering the possibility, she realized that Maya's excitement was catching.

"Maya, two months? What's the rush?" Katrina was twisting a clump of hair around her finger as she fretted over her friend's uncharacteristic impulsiveness.

"There's no rush. He asked, I accepted and now we just want to do this. We want to get started on our life together."

" 'Cause ya'll don't want to end up sucking exhaust fumes?" Katrina concluded.

"There you go! So, what do we have to do?"

"Look, I'm telling you right now, best friend or no best friend, I will not sit by and watch you get married in some tacky, thrown-together-any-kind-of-way affair."

"Okay, fair enough. So where do we start?" Maya asked.

"All right, first of all, how many people are we talking about?"

"Um, let me think," Maya said, drumming her fingers on the receiver. "Well, you know everybody on my side—that's about seven or eight people, tops."

"Wrong. You've got to invite a few choice co-workers. It's P.C. Then there's some of your parents' old friends and associates."

"I guess you're right. Okay, let's see." Maya paused, snatching a take-out menu from the kitchen counter and flipping it over to its blank side. She began quickly jotting down names. "All right, then make mine eighteen."

"Okay, then double that cause you've gotta account for their guests." Katrina quickly scratched a figure onto the notepad on her nightstand. "Now what about Vic?"

"Well, Phyllis said she'll get the list of their family together, but estimated the number to be around thirty. Vic thought his friends and business associates would account for about twenty. Double those figures to include guests." Maya paused as she did the math. "Wow, there'll be triple the amount of people on his side of the church as there will be on mine."

"That's what you get for being a recluse," Katrina joked. "Seriously, though, erring on the side of more not less, let's say a total of one hundred and forty guests."

"Whoa, that's more than I expected," Maya said.

"Yeah, well, that's usually how it turns out."

Katrina drew a double line under the figures and then wrote the word *location*. "Moving right along, I assume you guys want to do this in New York somewhere?"

"Uh-huh. And I want it in a church. My mother would want that."

"Okay, does Vic belong to any church? 'Cause I know your heathen behind doesn't," Katrina said.

"No, neither does his father. Phyllis and Andre belong to a church out on Long Island where they live, but I don't think I want to do that. How about Mt. Carmel in Westchester County? My parents and I went there for years."

"All right, well, I don't think they tear up your membership if you don't attend for a couple of years."

"It's been more than a couple of years. I haven't set foot in that church since my father died. But I'll give the reverend a call tomorrow."

"Okay, now, if you have the ceremony in Westchester, you might as well have the reception there, too. Hold on a minute," Katrina said.

When she came back, she informed Maya that she'd turned on her computer and was surfing the Internet for suitable hotels and banquet halls in Westchester. They spent the next half an hour making a list of different places to call, which they would later narrow down to prospective places that had availability. They planned to make appointments for the upcoming weekend.

"All right, now. Who's going to be involved in this little love fest?"

"Well, I'd like Phyllis to be involved. And I'd love to have Shelly and Bonnie as bridesmaids, provided they can get here."

"If I had to guess, I'd say Shelly will definitely be here. Bonnie, I doubt. This is extremely short notice to try and pull somebody out of the jungle." Katrina laughed.

"Bolivia's not the jungle, you nut. I'll write to her tomorrow and ask. And you'll be my maid of honor and—"

"Oh, will I, now?" Katrina toyed. "I'm not sure about that. I mean, I haven't officially been asked yet."

"Katrina, cut it out. I don't have time for games," Maya said.

"I'm not playing games. If somebody wants another somebody to be in their wedding—stand up for them, witness the start of that somebody's new life—then somebody has to formally ask."

"Katrina Marie Brewster, would you please do me the honor of attending me in my wedding?"

"Ah, I don't know. When did you say it was again? I might be busy that day." Katrina giggled.

"Later for you, Kat," Maya stretched and yawned. "I think the lack of sleep is starting to get to you. Go back to bed and we'll finish this conversation tonight after work."

"Already there," Katrina said, switching off the lamp beside her. "Tell Mr. Smalls I said congratulations and that he and I will have to get together for a little schooling real soon. I gotta hip the brother to a few things about you that he might not know yet."

"I don't think so," Maya said, tucking the notes she'd taken into her briefcase.

"No, seriously, I've gotta make sure he knows the rules. I wouldn't want to have to end up boxing his ass in a couple of years, if he don't act right."

"Okay, Mrs. Holyfield, 'cause you can beat the world."

"And you know this!"

Maya laughed. "Bye, fool."

"Smooches."

Chapter Thirty-Two

Bahama Mama

"I'm coming, I'm coming," Maya called through the closed bathroom door.

"I can't go out there in this," she whispered to her reflection in the full-length mirror. She had been standing there for fifteen minutes, pulling and tugging at the one-piece electric-blue bathing suit that strategically covered the barest minimum of her body.

"What did you say?" Vic asked, pressing his ear to the door.

He turned the knob, already knowing the lock was securely in place. He was dying to see Maya in a bathing suit. Most of the time she was conservatively dressed, wearing business suits for work and long dresses, slacks or jeans when they went out together. She didn't even own any negligees. While he found her incredibly sexy regardless of what she wore, he secretly wished he could see her in revealing clothing more often. He'd tried to look in her suitcase when they'd first arrived in the Bahamas, hoping she'd packed a bikini, but she'd shut him down before he could get a peek.

"Nothing," Maya answered. "I can't believe I let Katrina talk me into buying this," she hissed.

The suit was by Victoria's Secret and, as far as Maya was concerned, was telling all the business. The top of it dipped low to show off Maya's ample bosom. The midsection was cut out to reveal her taut belly. The back dipped low before providing only partial cover to her considerable rear. Katrina had practically twisted her arm into buying it, convincing her that it wasn't too risqué. As she contemplated herself now, Maya made a mental note to slap Katrina the next time she saw her. This suit was well past being too much. It was downright dangerous. She was certain she'd get a ticket for indecent exposure if she stepped foot on the beach in it.

Unfortunately, this was the only bathing suit she'd brought with her and the stores in the area were already closed. Their flight's take-off had been delayed for an hour, due to a thunderstorm in the New York area, and they hadn't landed until ten o'clock local time that night. They rode by taxi from the airport to the private villa Vic had rented, stopping along the way for sandwiches and beverages, which they would eat later that night. If she planned to swim tonight, this suit was her only option.

She did a slow three-sixty in the mirror, considering what Vic's reaction would be. The longer she looked, the realization dawned on her that she was actually sexy. She released the band holding her ponytail in place, shaking her hair loose until it framed her face, then placed one hand on her hip, the other in her hair, her lips settling into a tiny pout. The sight of herself and the thought of Vic seeing her was a turn-on. She began imagining his hands fingering the flimsy bathing suit, wanting to get her out of it as much as he wanted to see her in it.

As the heat in the bathroom seemed to rise, Maya

shook herself reluctantly from her daydream. She took a deep breath and reached for the doorknob.

"Woman, the ocean is going to freeze over by the time you—"

Vic lost his train of thought as the door opened and Maya stepped into view. His overactive imagination paled in comparison to reality.

"Wow," he said as he plopped down onto the edge of the king-size bed.

"Do you like it?" Maya queried. She was almost timid in her demeanor as she moved toward Vic. She stopped in front of him and turned around slowly, pausing with her back to him for a moment before facing him again.

"Well, do you?" she asked a silent Vic.

"Huh?" he mumbled.

"Vic, come on. What do you think? I mean, it's not really me. It's a little too . . . too . . . little, right?"

"Uh-uh. No. I mean, it's all good." Vic struggled to speak. "Baby, you look incredible."

He pulled her to him, his hands reaching behind her to fondle each cheek.

"That's it—when we get back to New York, I'm burning all of your clothes. From now on, this is all you're wearing."

"Hold on, buddy. Don't you think I'll look a little ridiculous in court?" Maya laughed.

"So what? I bet you'd win all your cases," Vic responded. His mouth was nestled comfortably in Maya's neck as he began kissing and licking her while his hands massaged her back and rear. His arousal was apparent as he pressed himself against her thigh, his swim trunks unable to disguise his reaction to her outfit.

"Chuckle, chuckle," Maya said as she pulled herself away from him. "I thought we were going down to the beach."

"Nah, I don't even like water. Let's just stay here

and—" Vic reached for Maya, who backed away toward the door.

"I don't think so. Do you know how much I paid for this suit? It's going to touch some beautiful Bahamas saltwater or you're gonna have to pay me back," Maya joked.

"Here, take it all," Vic said, tossing his wallet at Maya's feet. "Now, baby, please come here."

Maya removed her matching cover-up from a hook near the door and slid into it. As she opened the suite's door, she said over her shoulder, "Come and get me," before slipping out of the room.

Vic picked up his wallet, grabbed a couple of large towels from the dresser and followed Maya down to the beach. It was dark, save for a few dull lights scattered along the border of the sand. There were a few couples out, lying on blankets or playing in the water.

Vic and Maya walked the length of the small beach, hand in hand, until they reached a secluded spot near the end of the hotel's property. Maya ran across the sand and into the water, her laughter ringing through the quiet night air. A few feet out, she dove under a gentle wave and emerged seconds later, her wet hair covering her face. Vic ran in after her, reaching her quickly. He smoothed the hair back from her face as his arms encircled her body. Her kiss was salty as his lips sought pleasure in hers.

At the water's edge, they lapped each other's sea-soaked bodies, pleasuring one another as warm tropical air and tiny rivulets of ocean teased their flesh.

"I love you, soon-to-be wife," Vic said as he lay on top of her, stroking her smooth, wet face.

"Do you know you are the best thing that's ever happened to me?" Maya asked. "I love you so much, Vic," Maya said, kissing the tip of his nose. "I love your nose."

"You're gonna make beautiful babies," he said,

imagining a son or daughter possessed with her smile and velvet-brown skin.

"Babies? How many do you think we should have?" Maya asked, her heart fluttering at the thought of having children to share with Vic.

"About four or five."

"Not hardly, Mr. Smalls."

"Okay, how about one girl, a pretty little princess?" he countered. "And then—"

"A handsome boy, who'll be strong like his daddy," Maya finished for him.

"Yeah, he'll be smart like his mother."

"And a poet like his daddy."

"I don't care how many kids we have. I just want you to know that I'll take care of you and them forever. I'll never let you guys down and I'll never leave you."

Vic's sincerity was something Maya knew she could count on. Instinctively she knew that he was a man who did precisely what he said he would do, no matter what the challenges were.

"I know you won't. I love you, Vic." Maya wrapped her arms around Vic's neck and held him as she stared up at the starless, blue-black sky. She knew she had come as close to finding perfection in this man as one could expect. That night, for the first time in more than three years, she felt like the past didn't matter.

Chapter Thirty-Three

Devil at Play

Mimi shook her long, fiery-red hair from side to side, gliding across the plush carpeted floor, keeping time with the throbbing bass of the salsa music blaring from her boom box on the desk. She had danced continuously through four songs already. Ordinarily, Peter would be all over her before the second song had finished playing. Tonight, he lay stiffly across the bed, his head resting against fluffy down pillows, seemingly watching her, but nonreactive.

Peter's mind was far away from the penthouse suite at the Four Seasons or the young dancing girl in front of him. He had problems, real problems. The Haynes case was not disappearing as quickly as he had hoped. Somebody at the SEC seemed to have a real boner for this one and his sources had been unable to uncover who it was. And Haynes was becoming a real paranoid pain in the ass. Peter knew it would be just a matter of time until Haynes crumbled, possibly implicating Peter in the fraud. Peter certainly couldn't allow that to happen. He'd worked too hard and come too far. He'd had the vision, the guts to go after what he wanted in life.

Those law partners of his were nothing but sniveling cowards. Their practice was marginal at best and it was his drive and daredevil tactics that had allowed the firm to prosper. He'd single-handedly built the reputation Madison Pritchard now boasted by taking on the hard-to-win cases and doing whatever it took to win them. He used his brains and hired the muscle whenever needed. There was nothing he wouldn't do to protect what he'd built.

His thoughts turned to Maya Wilkins. A beautiful young woman whose only unattractive quality was her nosiness. He chuckled inwardly to think that Maya actually believed all her snooping was incognito. He was aware of her every move. He had to admit that it was somewhat of a turn-on to have her sniffing around him. She was pretty and young, with a firm body, just like he liked them. Black, white, Asian, Hispanic—hell, American Indian—it didn't matter to him: a fine woman was a fine woman. But he didn't fool himself for a minute by thinking he could bed Maya Wilkins—well, at least not willingly. No, she was a fighter, not a lover.

"Petey, baby, what's the matter?" Mimi asked in a whiny babylike tone.

Peter ignored her, still lost in his thoughts. He had to get his affairs in order, fast and in a hurry, or he stood to lose it all. The thought of that made his stomach queasy. A nasty metallic taste rose from his throat into his mouth as his memory rewound to a time when he was a nobody who owned less than nothing.

He had grown up poor as a church mouse in rural McKeesport, Pennsylvania. His father was an alcoholic loser who blamed Peter's mother for the fact that he never had two nickels to rub together, rather than blaming himself for knocking her up every time he looked at her, fathering five babies in rapid succession, of whom Peter was lodged in the middle. He knocked her around just as much, as if it was her fault that he was a bum.

Peter vividly remembered the day when, at sixteen, he'd stepped in between his parents, determined not to allow his mother to suffer one more bloody nose or busted lip at the hands of his father. At first his father had laughed at him. Through his drunken haze, he couldn't see that Peter was no longer a scrawny little kid, but had become almost a full-grown man. He stood several inches above his father, his arms and legs now thick and beefy. Peter curled and uncurled his fingers into fists as he demanded that his father leave the house.

"What? You little punk. This is my goddamn house. You don't tell me to get out."

"I'm not gonna let you hit on Mama no more. Do you hear?" Peter yelled back.

"You're not gonna let me? Boy, I'll knock you into next week." His father raised a shaking fist but Peter didn't flinch. The tiny, neat kitchen was silent, except for the thudding of Peter's heart against his chest. His two older sisters, seventeen- and eighteen-year-old Martha and Angela, pressed themselves into a far corner of the kitchen, near the refrigerator.

They were both small and timid, the spitting images of their mother, and they were equally terrified of their father. Peter's brother, Jimmy, a wiry thirteen-year-old who, as a result of his father's constant bullying and cruelty, continued to wet the bed even at that late age, stood in the doorway, amazed and at the same time enormously proud of his older brother's bravery. The baby, ten-year-old Kalyn, sat wide-eyed in her wheelchair pushed up to the dinette, her useless legs dangling to the floor, her hairless baby doll tucked safely in her lap.

There had been other babies, a still-born boy after

Kalyn, and twins lost in the fifth month of pregnancy. After that, his father stopped touching his mother—unless he was hitting her.

Peter was glad there would be no more children in the house. They barely had enough to eat as it was. Not that it mattered much since his father remained just as mean as ever, constantly yelling at the kids for any minor infraction, real or imagined. They relished the hours when he was either out working some meaningless job or at the pub. It was the only time the walls of their small apartment didn't shake. It was the only time when they could talk and laugh with their mother. Each day they all dreaded the moment they heard the jingling of keys and saw the turning of the dead bolt. Peter, for one, had grown weary of the lives they led and, without making a conscious decision, had stood up as if to say *no more*.

Something in Peter's eyes caused his father to pause, reluctant to let his fist continue its drive toward his son. Icy-cold blue eyes stared back at him, much like his own, but filled with a malice the likes of which he had never seen before.

"Boy, you won't disrespect me in my house," he said. To his wife, he spit, "Do you see what kind of ungrateful scum you've raised? Worthless, just like you. Worthless."

"Don't talk to my mother like that ever again," Peter said to his father, taking a threatening step closer to the man. "In fact, don't talk to her at all."

Peter's father glared at his son one last time, still not daring to take a final stand against this stranger who defied him. He snorted his resignation and slammed out the apartment door, undoubtedly headed for another round at the local pub next door.

"Pete, my sweet boy, you shouldn't have done that," Peter's mother said in a deflated voice.

"It's about time somebody stood up to him. It's not right the way he treats you."

"I'm okay. Really, I am. But he's still your father. A boy should not go against his father. It's not right," she pleaded.

"Why do you defend him? Why? He doesn't care about you . . . or them," he said as he looked around at his brothers and sisters, all of whom were slowly coming back to life as they began to move around the apartment.

"One day you'll understand him. Life has been so hard for him. That's why he's the way he is. He doesn't mean to be," she began.

"Stop it!" Peter yelled. "Just stop it. I will never understand him. I hate him." He slammed out of the apartment.

He walked around for hours along the outskirts of town, contemplating his life. He despised his mother's weakness, but at the same time pitied her. He knew he had reached the point of no return with his father, and it would be just a matter of time before Peter either had to leave home or kill the man. That time came a mere six months later, days before Peter's seventeenth birthday.

Peter had come in after ten o'clock, having spent the hours after school delivering take-out for the Chinese restaurant across the street from home. The apartment was quiet, and on the way to the bathroom, he passed his parents' bedroom. Through the closed door he heard a muffled gurgling sound, like someone was drowning. He pushed open the door to find his father sitting on top of his mother's chest, his massive hands around her throat, choking the life out of her as she fought for air.

In an instant, Peter was on his father's back. He grabbed him by his neck and tossed him across the room. The older man, surprised by the attack and too inebriated to recover quickly enough, was beat to a bloody pulp by his son within a span of sixty seconds. By the time Peter's mother was able to subdue her son, the father was unconscious, his broken nose and bloody face almost clownlike.

Peter left that night. His mother sent him to live with her uncle, an aged factory worker, in nearby Pittsburgh. This turned out to be Peter's saving grace. In Pittsburgh, he finished high school and received a full football scholarship to Florida State University. A knee injury during an exhibition game in his senior year ended his football career, but with a three-point-five grade point average and glowing recommendations from college faculty, Peter was admitted to Florida State University School of Law.

During his college and graduate years, he received sporadic letters from his mother and siblings. The year Peter received his law degree, his father was stabbed to death in a bar fight. Peter did not go to the funeral, nor did he ever return home. When he began practicing law, he sent a monthly check that well provided for his mother and siblings' care, but he could not bring himself to see any of them again. He was determined to become a man of means who would never know hunger, fear or loneliness. He would become the complete opposite of the worthless man his father thought him to be. He accomplished this goal without ever looking back.

At the foot of the bed, Mimi began pulling the sheet from Peter's body, exposing his nakedness. "Don't you wanna come out and play with me tonight?"

"Huh? What?" Peter stuttered as the cool air startled him, thrusting him back into the here and now. "What are you doing?" he asked, snatching the sheet from Mimi's grasp.

"What's wrong with you tonight?" Mimi asked,

stamping her foot like an impatient five-year-old. "It's like you're not even here. Hello, earth to Peter. Paging Peter Fusco, are you in there?" she mocked.

"Oh, cut it out. Listen, I've got a lot on my mind. Something you'd know nothing about."

"Oh, yeah. Well, how about I just leave you alone with your thoughts. How about that?" Mimi hissed, coming closer to the bed.

Before she could react to the impeding threat, Peter had reached out, grabbed her wrist and yanked her forcefully to the floor beside the bed. Twisting her arm, he grimaced at her.

"What did you say?" Peter said through clenched teeth, tightening his grip on Mimi's wrist and taking a handful of her brilliant mane in his other hand.

Mimi whimpered but didn't respond.

"Oh, I didn't think so." Peter released his grip on Mimi's wrist; she immediately began rubbing it. "Now, that's a good girl. Stop being so feisty and come show Daddy why you love him so much."

While Mimi touched and caressed his body, Peter thought to himself what a shame it was that such beauty came in such a dumb package. He'd long ago stopped making love to his wife—it wasn't worth the aggravation. Besides, the missus was happy being able to shop until she dropped and throw back martinis every night. Mimi was just the latest little toy he'd acquired. She was a towel girl down at the Y, and, boy, did she know what to do with a towel. She was barely twenty years old and her voice had an annoying nasal sound to it, but she served the purpose. For a moment he let his mind imagine it was the brainy Maya Wilkins kneeling before him, ready to submit to his every whim.

"Hmm," he moaned. "Wouldn't that be something."

* * *

"Maya Wilkins." Maya had reluctantly picked up the ringing telephone on her desk. It was Friday evening and she had just locked her desk drawer, picked up her briefcase and was wearily headed out of the office for the night after a grueling day. The last thing she needed was another request, question or delay. Vic was in Miami for a big music festival and was scheduled to return Saturday night. Maya was planning to use the free time to catch some R and R, clean her apartment and then meet Vic for dinner at Sylvia's Restaurant upon his return.

"Uh, Miss Wilkins?"

"Yes," Maya answered, annoyed. "Who is this?"

"Uh, Miss Wilkins, you don't know me, but I need to talk to you." The woman's voice was barely a whisper.

"Can you speak up, please? Who is this?"

"Miss Wilkins, I need to speak with you. I have some important information regarding Peter Fusco."

"Can you tell me your name?" Maya asked, her pulse racing.

"No, I'd rather not . . . not over the phone. Can you meet me?"

"Yes. When? Where?"

Chapter Thirty-Four

Getting the Goods

Maya stuffed some paperwork into her briefcase, snapping the clasps shut hastily. Adrenaline coursed through her body, her heart racing as she speed-walked to the elevator bank. She pressed the DOWN button, checking her watch as she waited impatiently for the elevator. She had half an hour to get down to Battery Park and she didn't want to be late. The woman didn't sound like she would wait if Maya wasn't there precisely at the time agreed upon.

Maya was sure that if this witness could, as she insinuated, provide her with solid information, it might be just what she needed to blow Peter Fusco out of the water. While the thought that this could be some of sort of setup briefly entered Maya's mind, she wouldn't entertain the idea for more than a split second. As far as she knew, Peter felt there was no reason to be threatened by her. But if this woman knew something that could concretely link Peter to Haynes's ill-gotten gains, or any other criminal activity, then it was well worth the risk. Maya wanted to see that self-satisfied look of his wiped clean off his face.

The elevator arrived and Maya stepped in, pressing

the CLOSE button quickly. Just before the doors came together, a hand shot in between them, stopping them from meeting. Maya, aggravated by this delay in her departure, looked up to find Rashon standing before her.

The doors closed and the women began their descent in silence. Halfway down, Rashon, who had been staring intently at Maya, spoke.

"Maya, can I speak with you for a minute?"

"Uh . . . sure. What's up?" Maya asked.

"Well, I . . . just wanted to say that I'm happy for you and Vic. He's a great guy."

"Yes, he is."

"And, uh, if I seemed a little unsociable toward you, I didn't mean to."

The elevator reached the ground floor and opened. Maya followed Rashon out into the lobby area before responding.

"Listen, Rashon, I have to admit, I was a little disturbed by your attitude toward me. But I got over it. I mean, we're grown women. This isn't high school and there's nothing to be gained from us being catty. You made it clear that you weren't interested in getting to know me, and that was cool. I don't know if it had something to do with Vic or—"

"No, no, that's not it at all," Rashon defended. "I just didn't know what to make of you at first. I assumed you'd be all stuck-up like the rest of those associates. I guess I shouldn't have judged a book by its cover."

"No, you shouldn't have. But that's in the past." Maya glanced at her watch. "Look, Rashon, I've really got to bc somewhere right away. I appreciate what you've said." Maya turned to walk away.

"Maybe we could do that lunch you mentioned a while back," Rashon called.

"I'd like that. A lot. Later, girl," Maya responded as she zipped through the revolving doors.

Maya made a mad dash to the subway station and hopped on a downtown train on the Lexington Avenue line. Arriving at the Bowling Green station in record time, she ascended the steps and walked quickly in the direction of the park. She reached the last set of benches, the appointed meeting spot, and stole a glance at her watch. She was right on time. Nothing to do now but wait and hope the mystery woman showed up. A light rain began to fall, but Maya remained seated. Waiting.

Several minutes passed before she noticed a tall, slim woman walking hesitantly toward her. The woman was wearing a plain gray trench coat with a matching scarf covering her head and tied in a knot beneath her chin. She wore brown-framed sunglasses and carried a black shoulder bag. Maya rose from the bench, but did not advance toward the woman.

"Miss Wilkins?" she asked.

"Yes. And you are?"

"Please, let's walk while we talk," she answered.

Maya acquiesced, matching her stride to the woman's as they walked across the park.

"Miss Wilkins, you've got to know that this isn't easy for me. My mother thinks I'm crazy for coming here. Peter Fusco is a dangerous man."

"If that's true, then that's all the more reason he needs to be exposed," Maya explained.

"I assure you, it's true. I gave up my life and everything and moved clear across the country to get away from him."

"Miss . . ."

"Elliott. Francesca Elliott."

"Miss Elliott, why don't you tell me what your connection to Peter Fusco is?"

Maya secreted a look at Francesca, confirming her suspicion from the sound of her voice that she was a young woman, no older than her early twenties. In spite of the sunglasses and scarf, Maya could tell she was a very attractive woman—the type an old geezer like Peter Fusco would go for.

"I used to work at Wexton & Haynes. I was Allen Haynes's assistant for just under two years."

"I see," Maya said.

"In my position, I had access to virtually all the company's records. Every stock transaction, every trade, all correspondence and invoices. You name it, I knew about it," Francesca said.

"Shortly after I began working there, I had occasion to meet Peter Fusco. He was at our offices for a meeting with Mr. Haynes. It was late in the afternoon when he arrived and he and Mr. Haynes were behind closed doors for quite some time. When it was time for me to go home for the day, I went to the door, intending to knock and let Mr. Haynes know I was leaving. However, I could hear Mr. Fusco yelling and cursing at Mr. Haynes."

Maya stopped walking. "Did you hear what he said?" she asked.

"Not everything, but one thing I'll never forget: he said, 'You'll do it, just the way we've always done it, or I'll kill you.'" While Francesca spoke, her eyes darted around the park before coming to rest on Maya again.

"Anything else?"

"No, that was all I heard. I waited a few minutes before knocking. When I went in, Mr. Haynes was sitting behind his desk, his face flushed and sweating profusely. Mr. Fusco was sitting in one of the guest chairs, with his feet up on the desk in front of him. He greeted me warmly and introduced himself. . . . He's a very charming man."

Francesca's last statement made Maya's skin crawl.

"Don't tell me you dated him?"

Francesca didn't respond, but her eyes became watery.

"After hearing what he'd said, why would you go out with him?" Maya asked incredulously.

"I don't know. To this day, I don't know what possessed me. I was young and stupid, I guess. Easily impressed by the wrong things. I think I'll regret that for the rest of my life."

There was a moment of silence before Francesca continued.

"Anyway, I accidentally found that Mr. Haynes was stealing from the clients. I was afraid that by working for him, I might somehow be an accomplice. So I confronted him. He told me I was imagining things. But the next thing I knew, Mr. Haynes fired me. Told me I wasn't doing a good job."

"Did you know about Fusco's involvement at that point?" Maya asked, trying to fit the pieces together.

"No, not then. I was so mad and I wanted to get back at him. What he was doing was wrong. So on my last day at the company, I waited until everyone had gone home for the night. I searched his office and found proof that Peter Fusco was involved.

"I met with a Mr. Darden at the SEC and told him what I knew. He assured me everything would be all right. All I would have to do is testify when the time came.

"Then the phone calls started. Someone broke into my house. . . . Two men wearing masks threatened my mother, shook her up terribly. I was so scared. We packed up and left. When the government caught up with me, I told them to go to hell. There was no way I was going to put myself or my mother at risk again," Francesca said.

"What made you contact me? What makes you think I won't go back and tell Peter?" Maya asked suspiciously.

"Let's just say a little birdie told me you're one of the good guys. Look, Miss Wilkins, I have a couple of friends who still work at Wexton & Haynes and they've told me about you and the questions you've been asking."

"Is Brett Davis one of them?" Maya asked, remembering how helpful he had been.

"I'll say this much—there are people who don't like what Haynes and Fusco are doing, but they're too afraid to come forward. People don't want to risk their careers—or their lives, for that matter."

"And you?"

"I'm still looking over my shoulder. I feel like if I don't do something, I'll never get my life back."

Francesca reached into her shoulder bag and removed a manila envelope.

"This should help you."

Maya pulled two sheets of handwritten paper from the envelope. She read the first few lines of what appeared to be a confession from Haynes. In his letter he implicated Peter Fusco. Haynes had apparently written the letter in the event that anything happened to him.

"Would you be willing to testify now?" she asked Francesca.

"If you get him, yes. Here's the telephone number of a friend. He knows how to reach me." Francesca scanned the park again before walking away. "Good luck, Miss Wilkins," she called before getting lost in the swarm of the rush-hour crowd.

Chapter Thirty-Five

Close Call

The initial glow from the orange embers at the tip of the fat cigar subsided quickly, replaced by a gray ash. Peter Fusco twirled the smoke around his tongue, savoring the deliciously illegal flavor. He didn't give a damn what the government or the moral majority said, there were two things he would never be able to do without—a nice Cuban and a twenty-year-old piece of ass.

"Peter, I don't like the way this thing is shaping up. You said I would come out of this okay, but——"

"Allen, relax. I told you I'd take care of you, and I will, in spite of yourself," Peter replied nonchalantly.

"This is my life we're talking about." Haynes's tone was tight with trepidation.

"I know what the stakes are. Believe me, Allen, I want this all to blow over smoothly as much as you do."

"But will it? I mean, first there was Francesca. How do you know she won't resurface? Then you've got Maya Wilkins questioning my staff, looking through my records. She's one of your own and you can't even keep her on a leash. She's bound to turn up something—if she hasn't already."

Peter, enjoying the crackling sound his cigar made as he sucked on it, didn't respond.

"Peter, she works for you. Why can't you just tell her to back off?" Haynes whined.

He began pacing the short distance between the conference table and the door.

"Because she's a nosy little black bitch who's out to prove how smart she is. But don't worry," Peter grinned, returning his attention to Haynes, "I've got a trick for her ass."

"Look, Peter, I've been thinking. Maybe it's time to just come clean. I mean, if you can't control your own employees, why should I trust that you can keep me out of jail? Maybe I can strike a deal."

Wham! The room shook as Peter slammed Haynes against the wall on the other side of the door frame.

Maya flattened herself further against the door, biting her lip to stop herself from crying out and making her presence known. She pressed her back farther against the wall, melding herself into it. Her breath came in shallow spurts as she fought to regulate the sound of the air she exhaled.

She wanted to kick herself for being caught in such a perilous predicament, especially at this late stage in the game. She was very close to having a strong enough case against Peter Fusco to expose him for the snake that he was, and if caught now, there was no telling what he might do.

Maya cursed her current misfortune. She was supposed to be at Vic's house right now. Victor Sr. and Katrina were throwing the couple an engagement party and all she was expected to do was show up on time. They'd been pretty adamant that they wouldn't accept any excuses about work from her. She hadn't planned

on giving them any, but this weekend was the firm's an-
nual partnership retreat in Boca Raton, Florida. As
such, it provided the perfect opportunity for her to get
into Peter's office. She needed to get into his file cabinets. While most people wouldn't be stupid enough to
leave any incriminating evidence where anybody could
get to it, Maya was counting on Peter being cocky
enough to do just that, thinking no one would have the
audacity to invade his personal space.

She and Vic had spent the day shopping for wedding
rings. Afterward, she'd told him she had a couple of er-
rands to run. They went their separate ways, Maya promising to meet him at the brownstone by seven o'clock.
After showering and dressing at home, her plan was to
make a quick detour to the office, spend half an hour or
so going through the cabinets and have plenty of time
to make it to Vic's. Unfortunately, she hadn't counted
on Peter Fusco leaving the partnership weekend early
and coming into the office. Now here she was, stuck
like a mouse on a glue trap.

Maya listened to Haynes wince as his back hit the
wall. As messed up as the situation was, even Haynes
didn't deserve to catch a beat-down, she thought. Peter
Fusco was definitely a man on the edge, which Maya
knew placed her in even graver danger.

"Listen to me, you little shit," Peter hissed. "Don't
you dare threaten me, because whatever my part in all
this, I can guarantee you I'll fare a whole lot better than
you.

"Now," he continued, releasing a beet-red Haynes
and smoothing the wrinkles he'd created in the latter's
golf shirt, "why don't you go on home and let me handle this."

"What are you going to do?" Haynes whispered,
struggling to retrieve his voice from the dive it had
taken into the pit of his stomach.

"First, I'm going to take another look in Ms. Wilkins's office to find out exactly where she is with her little investigation. And then she and I will have one more little chat. A final tête-à-tête."

With that, Peter ushered Haynes out of his office and watched as he scurried down the hallway toward the elevator banks. Peter then returned to his desk, opened a drawer and retrieved a ring of keys. As he came from behind his desk and made his way to the door, he stopped abruptly. A cabinet drawer was ajar. He changed directions and went to the cabinet, snatching open the drawer and quickly surveying the files before closing it. He went back to his desk, pressed a number on speed dial and waited.

"Slatten, I assume you're on your way here. If you're not, you'd better be," he said in response to the voice-mail greeting he received. He slammed the receiver down and proceeded out of the office again, pausing once more at the doorway, scanning the room and then leaving.

Maya waited three full minutes before sliding from behind the door and peering down the hallway. The pungent stench of Peter's cigar made her nauseous, but she swallowed the bile rising in her throat, burning her esophagus. Her stomach roiled as she planned her next move.

Not quite satisfied that the coast was clear, but propelled by an urgent desire to get as far away from 438 West Fifth Avenue as she possibly could, she made a beeline for the elevator bank, pressed the DOWN button and, at precisely the same moment, a ding sound rang out, announcing an arriving elevator. An electric shock coursed through her fingers, her hand recoiling on impulse. She sprinted down the hallway, making the first turn she could, which landed her in the darkened firm library.

At first she stood behind a magazine rack just inside the entryway. After what seemed like hours—but was only four or five minutes—Maya summoned the courage to come out of her hiding place and try for the elevator again. She prepared herself mentally, mind and body steeled against whatever lay before her. Just as she was about to move, she heard voices advancing in the direction of the library.

"She was in my office—I'm certain of it. Not that she'd find anything in there."

"What do you want me to do?"

"Go to her apartment. Follow her around for a couple of days and make sure she sees you. But don't do anything until I tell you to."

The men entered the library. Peter reached into the inside pocket of his suit jacket and retrieved a white envelope.

"Here. A little something extra to get the job done. Don't disappoint me."

"Don't worry, Mr. Fusco. I've got it covered."

With a broad stroke of his beefy hand, Peter violently smacked a stack of newspapers off the library table. The papers scattered across the floor.

"Ms. Wilkins has no idea who she's messing with."

As the men slowly exited the library, Maya decided not to wait another minute to get out of there. She made her way to the back of the library, keeping her back pressed against the wall, its rough stucco texture scraping her shoulder blades as she shimmied along the narrow space behind the numerous shelves of legal publications. She moved as fast as she could along the confined path, not making a sound. It seemed an eternity before she reached the stairwell, but finally the large door lay before her. She said a quick prayer that she would not trigger an alarm or bell when she opened it and then pushed the heavy release lever. She was halfway down the first flight of stairs before the door clicked shut behind her. On the second flight she accidentally skipped a step and, in trying to regain her balance, broke the heel on her left shoe. In one deft movement, she slipped off both shoes, picked them up and continued sprinting down the stairs.

At the lobby level, Maya pushed the door open just far enough to stick her head out. As luck would have it, the guard was away from the desk, allowing Maya to escape unnoticed. She stepped out of the stairwell and jogged across the lobby, not breathing until she was through the revolving doors and outside. Whether the passersby on the street noticed her running in stockinged feet, she'd never know, because within twenty seconds she'd hopped into a cab and was headed uptown.

During the short ride, Maya replayed Peter Fusco's words. She tried to calm the raging fear coursing through her, sitting on her hands in an effort to stop them from trembling. It was then that she realized she'd left her purse in her office.

"Stop right here, please. I need to make a phone call," Maya said to the driver.

They were on the southeast corner of the block of the Smalls' brownstone.

"No, no, Miss. You must pay first. You no get out car before pay," the driver sputtered in broken English.

"Relax, I'm not trying to skip out on you. Look, I'm just going to use this phone right here. I need someone to bring some money downstairs," Maya persuaded the driver. "And, uh, I need to borrow a quarter. Please?" Maya smiled shakily.

As she dialed Victor Sr.'s number, she prayed that anyone but Vic would answer the phone; she did not want him to see her like this. Once again, lady luck shone on her.

"Smalls residence," Katrina said. She had just called Maya's apartment, trying to figure out why she was late getting there.

"Kat, is that you?" Maya asked.

"May—"

"Shh! Don't say my name!" Maya yelled.

"What's wrong?" Katrina asked, anxiety chilling her voice.

"Listen, I'll explain later. I'm on the corner of One-Thirty-Eighth Street. I need you to bring some money downstairs for my cab."

To the driver, who sat nervously peering out of the passenger side window, she said, "How much is it, sir?"

"Twelve dollar, please."

"Kat, bring me twenty dollars. And don't tell anyone I called. Hurry, please."

Maya hung up the phone and took a seat back inside the cab. She didn't want to chance it that anyone heading to Victor's place might see her. Three minutes later, she spotted Katrina coming out of the building. When Katrina saw the taxi parked at the corner, she began running down the street. Maya jumped out of the cab and grabbed her friend, who hugged her back just as desperately.

"Girl, what's wrong? What happened to you? Did somebody hurt you? Do you need to go to a hospital?" Katrina said all this in one breath as she snatched open the taxi's back door.

"Kat, chill. I don't need to go to a hospital. Did you bring the money?" Maya asked as she glanced at the anxious driver.

Katrina handed her a twenty-dollar bill, which Maya turned over to the driver.

"Thank you so much. Keep the change."

"Thank you, Miss. Thank you."

Maya pulled Katrina back from the curb to allow the driver to take off.

"Katrina, where are you parked?" Maya asked.

"Right there." A bewildered Katrina pointed across the street about three cars closer to Victor's place.

"Come on," Maya said.

Katrina followed silently, taking her car keys from her purse. Once inside the vehicle, Maya sighed heavily.

"All right, Maya, I'm getting pissed now. What the hell is wrong with you? There is a house full of people waiting for you, and Vic is starting to get antsy and you're sitting out here barefoot, sweaty, hair torn up and God only knows what else is wrong with you."

"I'm sorry, Kat. I'm all right, I promise. Give me a brush or something."

"Give you a brush or something? Have you lost your damn mind? I'm not giving you anything else until you tell me what's going on."

Maya told Katrina everything that had happened to her, starting with the phone call, the files and the chase. She told her about leaving her purse at the office and burst out in nervous laughter when she showed Katrina her broken shoe.

"This is not funny, Maya. Those men could have killed your ass tonight," Katrina scolded.

"Fusco's got too much going on for him to add murder to the list. I think he just wants to scare me," Maya said, trying to convince Katrina, as well as herself.

"You *think?* Okay, great. That's what I'll tell the news people when they're covering the story of your death. 'She just thought they were trying to scare her.' Maya," an exasperated Katrina snapped, "like you said, Fusco's got a lot to protect. No disrespect, but I'm not so sure taking out a little nobody like you would be a stretch for him. We've got to do something. And you've got to tell Vic about this."

Katrina was twisting her hair around her fingers, a sure sign that she was uptight.

"I know, but not tonight. Look, we can figure this out tomorrow. Right now I need to fix myself up and get in there with my man. He's probably calling all over the country looking for me by now. Did he see you slip out?"

"No, I don't think so. But Phyllis was near the door so I told her I was going to the store. Here," Katrina said, handing Maya a wooden-handled brush she'd retrieved from her glove compartment.

Maya brushed her hair until all the loose strands were in place. She used the bristles to roll several pieces of hair around until her ends had the appearance of a curl. Next she used Katrina's lipstick to cover up the faded shade she wore and sprayed a little Chloé under each armpit.

"Okay, now all I need are shoes."

It was Katrina's turn to laugh as she looked at her barefoot friend. "You are so lucky I travel prepared," she said as she reached under the backseat and pulled out a pair of black Kate Spade mules. "You know I'm a six and a half."

"Yeah, well, if I scrunch my toes together a bit, they won't hurt too badly," Maya said as she stuffed her size-sevens into Katrina's shoes.

Satisfied that she at least looked presentable, she got out of the car.

"Let's go," she said, taking a few deep, cleansing breaths and trying to rid herself of the sick feeling swimming around in her stomach.

She held Katrina's hand as they made their way to the brownstone, both women looking up and down the streets for a sign of any gloom or doom.

The party went well; of that Katrina made sure. The champagne flowed, the music pumped and Maya and Vic danced all night. After a couple of hours Maya was able to stop herself from sneaking glances out the window or jumping every time the doorbell rang. By the time the last guest was gone, Maya had filed away in her brain the evening's earlier events. Vic seemed not to have noticed that anything was amiss, and although she planned to tell him at some point, she wasn't about to let anything spoil their night.

"I'll call you in the morning, okay? And we will talk about this," Katrina whispered as she kissed Maya's cheek.

"Aren't you coming back to my place?" Maya asked, confused. "I know you aren't driving back down to D.C. tonight."

"Uh, well, no. I'm gonna hang out with Mark for a while and then . . ."

Maya looked squarely at her friend and then over to where Mark Mantale stood, chatting with Vic and his dad.

"What? . . . You and . . . When?" Maya stammered.

"Girl, pick up your lip. Mark and I kinda hit it off. I guess he finally realized he doesn't have a shot in hell with you. Anyway, we're just gonna hang out at his place. He offered me his couch."

"Katrina Marie Brewster!" Maya exclaimed. "You can't be serious."

Maya was shocked, to say the least. Not that Mark wasn't a great guy and all, but how could Katrina even think about hooking up with anyone? The final test results weren't back yet and Katrina was still too emotionally damaged for a relationship. For that matter, Maya felt she was the one too emotionally damaged to watch Katrina get involved with anyone so soon.

"Come on, Maya, bring it down a little. We can talk about it tomorrow," Katrina promised.

"You sure you know what you're doing?"

"Maya, I'm not 'doing' anything. And, yes, I'm sure. You be careful tonight, and I'll see you tomorrow." Katrina kissed Maya's cheek and hugged her tightly.

"Ready when you are," she called over to Mark.

Maya watched as Katrina and Mark headed out the apartment door and down the steps. Katrina's coquettish laughter sailed across the night air.

"What a night," Maya said to herself before glancing up and down the block and retreating indoors.

Inside the apartment, Vic and his father were seated in the living room, having what appeared to be a private moment. For this, Maya was happy, because since the night Mrs. Smalls had returned, things had seemed a little distant between father and son. She headed into one of the bedrooms to give them some privacy.

"Son, you're a grown man now. Too old for me to try and tell you what to do," Victor Sr. said.

"You're right about that, Pops."

"But you're not so old that you're too set in your ways to change."

"I'm not sure what you mean," Vic said. He leaned forward in his seat, his forearms resting on his knees, fingers locked together.

"Look, son, I know you're angry at your mother, and you have every right to be—"

"Not tonight, Pops. I don't want to talk about this," Vic interrupted.

"Just hear me out. I just don't want you to let stubbornness turn you into a hardened old man. That's not who I raised you to be."

"I'm not stubborn," Vic defended.

"Say what? Boy, you're as stubborn as a mule. You're so used to being mad at your mother, you don't know how to be anything else. But that's not good for you."

"So, what—I'm supposed to just forgive her and kiss and make up?" Vic said, rising angrily. He walked to the window, purposely turning his back on his father.

Victor Sr. got up and joined his son at the window. He placed a hand on the younger man's shoulder.

"No, that's not what I'm saying. All I want you to do is think about the situation, and maybe one day you can see things from her perspective. Things happen in life, man, and people mess up. This game didn't come with a rule book, so we've all got to do the best we can."

"But she left us." Once again, Vic was that pajama-clad ten-year-old boy.

"She had her reasons."

"What reason could she possibly have for doin' somethin' so foul?"

"Your mother was unhappy, son. Unhappy with her life. Unhappy mostly with herself. She went looking for something and it took her fifteen years to figure out that she was chasing a rainbow. That's her struggle to bear, though, not yours nor mine."

"Do you forgive her?" Vic asked his father plaintively.

"Yes, son, I do. Not for her, but for myself 'cause I don't want to spend the rest of my life being angry." Victor Sr. grabbed his son's other shoulder, making Vic turn to face him.

"You're about to marry a beautiful girl, and I wish you two nothing but happiness. I pray you never have to go through one moment of sorrow. But I also want you to go into your new life with a light heart, unburdened by old hurts. Understand?"

"Yes, sir," Vic said.

He looked at his father, once again reminded of how much courage and strength it took for the man to persevere and raise two children on his own. He was grateful for every bit of wisdom his father had ever imparted on him, even when he didn't want to hear it.

"Thanks, Pops," Vic said, hugging his father tightly.

"Aww, so much love," Maya said, reentering the room at that moment.

"Well, come on over here, girl, and get some of this," Victor Sr. demanded.

That night Maya pushed all thoughts of Peter Fusco

out of her mind and enjoyed being with her new family. Tomorrow would be another story—time to put up or shut up. Tonight, in the safe, strong arms of those who loved her, Maya would find the courage to do what she had to do, whatever that entailed.

Chapter Thirty-Six

The Eleventh Hour

"Is this woman, Miss Elliott, willing to testify?" Mark asked.

He was seated in one of Maya's two recliners. Vic was on the floor, his back propped against a wall. Maya sat in the other recliner, her legs tucked beneath her body, while Katrina leaned on the kitchen counter, poring over the documents Maya had assembled in her case against Peter. She had just finished laying out the events of the past few months, including the night of the engagement party, for Vic, Katrina and Mark.

"She said if I get enough on him, she'd be there."

"I don't know, Maya. I mean, I hate to be the voice of doom and gloom, but even with the dummy invoices; the discrepancies in both his personal financial records and Madison Pritchard's books; and the letter Haynes wrote, it's all still circumstantial," Mark said.

"I know that. I need more," Maya agreed wearily. It was the eleventh hour and time had all but run out. Peter Fusco had made it clear that he was done playing games with her.

"I'm about ready to just go and beat the truth out of him," Vic said, his fists in a ball. Ever since Maya had told them about being trapped in the office by Peter and his punks, he had been fuming. He didn't know how much longer he'd be able to contain himself before he exacted another kind of justice.

"Or," Katrina said, moving away from the kitchen counter and closer to the group, "Maya uses what her mama gave her and gets Fusco to spill his guts."

"Your mind is truly corrupt, but I like the way it works. Tell me more," Maya said.

"Well, from what you've told me, Fusco is a dirty old man always out chasing young tail. I'm sure if circumstances weren't what they are, he'd be sniffing behind you. So, toss him a smile or two, you know? Stroke his ego a little bit . . . till he lets his guard down. Then you get him talking. If he's as full of himself as you think he is, he'll talk. All you have to do is get him on tape."

"Bingo. And I've got just the thing." Maya went to the closet and retrieved her briefcase. She fished around inside for a moment. "Here it is," she said triumphantly.

"What the hell is that?" Katrina asked.

"A dictaphone. I use it all the time at work. What's the problem?"

"You can't use that. What do you think he's gonna do, hold his confession while you situate your little tape recorder on the table between you? Girl, please."

Katrina sashayed into the bedroom and returned to the living room carrying her overnight bag. She unzipped the bag and pulled out what appeared to be a cell phone.

"What is that?" Maya asked.

"It's a cell phone," Mark said.

"No, it just looks like a cell phone. This, my amateur little friends, is the latest gadget on the spy circuit. See, all you do is turn on this little button here and then it's in a special spy mode."

Maya laughed. "You can't be serious?"

"I'm dead serious. Watch. Now all I have to do is dial the number from another phone and it will automatically answer without any ringing or lights or anything."

Katrina dialed the number from a real phone.

"Nothing's happening," Maya said.

"Exactly," Katrina said. "But look at the display. It's in STANDBY MODE. Now talk."

"Talk about what? Oooh, I know. How about the fact that you've apparently watched one too many James Bond flicks. I hate to tell you this, Miss Brewster, but you ain't Halle Berry, code name Max. Not in this lifetime."

"It's Jinx," Mark corrected.

"Max, Jinx, Storm, whatever. This is silly."

While Maya and Mark talked, Katrina held the receiver to Vic's ear. A slow smile spread across his face.

"Baby, you're gonna have to take that back. Jinx here has got skills."

Vic handed the phone to Maya, who listened skeptically. Vic began humming the theme song from 007. The sound of his voice was coming crystal clear through the handset. Maya rose and moved away from the group, not quite ready to believe that she was hearing his voice through the phone.

"Well, I'll be damned. That's a handy piece of equipment, Katrina," Mark said.

"Thank you, thank you." Katrina beamed.

"Only you," Maya said. "You can tell me later why you have something like this."

"What?" Katrina's wide-eyed look of innocence was lost on Maya. "I confiscated it from one of my students."

When Maya cocked her head to one side and held her eyebrows arched in skepticism, Katrina sucked her teeth.

"Okay, don't believe me. Wherever I got it from, it's just what we need, right or wrong?"

"You think you're so cute, don't you?"

Maya playfully pulled at the back of Katrina's ponytail.

"How much does something like this go for?" Vic asked Katrina.

"Hundreds, probably, but worth every penny. And I've got this."

Once again Katrina reached into her bag of tricks. She retrieved a mini tape recorder with a suction cup attached by a chord.

"We attach this to the actual telephone we're calling from, and voilà! We get the bastard on tape."

"And he's none the wiser," Mark added.

"This is all good and everythin', but I still don't think it's a good idea for Maya to be alone with this guy. I mean, he's got a lot to lose, and who knows what he might try if he feels threatened," Vic said.

"Vic's got a point, Maya. Besides, what makes you think he's dumb enough to say anything incriminating?" Mark asked.

"He's a cocky son of a gun and he's been enjoying playing this cat-and-mouse game with me. He'll say something," Maya said confidently.

"All right, then. I say we go for it. Maya'll get that bastard to confess to something, anything, and then we'll throw his trifling ass to the wolves," Katrina concluded.

Maya spent the next few days hanging around Peter's office, attempting to get a moment alone with him. He brushed her off more than once, and she grew ever more frustrated. Four days after putting the plan into motion, she was no closer to her goal. Then Peter came to her himself, setting up a golden yet dangerous opportunity.

"Maya, hope you're not too busy because I need you to take a ride with me downtown," Peter Fusco said, bursting into Maya's office without knocking.

Flustered by the startling interruption, Maya fumbled with the papers she had been reading on the desk in front of her and nearly knocked over a cup of water.

"Downtown? For what?" she answered, annoyed.

"Jeffrey Rayne over at Winston Sprager & Berkowitz wants to meet with me on the Bucktown case. They're ready to settle. Katherine Parker is out today, something with her kid. Anyway, you helped her with the due diligence, so I need you to fill in."

"Peter, I'm not up to speed on that case. I haven't put in any time on it all month," Maya protested. The last thing she wanted to do was go anywhere with Peter Fusco.

"No matter. I just need someone to second chair—a single lawyer appearing at settlement talks isn't threatening. Appearances are everything. You can just shuffle some papers around and try to look like you know what you're doing."

Maya wanted to slap the smug look off Peter's pockmarked face. He was so damn condescending, it made her stomach hurt. She couldn't wait until the moment when she caught him with his pants down. Maybe today would be that day.

Maya smirked. "I think I can manage that."

She snatched her briefcase and purse off the chair in front of her desk and marched out the door, brushing past Peter with a steely gait.

"I need a minute to freshen up," she said as they walked down the hall.

"Women," Peter muttered. "I'll meet you in the lobby."

He had every intention of setting the record straight with Miss Wilkins once and for all. She would either see things his way or she would find herself in a world of trouble.

As soon as the elevator doors closed behind Peter, Maya snatched up the telephone in the reception area. She called her apartment.

"Hello," Katrina answered.

"Katrina, great, you're there. Look, Peter's got me going downtown to a meeting with him. I think this might be the opportunity we've been waiting for."

"Yes!" Katrina exclaimed.

"We're going to a firm named Winston Sprager & Berkowitz. Look them up. And call Vic for me."

"Right. We'll meet you down there. Be careful," she warned.

They rode downtown in a car service ordered by Peter's secretary. The meeting went as predicted. The guy from Winston Sprager & Berkowitz was falling all over himself trying to stay on Peter Fusco's good side. The offer he put on the table was more than generous, but of course Peter didn't accept it immediately.

He told the guy he'd have to get back to him after conferring with his client, but that it was entirely possible his client would prefer to continue into litigation. He reiterated the damages suffered by his client, and by the time he finished laying it on nice and thick, the other side was offering to have their client take another look at their numbers to see what they could do.

When Maya and Peter reached the lobby and exited into the street, she pulled the Nokia phone from her purse.

"What are you doing?" Peter snapped.

"Checking my messages," Maya returned with the same amount of roughness in her tone.

"No time for that now. We need to talk. Get in." He opened the door to his waiting Cadillac.

Maya did not return the phone to her bag, but rather held it in her hands.

"What's this?" Maya asked nervously. "Where's the car service?"

"I told him not to wait. This is my private car. I'll have my driver drop you off."

When Maya didn't follow, Peter grew more annoyed.

"Let's go. I haven't got all night."

Maya glanced across the street, spotting Katrina's car. She slid into Peter's car, immediately swallowed by the dark interior. Peter slammed the door and, without a word, the driver pulled away from the curb. Vic eased Katrina's BMW away from the curb also and proceeded to follow. He was careful to remain two car lengths behind the Cadillac.

"You know, Maya, under different circumstances I think you and I could have made quite a team," Peter said.

"I don't know what different circumstances you're referring to, but I doubt it," Maya retorted.

Peter chuckled heartily as he admired the young woman's guts.

"What will it take for us to reach a truce?" he asked.

"We don't need to reach a truce. You've made quite clear how you feel about me. And trust me, the feeling is mutual."

Peter looked at Maya for a moment, his anger at her impudence rising dangerously close to the surface.

"I don't think you're as tough as you make out, Miss Wilkins."

"Well, I *do* think you're as slimy as you make out."

A spark flashed in Peter's frigid eyes. Maya nervously glanced out the back window, no longer able to see Katrina's car behind them. Could Peter's driver have lost them on that last turn? Maya didn't want to think about that possibility. She tried to remain calm, but sweat had already begun sliding between her breasts and slipping down her armpits.

"You should have just minded your own business."

"So you could just go on getting rich off other people's losses?"

"You act like it was your damned money."

"What about your partners? Those people trust you."

"What about those idiots? That firm would be nothing without me. I brought Haynes's money in and took it back out, right under their stupid noses. I don't owe them anything."

"You've jeopardized their livelihood, their reputations. These people consider you a friend." Maya's rage had taken over her senses. She was sick and tired of the Peter Fuscos and the Andrew Paynes of the world just arbitrarily changing the courses of people's lives with no regard. "What a lowlife," she spat.

Peter suddenly reached for Maya, grabbing her roughly by the arm. At that moment, the car slowed as it approached a red light. Without hesitation, Maya grabbed the door handle and jumped out of the vehicle before it completely stopped moving.

In a scene straight out of the Fox television series *Cops,* Vic swerved from behind the car, screeching to a halt a hair away from the driver's door. He jumped out, climbed over the hood and pulled Peter through the open window. Fusco's driver, unable to open his door, climbed out of the passenger's side, but before he could reach Vic and Fusco, Mark had intercepted him and threw him against the hood of the car.

"Vic, Vic, no!" Maya screamed. "Not like this!"

"Kick his ass, Vic!" Katrina yelled. "Kick that son of a bitch's ass!"

"No, Vic. Please."

Peter's face had turned bright red as Vic held him

tightly by the collar, cutting off the oxygen to his lungs. The lower half of Peter's body was still inside the vehicle, while the upper half was outside. Vic looked Peter squarely in the face, his angry eyes penetrating into the cold empty blueness of Peter's.

"If you ever come near her again, it'll be the last thing you do. You got that?" Vic hissed.

"Yeah," Peter gasped.

"What?" Vic screamed into the crimson face.

"Got it. I got it," Peter sputtered.

Vic released Peter, shoving him almost completely back inside his car. On cue, Mark released the driver, who took a threatening step toward Vic.

"You want some?" Vic shouted at the driver.

"Filipe, get in the damned car. Get me out of here!" Peter yelled.

Filipe looked from Mark to Vic before climbing back into the car, over the passenger's seat. He backed up the vehicle a few feet, made a U-turn and sped off back in the direction they'd come. Maya ran over to Vic, who was staring after the car, his fists clenched.

"They're gone, baby," she said as she reached him.

Vic pulled Maya into his arms, hugging her briefly before releasing her again. Holding her by the shoulders at arm's length, he looked her up and down.

"Are you okay? Did he hurt you?"

"No, I'm fine."

His skeptical gaze was unwavering as he continued to examine her from head to toe.

"I'm fine. I promise."

By now other drivers had begun blowing their horns at the group. Katrina's car was blocking part of the street and the scene had created a traffic jam.

"We'd better get out of here," Mark commented.

They jumped into the car, Vic behind the wheel, and sped off to a chorus of irate honkers. Katrina retrieved her regular cellphone and the attached tape recorder from where she'd tossed it on the car's floor and examined the tape.

"Did we get it?" Maya asked.

"Yeah, we've got that maniac."

Chapter Thirty-Seven

Dragon Slaying

"James, thank you for agreeing to meet with me," Maya said once the waitress was out of earshot.

She and James Pritchard were seated at a table near the kitchen at the Grill on 45th Street.

"I must admit, Maya, I was a little surprised by your request that I meet with you outside of the office. Surprised and concerned by its urgency. Is someone at the office giving you a problem? You know we don't tolerate harassment of any sort."

"James, it's nothing like that. However, I didn't feel I could speak freely with you in the office. I'd like to preface everything I am about to say with this: My first and foremost loyalty is to the clients we represent. The oath I took forces me to act in the client's best interests at all times. Second, my obligation to you and to the firm is that I act at all times with integrity and honesty."

"Well, yes, Maya. We all adhere to those same high ethics. We have to."

"Unfortunately, James, not every attorney operates in sync with the duties bestowed upon them."

"Maya, let's get specific. What exactly are we talking about here?"

"Several months ago I was assigned the Haynes case after Roger Perkins left the firm so unexpectedly."

"Right, right. Roger's departure was our loss."

"Well, I now know why Roger decided to return to his hometown so hastily. It seems he uncovered some startling facts about the Haynes case."

"Really? Such as?"

Maya took a deep breath. The moment of truth had arrived and it was time for her to do as her father always said: either piss or get off the pot.

"The missing client funds derived from Haynes's shorting of stocks didn't just disappear. Haynes had an accomplice who has been funneling the funds through his company in phony escrow accounts."

James Pritchard silently sipped from the glass of water in front of him. He took a quick glance around the crowded restaurant before settling on Maya.

"Who is this accomplice?" he asked. Maya watched a fleeting look pass through his eyes, which she could not read.

"It's Peter Fusco. He's been funneling the money through the firm," Maya said.

The air in the space across the table between them evaporated, leaving them momentarily in a vacuum. Maya waited for James to either digest the grenade she'd just dropped in his lap or toss it back at her. Beneath the table her left leg did double-time.

"That's a very serious allegation, Ms. Wilkins."

"Yes, sir, it is. But I assure you, it's true."

James Pritchard slumped backward in his chair, sighing heavily. His eyes shifted uneasily around the room before resting on Maya again. Maya's heart began to beat harder as she feared she'd made a mistake. Could James Pritchard have already known about Peter's misdeeds? If so, could he be involved? Maya's legs tensed as she poised herself to make a quick exit, if need be.

"How do you know all of this?" James asked quietly.

Maya hesitantly retrieved the envelope from her briefcase and slid it across the table to him. James morosely reviewed its contents. Everything was there, including the invoices and a transcription of Peter's confession, along with the original cassette tape, the letter written by Allen Haynes and a signed statement from Francesca Elliott. When he had finished, he returned the documents to the folder, clasped his hands in front of him and stared at the water glass.

"Have you told anyone about this?"

"No one I can't trust."

James leaned back in his chair. "Hmph. That's an ironic choice of words—'No one I can't trust.' . . . Is there really such a person?"

"James, why do I get the sneaky impression that this isn't quite a surprise to you?" Maya dared ask.

"Because it isn't. You have to understand something, Peter Fusco and I have been friends since college. That's more than thirty years of weddings, baby christenings and family outings. Our wives play bridge together weekly. He's closer to me than a brother."

James Pritchard suddenly looked old as deep creases appeared around the corners of his mouth and eyes.

"Peter has changed lately. He's been argumentative, even with me. His lifestyle has become flashy, his mannerisms callous. And the money he's been spending . . . I have to admit, I've been suspicious of him for quite some time now. But I didn't want to believe he was capable of anything . . . anything like this."

"Look, James, I'm sure this must be difficult for you and I'm sorry to have placed you in this position. I haven't known you very long but I get the sense that you're about doing what's right. Believe me, I wish I had never found out about any of this. But I did, and I had to do something about it . . . I had no choice. And neither do you."

"Maya, I'm at a loss right now. I have spent more than thirty years in this business and I've seen good people do bad things and bad people do even worse. I'd say I can't believe it, that the Peter I know, or knew, wouldn't do these things, but that's too cliché. I'm not that naive. The evidence is hard to refute. And Edna Tully? She might not have been an accomplice, but she was at the very least negligent in her duties. It just goes to show, you never know what people are capable of."

"If I didn't know that before, believe me, I know it now," Maya said, shaking her head.

"What do you mean?"

"Let's just say that while he hasn't come out and confronted me, he knows I'm on to him and he's made some pretty strong suggestions that I mind my business."

A worried expression cloaked James's face as he patted Maya's hand.

"Look, Maya, I want you to take the next couple of days off. Go home ill. There's no reason for you to be exposed to any further danger. Peter's scheduled to attend a conference in Los Angeles until week's end. The other partners and I will have to figure out how best to handle this situation by then."

"That's fine," Maya said, standing to leave.

She walked out of the restaurant with a lighter step than when she'd entered. She felt relieved that this whole mess was near its conclusion, and while she was anxious about the outcome, she was confident she had done the right thing. It was out of her hands now.

Late that evening the partners called an impromptu partnership meeting where James Pritchard laid out all the facts. By the time Peter returned to the office on Friday, his office had been cleared out and the partners were seated around the large conference-room table, waiting for him.

"The way I see it, you've only got one real choice, Peter," James said. "Either you take the plea, and then, because you'll surely be disbarred, leave the firm now, or do nothing and the government will surely take you down the hard way. Taking the plea, you'll pay a large fine and have a few years probation, but no jail time. If not, you crash and burn and run the risk of taking the firm with you. Surely you don't want that."

By now Peter Fusco's inflated, pockmarked cheeks were red and little pellets of sweat veiled his pasty forehead. He couldn't talk. Couldn't look at the faces of his partners. He just sat there staring into space and translating what was being said to him. What they really meant was they wanted him out and if that meant feeding him to the lions, so be it.

"Look, Peter, I'm sure you understand that ordinarily we'd be behind you all the way. However, there is a lot more at stake here than just you. The firm will not survive the scandal of being publicly implicated in this mess," James Pritchard said.

"So I guess I'm on my own, then, huh, James?" Peter's voice quivered as he clutched the armrests of his chair. In spite of the fact that he had been a partner with one of the most renowned firms in New York City, Peter had wanted more. Greed had been the motivating factor for Peter Fusco to get involved with the crimes he was being accused of, and now that all was said and done, he would end up losing everything.

"Well, Peter, we've got to do what's best for the firm. Should I put a call in to Vergo & Rhodes to get you some representation?" asked Faye Rosen.

"Yeah, go ahead."

The brief conference ended, Peter Fusco a beaten

man, resigned to his fate. As he departed, under escort
by two hired security guards, he made one final request.
"Tell Maya Wilkins that I said, 'a job well done.' "

Maya had waited nervously all day on Friday for the
call. Shortly before five o'clock, the telephone rang. It
was James and Marjorie.

"Maya, it's all over with, dear," Marjorie said. "Effec-
tive immediately, the firm name has been changed to
Madison & Pritchard."

"That's certainly good news."

"I realize this is a very awkward situation for you,
but I hope we can reach some sort of accord. You're a
great attorney, and we appreciate your loyalty to the
firm."

"Marjorie, Jim, don't misunderstand—I didn't do
this just for the firm, because I still believe you guys
should have known what he was up to."

Maya's assertion was received with a silent accep-
tance of its truth.

"I put myself on the line because I am a good attorney, and I had to because it was the right thing to do,"
Maya continued.

"Yes, well, uh," James interjected, clearing his throat.
"We, uh, hope that you plan to stay on here at the firm.
We see great things for your future here, Maya."

Maya quietly weighed his words. She had already
decided she would not make it easy for the firm to
sweep the incident under the rug by leaving. But she
also thought seriously about what would have happened to the firm had Peter's crimes remained unde-
tected. Even if he'd gotten away with it, eventually he
would have done something else to bring dishonor to
the firm's reputation. It was obvious that they were, on
many levels, glad that Maya had brought Peter's deeds

to their attention. It was also apparent that one bad apple had not spoiled the whole bunch.

"Yes, James, I do intend to stay on at the firm. I hope we can all put this unfortunate business behind us and get back to the business of giving our clients solid, dependable representation."

"Amen to that," Marjorie agreed. "And one more thing, Maya, we would like to reward you for your loyalty and fine work. When you come back to work, let's discuss a senior associate position."

"Sounds good to me. See you both on Monday."

Maya hung up, pumped by the positive outcome. She'd done it, despite the odds.

"Driver, pull over at the front gate, please. We'll walk from there. Thank you," Maya said, sliding two bills into the little window of the cab. Tugging at Vic's hand, she got out of the taxi.

"You sure you're up to this?" Vic asked as they walked up to the winding path of Whitmore Cemetery. "You've had a rough few weeks."

"I know, that's why I needed to come here. You don't mind, do you?"

"Never," Vic said. He stopped walking to kiss Maya's forehead, then searched her face, certain that the familiar veil of sadness would have descended by now. To his surprise, she was smiling at him, her eyes bright and clear, her face radiant and beautiful.

Maya kissed him deeply, letting him know that everything was okay. They continued on to her parents' graves. Maya stooped in front of her mother's headstone and carefully placed a single white rose against the marble block.

"My parents would have really loved you, Vic," Maya said, her back to him.

"I know I would have loved them, too."

"Mommy would have opened her arms and said, 'Welcome to the family, Victor,' and Daddy would have offered you a cigar and a sip of brandy before warning you to take care of his baby." Maya laughed.

Vic puffed out his chest, feeling protective of the woman who had changed his life so completely.

"I would have promised them both that they don't have to worry 'cause I will love and cherish you forever. It's you and me baby, always."

Maya turned her head so she could see Vic's face, the sincerity that was etched into it warming her soul. He walked behind her, wrapping his arms around her body, and Maya let herself rest against Vic as she looked up at the sky. It was the bluest sky she had ever seen. She felt her parents' kisses brush her cheek as a gentle wind rustled the trees above them, and she thanked God for the life of love and happiness she'd found.

"I don't know what tomorrow holds, Vic, but I do know that I don't want to face it without you. That scares me . . . being dependent."

"Me, too. But you know somethin'? It doesn't matter if we have a day, a month or fifty years together—my dreams have already come true."

"Mine, too."

Chapter Thirty-Eight

No More Drama

"What's up, girl? I was just throwing some things into a bag. I'll probably catch the four o'clock shuttle."

"Then I'm glad I caught you," Katrina said. "You don't need to come down here."

"What? Of course I do. I'm going with you to the doctor's office tomorrow, remember?"

"No, listen, Maya. I just want you to know that I appreciate everything you've done for me. You've been a rock . . . through all of this. I don't know what I would have done without you."

"Kat, you don't have to thank me. You've always done the same for me. But why don't you want me to come tomorrow?" Maya asked.

" 'Cause I've already seen my doctor. I went in this morning. Told him I couldn't take the suspense any longer. He got the lab to send the results over today. Six months is six months, give or take a day, anyway."

Maya stopped folding the pair of khaki shorts in her hands and clutched them to her chest instead. She eased herself down onto her bed and waited. She had known this moment was coming since that dreadful night and she had told herself and Katrina that no matter what happened, they'd handle it. But now she wasn't so sure.

Could she bear to hear that her best friend had been handed a death sentence? How could she help Katrina through that? It would be hell all over again, just like her mother's cancer. But wasn't she stronger now? Hadn't this past year proven that? Maya closed her eyes, waiting to hear whatever Katrina had to say and praying that God would give her the strength to deal with it.

"Negative," Katrina whispered.

"Negative?" Maya asked.

"Negative," Katrina said again, a little louder this time. "I still can't believe it. I keep saying it over and over again, keep reading the printout, scared that it's gonna change. But it hasn't. It's negative, Maya."

The two women were silent, each considering the righteousness of a word that normally did not translate into good news. Maya released the breath she hadn't realized she'd been holding and allowed her fingers to relax the death grip they'd held on the receiver. All of a sudden it was as if the earth had started spinning again and the sun had decided to come out of hiding. Maya began to cry a river of tears, released from the dread she'd felt since the night she'd been forced to face the possibility of losing her best friend.

"Kat," she began, her voice cracking under the weight of the relief she felt. She couldn't control her vocal chords, the vessel for the thoughts that continued springing forth in her mind, wanting this woman, her sister, her friend, her family to know how much she meant to her.

"I know, Maya," Katrina whispered. She didn't need to hear the words to know their meaning. She felt the same way. Her friendship with Maya was one of the most beautiful things in her life, and the prospect of being separated from that friendship was equally as troubling as the fate that had almost claimed her. The silence between them was a time of quiet reflection, during which the bond between Katrina and Maya revealed itself to be impregnable and limitless. The two hundred–mile distance between them dissolved as their spirits embraced.

"Look at us," Katrina said finally. "Acting like two big babies."

"I know." Maya sniffed.

Katrina had been floating on a cloud since getting her final test results. Now that the nightmare was over, she vowed to never put herself in such a scary predicament again. This threat had forced her to appreciate everything in her life she had always taken for granted. Maya's friendship was one of those things.

"Enough of this. We've got a wedding to get ready for, in case you've forgotten."

Maya laughed. "I haven't forgotten."

"Where's that man of yours? He was supposed to send me a copy of his vows more than a week ago. If he waits until the last minute, I won't be responsible if they turn out looking like chicken scratch instead of calligraphy. I'm good, but I'm not that good," Katrina complained.

"All right. I'll get on him."

"Good. And by the way, I spoke to Mrs. Armstrong again yesterday. That lady is a riot." Katrina laughed.

"What'd she say?"

"First she talked my ear off about how she and your mother used to paint the town red back in the day. And how she's the one who hooked your parents up in the first place. Then she went on to talk about how you had the buckiest front teeth she'd ever seen, and how she was so glad the braces worked out well for you."

"That's not true!" Maya exclaimed indignantly.

"Girl, you forget I've seen the pictures. Anyway, she's expecting us at her house Friday night before the wedding. And I hooked her up with my mom."

"Uh-oh, that's twice the fire." Maya laughed.

"Tell me about it. My mother has been looking over my shoulder, double-checking all the wedding arrangements I've made. Anyway, those old birds say they've got everything at the house covered."

"Oooh, it'll be nice to see Mrs. Armstrong again. It's been so long. I wonder if that old dog of hers is still mean. He was a nasty little so-and-so, always nipping at my feet," Maya reminisced. "I'm gonna kick him if he messes with me."

"Haven't you kicked enough butt lately?" Katrina joked.

All worries aside, Katrina and Maya were able to throw themselves into planning for the wedding. It was almost as if the trials of the past year hadn't happened at all, yet the lessons learned would last them a lifetime.

Vic and Maya strode hand in hand into Nell's Night Club, where Pierre, a recording artist, was holding his album release party. Pierre's recording of Vic's song "Wings" had already reached the top of the R&B and pop charts, making tonight both a celebration for Vic as well as the perfect opportunity to network.

Moët & Chandon and Dom Perignon flowed endlessly as music executives, entertainment lawyers and recording artists of various levels of notoriety mixed and mingled. Maya had never seen so much glitz and glamour in one room at one time. Diamonds and other extravagant jewels dripped from ears, necks and wrists everywhere she looked.

At one point in the evening, Pierre called Vic over to

the mike where he publicly thanked him for writing his hit song and cemented his desire for a long-term business relationship with Vic. Maya watched Vic from across the room, looking svelte in his Armani suit. Her pride in his talent and success warmed her from head to toe.

When Vic left the stage, he was approached by several executives and artists. He greeted each with a handshake and a smile, and, without making any commitments, slipped their business cards into his pocket with a promise that they'd talk. At his side, Maya interceded between Vic and several lawyers offering their legal services.

"You're scaring people. They think you're just a sexy lady until you open your mouth and start talkin' legalese," Vic teased.

"Yeah, well, they need to back up. I'm taking care of you," Maya replied. She planted a tender kiss on Vic's lips.

"I've had enough of this," Vic said, looking around the crowded room. "You?"

"I'm having fun." Maya laughed. "Look over there." She tried to be discreet as her eyes darted to the left.

"Isn't that the girl from that movie we saw last week? In the blue dress?"

"Yeah, I think so." Vic responded.

"I thought she was married to that football player you like?"

"So, what about it?"

"Well, the guy she was just swapping spit with surely wasn't her husband. I tell you, these celebrities are something else. I hope you don't get famous and start acting like you've lost your mind. I'm not having it," Maya said.

"Woman, please. You know you're the only person I want to swap spit with."

"That's what you say now—ooh, look at him."

"That's it—I'm getting you out of here right now," Vic said, tugging a reluctant Maya toward the door.

She took one final sip from her glass of champagne and placed it on an empty table. They made their way through the crowd, stopping to speak to a few well-wishers.

"You are so bad," Vic said once they were outside.

"So take me home and punish me," Maya said wickedly.

Chapter Thirty-Nine

Wedding Bells

Maya's gown was strapless, made of satin and organza fabric, and was from the Ilissa collection by Demetrios. She was a little worried because at the last fitting on Monday, it felt a little snug around the mid-section, but she refused to let it out one bit for fear of ruining the look. She'd spent the better part of the morning in Ramona's chair at Hair Haven uptown, the only place to go if you wanted to get your hair hooked up for an occasion. Ramona followed up a deep-cleansing shampoo and moisturizing conditioner with the placement of drop curls all over her head and a feathery bang across her brow. The softness of the hairstyle gave Maya's already angelic face an added radiance.

Maya and Katrina returned to Mrs. Armstrong's house, where they were greeted by a crew of multicultural technicians. This talented crew had been borrowed by Katrina's mother from a chic full-service spa on Long Island. There was a Latin Antonio Banderas look-alike named Miguel, who gave Maya the massage of a lifetime. He rubbed eucalyptus and lilac oil all over her body, beginning between her shoulder blades and moving to her outer thighs, calves and feet until she felt like butter. In the end, her body felt like hot liquid chocolate and she had to be assisted to her feet.

She was then treated to a scrumptious snack of buttered croissants baked from scratch, assorted sliced fruit with freshly whipped cream, juice squeezed from orange and grapefruits and mocha cappuccino. The caterers were a petite duo comprised of a quiet brunette named Sally and a chatty Filipino named Christine.

As soon as she swallowed the last morsel on her plate, Maya was whisked in front of a traveling vanity manned by Desmond, a fine and unmistakably homosexual brother who mixed, matched, tested and retested, applied and reapplied every color on his palette. Finally, he turned a tortured Maya around to face her reflection in the mirror. She gasped, unable to recognize herself.

"Oh, my God! Is that me?" she asked incredulously as everyone gathered behind her in the mirror, beaming.

"Girl, you got it going on!"

"Strangé!"

"Beautiful!"

The heartfelt shouts of admiration echoed around Maya as she stared at herself. Katrina grabbed a camera and shot an entire role of film while Maya struck pose after pose, egged on by an adoring crowd. The hoopla continued until Katrina's mother, Mrs. Brewster, finally went rodeo and corralled everyone together. She had them packed up and out the door so fast, they were in a cheerful tailspin.

"Come on, now. Out. Everybody out. Maya's got just a little while before the limousine arrives. Skedaddle."

"Listen you guys, Miguel, Sally, Christine, Desmond . . . you guys are amazing. I can't thank you enough for all this!"

"It was my pleasure, lovey," said Desmond, hugging Maya.

"Make sure you send us pictures," chirped Christine as she and Sally rolled their gourmet carts out the door.

"Yes, Mami. That man is gonna flip when he sees you!" Miguel said, giving Maya a light peck on the cheek.

Mrs. Brewster followed Mrs. Armstrong out, the latter in a complete tizzy because she couldn't find her grandmother's antique broach she just *had* to wear today.

"Come on, dear, I'll help you locate it. If we put these old eyes together, I'm sure we'll be a success." Mrs. Brewster cackled.

Once Maya, Shelly and Katrina were left alone, Katrina turned on Erykah Badu's *Live* CD and the women spent the next half hour singing along, pinching off of leftovers and laughing.

"So Shel, I know I already said this, but you're looking good these days. Californian life definitely agrees with you," Maya complimented. She was so happy Shelly had made it to the wedding.

"Thank you, thank you," Shelly replied, showing off her figure.

"Yeah, I'm glad to see you've come out of those damn oversize man clothes you used to wear," Katrina barked.

"Don't listen to little Miss Tacky Pants over there."

"Please, have I ever let Ms. Brewster ruffle my feathers?" Shelly laughed, mussing the back of Katrina's head.

"Oh, I forgot to show you this. Bonnie sent it from Bolivia," Maya said, lifting a small, handblown bowl from a mound of protective tissue in a box at her feet. "And she promises to visit next year."

"It's beautiful," Shelly said, delicately turning the dish around in her hands.

"Isn't it? And look at the inscription on the bottom." Maya smiled. " 'May life's bounty always nourish your soul.' She made this herself."

"Remember that time she made those ugly-ass dresses for us?" Katrina hooted.

"Yeah, and she really thought we were going to wear those hideous things to her sister's wedding!"

The women barked with laughter until tears threatened to ruin their makeup. Phyllis arrived a short time later, bringing the bridal party's bouquets.

"Hey, Phyllis. How'd the church look?" Maya said, kissing her.

"The florists did a wonderful job," Phyllis said, preparing a small plate of fruit for herself. "They didn't miss a beat."

"Great."

"How are you doing? Girl, you look fierce. Them curls are gorgeous. I know you went to Harlem to get those done 'cause there ain't a single decent stylist in this neck of the woods."

"Yeah, you know it. Listen, Phyllis, thanks again for handling everything at the church for me. Was the traffic bad getting up here?"

"Not at all. It only took me about forty minutes. And you're welcome, Maya. It ain't every day that my baby brother gets married, you know." Phyllis hugged Maya. "And he sure picked a beautiful bride. Now, you keep him happy, hear me? He deserves it."

"I will, I promise." Maya's cell phone rang and Katrina snatched it up before Maya could get to it.

"Hello, Victor. How can we help you?"

"Hey, Katrina. How's she doing?" Vic asked.

"Well, she hasn't broken out in hives yet, like she did during finals week at Albany U, so I guess she's okay," Katrina joked.

"Cut it out, Kat. Give me the phone," Maya yelled.

"Hold on, here she is."

"Hey, you," Maya whispered into the phone as she stuck her tongue out at Katrina.

"Hey, baby, how are you?" Vic asked.

"Wonderful. You?"

"I'm good, cool. You ready?"

"Almost. I can't wait to see you in your tux."

"What tux? I ain't wearin' a tux," Vic said with as much sincerity as he could muster.

"Victor!"

"Nah, baby, I thought I told you. I decided to come in my Timbs and—"

"Victor, you don't want me to have to knock you out on your wedding day, do you?" Maya warned.

"You knock me out every day."

"Aww." Maya melted.

"Okay, okay," Katrina broke in. "Y'all got plenty of time for that mess later. Right now, it's show time. Say good-bye, Victor."

"Good-bye, Victor," Maya mimicked.

"Later, baby."

"All right, ladies, it's time to get your butts into those dresses," Mrs. Brewster said as she and Mrs. Armstrong fluttered into the room. Mrs. Armstrong alternated between blowing her nose into a handkerchief as she cried over how beautiful Maya looked and how proud her mother would be, and picking at the remaining trays of snack foods.

Not only were Katrina and her mother, Mrs. Penelope Brewster, the spitting images of one another—they were two peas from the same pod. Mrs. Brewster took charge of the final grooming, whipping the girls into shape like a drill sergeant, but with much love.

After zipping, tucking and straightening Katrina, Phyllis and Shelly into their dresses, Mrs. Brewster assisted Maya as she got into her stockings, shoes and accessories. Maya was wearing her mother's diamond stud earrings, the ones her father had given her at their 25th anniversary party. Katrina had given her a sapphire and diamond hairpin and Phyllis commented that the dress took care of the something new. Maya had something else in mind for the new, but that would have to remain a secret for now.

"And for the something borrowed, here you are, sweetie," Mrs. Brewster said as she opened a small box and removed a diamond tennis bracelet. The doorbell rang just as Maya was zipped into her gown.

"All right, the limo's here. Let's do this!" Katrina called from the window.

They arrived at the church promptly at the appointed hour. The hustle and bustle of the day and of the past few months seemed to melt away. As the music began, serenity settled over Maya. It was strange how calm she felt as she waited for the moment when she would join the man waiting for her at the end of the aisle. It had been just under a year since they'd met, too soon some people would say for them to be getting married. Although the past year had been filled with lots of intensity and change, Maya knew this was the love of her life—her soul mate.

All her life she had prayed to God that she would one day know a love like her parents had, and in answer to her prayers came Vic. Day by day he'd peeled away the layers of pain and found her hiding, scared and uncertain but wanting to be found just the same. An unlikely suitor, yet one who'd instantly burrowed his way deep into her heart and soul. Everything made sense now—all the pieces fit, and this Maya knew as certainly as she knew her own name.

"Girl, you are absolutely beautiful. I never knew what people meant when they say a woman has a certain glow at different times in her life until now. You look so happy," Katrina said as she patted the corners of her eyes with a tissue.

"I am, Kat. I am so very, very happy."

"Ooh, I can't stand you, girl," Katrina said, hitting Maya's hand playfully.

"Neither can I." Maya laughed. "Hey, listen, Kat, I've got something to tell you later, after the ceremony."

"What?"

"Nothing, nothing. I'll tell you later."

"Maya, you know how much I hate it when you tell me in advance that you've got something to tell me later. Now I've got to spend the whole ceremony waiting. Ooh, you make me sick," Katrina said, stamping her foot like an impatient two-year-old.

"Yeah, but you love me anyway."

"All right, then, come on . . . this is it. No backing out now. Give me a hug." Katrina reached for Maya and the women embraced each other.

"God only knows what I did to deserve a friend like you," Maya whispered into Katrina's ear.

"Back at you." Katrina smiled.

From the doorway of the sanctuary the organist motioned for Katrina to begin her march down the aisle.

"Ooh, girl, he's looking *good*. You'd better come on behind me and marry that man or you know I will," Katrina whispered over her shoulder.

After Katrina had walked to the altar, a former classmate of Vic's from NYU began playing Lauryn Hill's "Tell Him" and Phyllis sang the lyrics as Maya walked slowly down the aisle alone.

Another wish came true as she felt her daddy's arm loop into hers and his strong stride paralleled hers. She smiled and continued down. Maya marveled at the happy faces filling the church on either side of her.

When her eyes met Vic's, they held, and she watched as a tear slid from the corner of his lid. She reached his side and wiped that tear from his cheek, taking his hand in hers. Vic spent the entire ceremony looking at her instead of the reverend, and the reverend had to repeat Vic's name twice before Vic heard him. Their friends and family laughed with them. As the reverend pronounced them husband and wife, Victor lifted Maya's veil and whispered, "I got you now."

"You sure do," Maya answered.

They kissed amid claps and cheers, none of which were heard by the happy couple, lost in each other's arms. Over Vic's shoulder Maya spotted his mother standing by herself. Their eyes met and the tears in Mrs. Smalls's slid down her light reddish-brown face, much more like Vic's than Maya had first thought.

"Your mother looks a little lonely. Maybe you should go and talk with her."

Vic turned to look in the direction of his mother and nodded at her. He returned his gaze to Maya.

"Maybe later."

"You're doing the right thing, you know. It's time both of you put those heavy bags down for good."

Vic laughed. "Now where have I heard those words of wisdom before?"

"Yeah, I know. Maybe you should learn how to take your own advice, Dr. Phil, instead of always dishing it out to others."

"Thank you."

"For what?"

"For makin' me believe I could live each day of my life in the springtime," Vic said, knowing in his heart he would love this woman forever.

"And thank you, too. For making me feel safe again."

At the reception, Maya turned down three offers of champagne before Vic noticed she wasn't drinking.

"Are you okay?" he asked, concern lighting his eyes. They were standing in the middle of the dance floor, having just finished their first dance to Prince's "Adore."

"Yep. Couldn't be better," Maya responded.

"You sure? I mean, I know everythin' has been happenin' all at once and I know you and I . . . Well, this is all so fast. But I promise you, Maya, it's all good. I'm gonna make you happy."

"You already have, Vic. Besides, it's a little too late to be second-guessing us now, don't you think?" Maya laughed.

"I just want you to know that we're gonna be all right."

"I know that. We'll all be fine. Katrina's doing great. Your dad is the best father-in-law a girl could hope for. Look around. Everybody's happy for us and having a good time. Yeah, we'll be fine, especially you, me and . . . this little baby." She smiled, placing her hand on her belly. Vic couldn't speak as he stood there feeling the overwhelming joy deep inside him triple until his chip-toothed half grin erupted into a raucous laugh.

"Serious? he asked as he moved closer to her. "How?"

"Remember the night of Pierre's party?"

"Oh, yeah, when we slipped up because you were so impatient." Vic laughed.

He rubbed his hand across the place where their baby was growing and rested his face in the small of Maya's neck where he could smell her sweetness.

From across the room Maya spotted Katrina, the center of attention as usual, holding a small group of people captive. She tossed her head back as she laughed, and when she saw Maya watching, blew a kiss in her direction. Maya couldn't wait to tell her best friend she would be getting a godchild sooner than any of them had planned. But right now, she wasn't quite ready to pull herself away from Vic's arms. In fact, she was certain it would be an eternity before she'd want to do that.

"When everything was wrong
and nothing seemed right,

you came into my life,
now my heart feels light.
I owe you everything,
I'll give you anything,
I'll deny you nothing,
for you are my queen."

Maya stared into Vic's eyes for a long time after he spoke those words to her. She couldn't believe she was really there in this moment.

"Is that new?" she asked.

"Yep. I wrote it just now, just for you," Vic answered.

"I finally know what it was my parents shared that made them seem so special—love everlasting." Maya closed her eyes for a moment and said a silent prayer of thanks. "I love you, Mr. Smalls." She smiled, and they danced the night away.

Dear Reader:

Thank you for letting Vic and Maya into your lives. I hope their story inspires you to become more romantic, more loving and more forgiving in your own relationships.

I enjoyed writing about this particular couple because it gave me an opportunity to remind society that black folks are multifaceted, colorful and compassionate.

I began writing as a child because I enjoyed bringing characters to life. I continue writing because it is a vehicle with which to make a statement, take a stand or just show a different side of things.

With your support, I will continue to bring you people whose stories will inform and entertain. For updates and information regarding my other works, please check my Web site, http://www.kimshaw.net.

In the meantime, take care and keep reading.

Yours truly,

Kim Shaw

About the Author

Kim Shaw holds a bachelor's degree in English—creative writing/journalism. Originally from New York City, she currently resides in Roselle, New Jersey, with her husband and two children.